TEN
Righteous
PEOPLE

TEN
Righteous
PEOPLE

Danny Rittman

iUniverse, Inc.
Bloomington

Ten Righteous People

iUniverse books may be ordered through booksellers or by contacting:

iUniverse
1663 Liberty Drive
Bloomington, IN 47403
www.iuniverse.com
1-800-Authors (1-800-288-4677)

ISBN: 978-1-4759-6394-6 (sc)
ISBN: 978-1-4759-6395-3 (hc)
ISBN: 978-1-4759-6396-0 (ebk)

Library of Congress Control Number: 2012922414

Printed in the United States of America

iUniverse rev. date: 11/27/2012

"Light need not combat darkness in order to overpower it. Where light is, darkness is not. A thimbleful of light will therefore banish a roomful of darkness."

The Rebbe

"וַיֹּאמֶר אַל נָא יִחַר לַאדֹנָי וַאֲדַבְּרָה אַךְ הַפַּעַם, אוּלַי יִמָּצְאוּן שָׁם עֲשָׂרָה, וַיֹּאמֶר לֹא אַשְׁחִית בַּעֲבוּר הָעֲשָׂרָה." (בראשית פרק יח)

"And he said, 'Oh let not the Lord be angry and I will speak just this once: Peradventure ten shall be found there?' And He said, 'I will not destroy it for ten's sake.'"

(Genesis 18:32)

*   *   *

"The world must be destroyed." said the dark angel. "There is no doubt about it." The light angel was deep in thought. Both angels stood at the bottom of a large cathedral. It was huge and made of old brown wood. The top of the cathedral could not be seen as it rose above a cloud into the skies.

"No," the light angel said eventually. "We cannot destroy the world. There is good in it."

"Oh, we cannot consider children, religious people and the elderly." The dark angel claimed with arrogance. "We know that they are not capable of doing evil but the rest of the world has proven differently." He raised an eyebrow and directed a half smile at the light angel. "The rest of the world is corrupt. The rest of the world has been performing acts of extreme evil." He paused to increase the impression of his words. "And they have been doing so intentionally." The light angel remained silent. This gave the dark angel encouragement to continue. "I do not need to tell you what they have been doing for the past few hundred years. They have butchered each other. They have neglected and abused children and elderly people. They have murdered each other en masse using a wide variety of methods. They even created a system for the organized elimination of their own race." He apparently enjoyed indicting humanity. "It is revolting." he concluded in a whining tone. "It has to be stopped. We cannot continue doing nothing about it."

"We have to consider their acts of goodness as well." The light angel spoke in a steady tone. He did not seem to be impressed by the dark angel's speech. "How can we destroy the world if there are also good people in it?" He raised his hand in a questioning gesture.

"You are not the one to make this decision." the dark angel teased. His dark eyebrows were raised in amusement. He clearly enjoyed discussing matters of evil.

Both angels stood silently as a loud voice sounded. "The course of action has yet to be determined." After a pause the voice continued from above, "I do not intend to destroy an entire world without significant proof that it deserves such punishment. I would like to hear some ideas." There was silence for a short while.

"I have one my Lord." said the light angel raising his hand. "I have an excellent idea to prove that there is good in the human world . . ." The dark angel looked at him with curiosity. He was sure that he had been winning this argument.

"I will find ten righteous people in this world. These righteous people will be neither infants nor religious people. They will be people who had done evil but have changed for the good. These people have listened to the light inside themselves amid the darkness that completely surrounds them." He stopped for few seconds and then continued "These people are righteous."

Ah," The dark angel protested. "This will bring nothing. It will not prove anything. Anyone knows that in a world of few billion you'll always find few who are exceptional." Then he remembered something and an evil smile spread on his face. "Besides, this sounds familiar." He directed an evil look at the light angel. The light angel nodded silently. He knew what was coming. The dark angel reminded him of this occasionally. "Didn't I already win this? Many years ago . . ." His evil laugh rumbled throughout the clouds. "The same scenario occurred with those twin sin cities. What were their names?" The light angel rolled his eyes. He knew that the dark angel well knew the names. He simply enjoyed bragging about his victory. "Oh yes, Sodom and Gomorrah, were they?" He straightened his look at the light angel. "What happened then? Didn't I prevail? Do you want to play the same game again?"

"No." proclaimed the light angel with a smile "I am talking about purely evil souls; humans who conducted their lives committing heinous acts, people who knew nothing other than evil. These people have to prove that they have changed their ways of thinking, changed their morals, and changed their perspectives." He rested for a while and then continued "Their souls already belonged to the dark side with no expectation of changing yet they decided to crossover. They coherently made the quantum leap and turned toward the good. Their hearts and souls transformed into good." He breathed deeply. "That is what I am talking about."

He then turned towards the dark angel with white flames sparkling in his eyes. "I am talking about ten truly righteous people who have banished the darkness from within their souls. I am talking about change and atonement."

The dark angel did not smile anymore. His eyes lit in red flames "It is never going to happen. Those who already belong to me will never crossover to your side. It is not possible."

There was a complete silence which stressed the intensity of the moment. Then a loud voice sounded.

"So it will be written, so it will be done. Ten righteous people will be found. Otherwise the world will be destroyed."

The dark angel laughed. "I am going to win again and your defeat will haunt you for thousands years."

The light angel smiled with light in his eyes.

"Ten righteous people."

Chapter I

INNOCENCE

*   *   *

"Dealing drugs is a tough business." said Boris Hess to his assistant Rudolph Morin who brought him the news. Then he poured himself a glass of whiskey and scratched his head. Rudolph had just told him that the village which was earning him a multi-million dollar annual income from the manufacture of cocaine was rebelling. The local people did not want to cooperate anymore. He had made lots of money from this village in Colombia and could not think about the possibility of giving it up. Trouble started few months ago when all of a sudden locals came up with the idea that they were being used as extremely cheap labor to manufacture drugs and did not want to cooperate anymore. The rumors passed through the village like wild fire in a dry field. At the beginning he simply gave the order to kill those few men who mentioned something about cheap labor and thought that the problem was solved. It happened, he thought at the time and figured it would be only one incident but it seemed to have escalated. The entire village; all the men, women and even the elderly refused to do any work for his people. This was such a shame. He was not too worried though. As a person who was always thinking ahead, he had seen this coming and for the past few months quietly worked to prepare another village to do the work. The other village was small and very poor which made it excellent for his purposes. His personnel had already closed all the technical details regarding redistribution of the land belonging to the rebellious village to the poorer one and they were very happy. In exchange, they would work for minimal salaries but would be owners of plentiful land. In addition, his people reported that the new village included many young, beautiful women. This by itself was a great incentive, thought Boris and worth the exchange. He could bring few women over to his mansion in Los Angeles. It could not hurt. Regarding the rebellious village, they were expendable. That was a sacrifice he was willing to make.

He looked at Rudolph who always stood erect like an army officer. It must have come from the fact that Rudolph was a true believer in Nazism, thought Boris to himself. Oh well, it was always a beneficial characteristic for a guy in his position. After all he was Boris's best man. Boris had found him in the lowest bar in Los Angeles many years ago. At the time he was looking for a person to make him the ruler in his domain. He knew that only through real terror could he make his way in. When Boris came from Russia he was determined to be the leader in this industry, as he had been in Russia. He wanted to dominate drug dealing in America, starting in Los Angeles and eventually expanding to the entire continental USA. He had brought a few hundred thousand dollars from Russia and knew that he would have to use these funds wisely in order to establish his new kingdom. He had gotten some information about all kinds of characters who could be found at this bar so he went there late one night. The first person who attracted his attention was Rudolph. As he entered the bar he could tell that the majority of the people there were criminals of some sort. They were drug dealers, hit men and people who did not hesitate to commit crimes for the right price. Yet Rudolph was different. His large build, the way he handled himself and the expression on his face did not leave any room for mistake. He stood out. He had no fear of anything. He had no boundaries, not ethically, not morally and not of any other type. That was exactly what Boris was looking for. He remembered clearly how he had sat near him and approached him with a cigarette.

"I need a reliable man to handle my business." He told him straight, lit his cigarette and blew the smoke in his face. Rudolph did not even blink. Nor did he utter a word. "I recently arrived from Russia." he continued as he was blowing smoke circles into the air "I want to establish my drug cartel here. I can guarantee you a salary of six figures within a few months." He then looked briefly at Rudolph. "Would you like to join me?" Rudolph still did not say a word but instead took a big sip from his huge glass of beer. Boris looked at Rudolph and felt that he was the right one. Something inside him told him that he was the right one. There was only one thing to do. One thing would finally determine if he had found a match for this job; a test. "What can you show me?" he asked Rudolph and looked straight into his eyes.

Rudolph did not answer. Instead he finished his beer in one gulp and banged the mug down on the bar with a loud noise without breaking the glass. Then he stepped off his seat and looked over the bar. He identified someone and walked over to him, whispered something in his ear and they both left for the bar's restroom. That's awkward, he thought then. He simply left with this man, just like that. Maybe I made a mistake after all. He wondered since he did not usually err regarding people's character.

A few minutes later Rudolph returned and sat near him putting a plastic bag on the bar. Boris would never forget what happened next. What was it? What did he bring me? A bag? He got the urge to look inside the bag. He briefly looked at Rudolph who sat quietly near him. No expression was shown on his face. He ordered another huge mug of bear and started to sip it slowly. "What's in the bag?" he asked him but got no answer. He took it as permission to look. Slowly he opened the bag and felt his blood freeze inside his veins. Inside there was the head of the guy Rudolph went to the restroom with. Blood dripped out of the head and slowly filled the bag inside. Quietly he closed the bag and inhaled a long drag of his cigarette.

"Who was this man to you?" he asked him without looking at his face.

"Just a man in the bar." he first heard his voice, loud, deep and emotionless as Rudolph looked straight into his eyes without a blink. He then smiled. He was the right guy after all. He had picked the right man.

"I am Boris." he said.

"I am Rudolph and I believe in Hitler". Said Rudolph in a monotonic voice.

He laughed; He made a perfect choice. "Good for you." That's how he hired Rudolph. Since then they had been together.

"Give the order to initiate the exchange plan." he told to Rudolph and yawned widely. It was early in the morning yet he poured himself another glass of whiskey. It is going to be a good morning he thought.

"Sure, I'll contact our man there. Should we do the full operation?" he asked. Boris rolled the whiskey in his mouth for few seconds. "Am I rushing here?" he thought to himself. After all there are children in the village. There are elderly people. The full plan means killing them all. They had talked only about the extermination of men. Women, children and the elderly could still work. Most likely they would be so scared seeing all men massacred that they would continue working without any problems. But this morning he did not have any patience for thinking about the human factor. "What the hell?" he thought. "We have the entire new village to replace them anyway."

"Yes, you can exterminate them all." he instructed Rudolph and looked through the window. Rudolph stepped out without a word and Boris knew that the task would be done perfectly. That was Rudolph's nature. That was why he had been working with him for the past ten years. In a short time the entire village would be killed and burned to the ground. Men, women, children and elderly people would be wiped out. A thought snuck into his mind. "How can I do something like that? There are children in the village; innocent children who worked only for me for the past few years." Then he kicked the thought away. It was not his problem.

*   *   *

The small village was still sleeping when the artillery started to hit it. A few Hughes helicopters equipped with Vulcan 20mm cannons approached the village from the north and started launching Napalm bombs that created huge flames in the hey based village houses. Men, women and children who woke up to this horror ran outside screaming at the top of their lungs. They did not have too much time to scream. The helicopters that were capable of slow hovering motion smoothly and accurately opened fire from their Vulcan cannons and killed every living person who was out. The massive blizzard of bullets that the Vulcan cannons produced did not leave any chance for anyone. Within a few minutes the entire village was in flames and a few minutes later all the people were dead. The helicopters continued hovering above the village for about an hour more, searching for survivors who were hiding. After an hour a group of twenty people arrived via army trucks. They searched the village, killing those who were still alive including babies, children and elderly people. After a while all was quiet and only the crackling of flames was

knew that a night like this was something she would never have dreamed. He went to her and hugged her. They both watched the magnificent view silently. It hypnotized them for a while. Ronny had to recruit all of his efforts to disconnect from the flickering lights and turn to Tina. "So, what do you say? We are going to have a fun night." His hands easily found her dress buttons on the back of her dress and opened them. The silky, black dress simply fell to the floor.

"You are quick." Tina hummed towards him with a seductive smile. Her eyes misted and they kissed passionately, ripping each other's clothes with intense hunger. He removed her bra and her full, young breasts erupted towards him like a challenge. He sank his face into her as she moaned with lust for him. He threw her on the huge bed and in a quick move she was on top of him. As she was licking her full lips and looking straight into his eyes she slowly opened his belt buckle. Her hands found what she was looking for and now it was his turn to moan. Soon enough they embarked on a sensual trip of taste, touch and smell as their bodies joined together in wild passionate love. Afterwards they lay in bed in each other arms looking through the huge wall window. "What an amazing evening Ronny, Thank you.", she whispered.

"My pleasure. I love you." He mumbled, "I want to live with you for the rest of my life."

A knock sounded on the door. "Room Service."

Ronny looked at her as his forehead wrinkles. He was surprised. "I did not order anything." He put on one of the fancy robes that were available for them and went to open the door.

A well dressed, tall, wide shouldered waiter stood there erect. "Wine service sir," the waiter said and quickly added "Complimentary of the presidential suite sir," He stood erect and knocked with his shoes.

"Wow", thought Ronny, "This room is really fancy. Anyway, what is it with this weird waiter? He acts like he is in the military." "Thank you, please do come in." he invited the waiter to their room. The tall waiter lightly bowed and pushed a large cart into the room. The cart had a huge, shiny round dish cover. Near it were a few covered large plates. Two wine bottles were in the middle, surrounded by crystal champagne flutes. "Looks good", thought Ronny with joy as he followed the waiter into the room.

"Honey, who is it?" Tina called from the bedroom.

"My girlfriend." Apologized Ronny with a shy smile. "We are having an anniversary tonight."

"Of Course," Smiled the huge waiter, who pulled out a cork screw and started the procedure of opening the wine. "One of our best wines, Romanée Conti French wine, vintage 1957."

"Impressive," Ronny had no knowledge of wine but what the waiter said sounded remarkable. He patiently waited until the waiter opened the bottle and poured the burgundy wine into two crystal glasses. The dark red wine smoothly slid into the goblets, creating small waves as drops lightly splashed into each curved glass. Fascinated, Ronny watched at the procedure until it was complete. The overdressed, over mannered waiter stood erect again and knocked with his shows like a soldier.

"Would you like to be the first to taste, sir?"

"Sure," Ronny was a bit embarrassed but politely cooperated. No one before had offered him wine with such a ceremony. "This is due to this fancy suite", he thought and took the wine glass. As he had see other people do before, he shook the glass slightly, pretended to smell it gently and eventually took a small sip. The wine was silky and round. "The dam thing actually tastes good." The thought crossed his mind as he swallowed his first sip. Then he took another sip and nodded. "Perfect, thank you." he approved with a smile.

"Very well then." the waiter seemed to be happy and started to close his gear as he wiped it meticulously.

"Let's get over with this," Thought Ronny. He wanted to be back in bed with Tina. Then he got curious. What was in the large dish that was covered with a giant, shiny cover? "What's inside?" he asked the waiter.

The waiter gave him a long look as if it were weird that he asked the question. This was the first time that he actually looked into the waiter's eyes. He had large ice-cold blue eyes that that seemed stuck into him. All of a sudden Ronny felt fear. Those eyes looked at him in a predatory way, like a killer animal about to

13

hunt its prey. The eyes were hostile and merciless. Instinctively he stepped backwards.

"Do you mean this cover?" The waiter pointed at the metal cover as his tone changed. He did not talk like a waiter anymore. He sharply turned towards Ronny and without any further notice removed the dish cover exposing what was on the dish. "It is your mother's head."

Ronny saw the world turning around. On the dish was his mother's head. Her eyes were still open and looked straight at him. He thought he would pass out but the waiter quickly grabbed him and put him gently on the wooden chair. There was a knock on the door and the waiter rushed to open it. A man stepped inside dressed in a black business suit. He looked short and chubby. His face radiated unhappiness and anger. His fat nose matched his thick neck and full lips. His small black eyes were sunk into fat rolls of skin that gave them a look of a pig's eyes. He quickly stepped inside and stood in front of Ronny who was in shock.

"You were stealing my drugs and money from me." He spit into his face. "You are just a kid." He grinned to himself. "You are just an ambitious kid." He slapped Ronny's face. "I can't believe it," he turned towards the waiter. "A kid robbed me." Ronny had difficulty catching his breath. Seeing his mother's decapitated head caused him to panic. He tried to regain control.

"What did you think would happen?" The chubby man walked around him slowly as he was clearly enjoying Ronny's panic. "That you'd be able to steal from me?" He then looked at the suite. "Stay in fancy hotels with my money? Ha!"

Screams sounded from the bedroom and Ronny saw in growing panic how the waiter brought Tina terrified into the room. "What is going on Ronny?", she screamed in panic and then noticed his mother's head on the large dish. She opened her mouth to scream but the waiter quickly covered her mouth, silencing her.

The fat man walked towards Tina. "So you thought that you could have a good life by becoming a dealer by yourself. Not too bad, I actually respect this but why steal from me? This was not a smart move." He approached terrified Ronny. "Now your mother, your girlfriend and you will suffer." He stopped for a second and grinned for a second. "Well, your mother does not suffer anymore." The waiter pulled out a gun with a silencer. He approached Ronny and looked at his face which expressed hopelessness and devastation. Then he shook his head. "You should not have played with the big boys. It is way beyond your league."

He then turned to Tina who was screaming hysterically as Rudolph held her by her hair. Rudolph had no problem silencing her with his large hand on her mouth. Her eyes rounded with frantic fear as she saw Ronny's glazed eyes. He seemed to be in shock and did not respond. It was too much for him.

Boris looked at both of them and reached a conclusion. "Just tie them together and torch the place." He mumbled. He realized that they needed to destroy evidence. He did not care that they would both be burnt alive. That was their punishment. He wiped a small hair off his suit, gave Rudolph a last, brief look and stepped out of the room. He knew that Rudolph would complete his job perfectly.

The next day the headlines in the newspapers were about a severe fire that had completely destroyed the presidential suite in one of the most prestige hotels in Los Angeles. Two guests perished in the fire.

*   *   *

"I love helicopter rides." Boris sat on his comfortable seat in the new helicopter he had recently purchased. "Especially in my brand new one." He grinned at Rudolph who sat in front of him chewing on a huge bologna sandwich. Rudolph just nodded and gave him a tiny smile. He was busy with a huge bite. Boris looked at him with an expression of disgust. "I do not know how you eat this crap, but then again you are a special human being." he said to Rudolph sarcastically. Rudolph did not care. He was used to be treated that way but only by Boris.

Boris had purchased the new helicopter last month for the astronomical amount of twenty million dollars and he planned to use it on every visit to Columbia. The fully equipped, brand new BELL 430 helicopters was fully loaded with the most recent electronics that money can buy. It provided its passengers with all the information needed for just about everything, starting with the weather in every city around the globe and ending with global news and military information in all countries and locations. In addition the helicopter was equipped with special extended fuel tanks that significantly increased its trip range and enabled it to reach many desired destinations worldwide. Boris picked its electronics personally using an aviation expert who consulted with him about the available systems. In addition he picked weaponry systems that were nicely installed and hidden within the aircraft's structure so no one could identify them. The helicopter had the capability of producing a serious bullet storm using its sophisticated, hidden canons. Boris wanted to have these systems installed especially for dealing with villages and competitors in Columbia. The peaceful appearance of the helicopter was completely deceiving. It had the weapon potential of a full combat aircraft excluding missiles.

Boris enjoyed the passing view of the green forests below. He wanted to visit the new village to see in person how the drug production was going. Rudolph reported that Cocaine production was going well and the profits supported his reports. Yet, Boris liked to check things personally to make sure that no one was stealing from him. That was his nature and that is why he survived in this business for so long. Boris was extremely rich. Over the past few years he became the main drug supplier in Los Angeles metro area and even expanded his activity to other major cities like Miami and New York. He was always careful to pay respect to the local dealers and to make sure to give them the feeling that they were working together. He made sure that they even gained more income due to the new business that he brought with him. In this way, he used to say, we are all benefiting from our joint cooperation. They loved it. His business approach was cold, accurate and efficient yet very appealing and he slowly expanded his successful empire like an advanced spider web throughout the United States. He had charm combined with a frightening capacity to demonstrate extreme cruelty and functioned at high efficiency and high profit. This was very appealing to all the other major dealers who worked with him. It was also very scary. They knew that behind his smile there was a definite death threat if they refused to work with him so they chose to join him. Knowing that he had become the ruler in this field did not leave them many choices. He became infamous for his brutal methods that were implemented on people who refused to work with him. Human life was worth nothing in his eyes. Given the fact that he spent millions of dollars paying off chief police officers, judges and legal officials gave him almost endless power. Slowly but surely Boris became the leader of all drug activities in the continental United States.

*   *   *

The helicopter landed in a secluded area on the far side of the village. A group of about twenty, armed men waited silently for Boris and Rudolph. Boris always insisted on getting full protection when visiting his villages. He knew that many people would be eager to kill him and take over his workers. This village was the largest one and brought him the majority of his drug supply. The previous village had been destroyed and all of its people killed according to his instructions as a penalty for their rebellion. He kept a small mercenary army in this village to ensure that no similar phenomenon would occur here. In the previous village the locals had instigated resistance against his people, claiming that they had turned the natives into slaves. He had to search for a replacement village and get rid of the old one. Now there were at least a hundred fully armed guards on the village premises at all times, supervising the smooth operation of drug manufacturing. According to Boris' instructions his military was involved in every small detail of the drug making process from tending the coca plants to the final chemical processing and packing. Boris invested a significant amount of money building an underground manufacturing lab that was fully equipped with the most hi-tech electronic security and protection systems. There were engineers, chemists and a maintenance person on site around the clock to maintain high quality production of the drugs. Recently, he expanded the village's drug production capabilities and now produced few new types of drugs besides a high quality line of drugs. The procedure itself was completely automated and required only few people mainly to supervise the machinery. A large set of modern generators produced electricity for the underground machinery and the plant operated smoothly, to Boris' great satisfaction. "I own all of this?" Boris could not stop himself from asking as he was walking among the sparkling, brand new machines, touching them and nodding in astonishment. "Well, this is an industry that rolls billions of dollars, he thought." There should be such machines to do all the necessary work. After an hour in the plant they went to see the huge fields that were full of all types of plants. These were the raw material to be collected at a certain time for the underground plant manufacturing. They could see rows of men and women working in the fields. The rows of people progressed slowly, doing their jobs quietly. They also noticed a line of armed soldiers escorting the workers along their territory. "Efficient", Boris thought and lit a joint. He actually needed at least one or two of these cigarettes every day. It relaxed him and helped him pass the night. He even had a medical permit to smoke them any place. So far he was quite happy with what he saw. The new village was well disciplined and working well without any local resistance as had happened in the previous one. Things seemed to be working smoothly, almost too smoothly. Something did not feel right to him but he could not put his finger on where the problem was. "What about the previous village?", a thought snuck into his head. They were supposed to have been exterminated. "Is the last village far away from here?" He sent the question into the air.

"Not at all," Rudolph was the first one to answer. "About ten minutes walk to the south."

"Indeed." confirmed Armand. "But it is completely empty. The last time we were there was few months ago after we had killed everyone." He grinned "Not a view for weak stomach.

Boris thought for a while. It may be only slight paranoia, he thought as he took long drags of his cigarette. The yellow smoke he exhaled looked pretty to him and he observed it fading into the air with satisfaction. He always liked the process of smoking marijuana. It was almost like a ceremony to him. That was why he always smoked before having sex. It became his ritual. "I would like to see where the old camp was. "Check on the rebels." Boris smiled with evil.

"I'll lead the way." Armand said with great enthusiasm.

"No need, I'll take him to the place." Rudolph waived with his hand to cancel Armand's offer. "I know the way and anyway there is no one there."

"Sounds like a plan to me." Boris agreed. Rudolph quickly checked his weapons and ammunition. He was always armed like a damn platoon, thought Boris as he observed how many guns and grenades and other ammunition Rudolph carried.

"You," Rudolph pointed toward a short guy. "Come with us in case we need your language skills." He turned towards Boris and explained "This guy knows the language here. We may need him in case we meet someone although I doubt we will." Boris nodded. "We are all ready boss." Rudolph barked and Boris smiled.

"Yes, I can see that. Off we go. We will be back soon." Boris concluded. Rudolph led them into the forest and they soon disappeared among the trees.

*   *   *

The previous village was a gruesome site. Although a few months had passed since the entire village was massacred many bodies were still scattered around in progressive stages of decomposition. Rudolph simply walked among the rotting bodies as Boris covered his entire face with his handkerchief due to the horrific stench.

"Do not walk so damn fast." Boris and the other guy had difficulty to catching up with Rudolph who walked quite fast inside the village.

"OK Boss." He slowed his pace. "But I see that we did a good job here. There is no one left." Rudolph looked quite happy.

The other guy looked calm. He was used to seeing villages in such condition. It was not the only one massacred by drug cartels.

"I can't believe that you can walk like this without covering your face." Boris mumbled under his handkerchief. "I've seen long, burning needles. From within the clouds he saw the snake biting again and again many times. Then the snake retreated. Boris's blur started to fade away but he was still too weak to scream or move. He lay there and tried to assess his condition. There he was, bitten by a snake, most likely a very poisonous one without any capability to call for help. All he could do was to lay there. He could feel the area where the snake had bitten him getting numb. Slowly he regained clear vision in his right eye. He thought that this was a sign that his powers were back and tried to move but without success. He realized that he could not even call for Rudolph or the other guy for help. His brain did the calculation. He had stepped not too far from them but fell into a dead spot behind thick bushes. It may take some time for Rudolph to find him. In the meanwhile the poison was moving within his body. How long he could survive? He knew the basics about snakes. If it was a deadly type he had very short time to reach to a hospital. Even if Rudolph would carry him to the other camp it would take at least another thirty minutes or so. He closed his one functioning eye when he reached a conclusion. Most likely he would never make it on time to a hospital. He was going to die.

*   *   *

Something stepped into his vision. Boris looked at the image with great surprise. Has the poison started to affect my mind?

He continued watching. Yes, the image was still there. A young little girl in faded red clothing. She looked about seven or eight years old. She was filthy and her clothes were decrepit. Her cheeks were almost dark from dirt and her long hair looked like she had not combed or washed it for many days. She looked like one of the local children who had been working for him in the village. Typically they used children to pick the plant leaves. "What is a little girl is doing here?" The thought flashed in his head. He wanted to say something but could not make a sound. The little girl looked at him and then at the snake that was still near him. When she saw the snake she quickly disappeared into the thick bush behind her. "Well, a vision is expected given the circumstances", he thought bitterly. "After all, what did I think that she would be able to do something for me?" To his surprise after few seconds she appeared again, this time with a long stick in her hands. With a quick movement she pulled the large snake away from him. She looked like she knew what she was doing. After she had gotten rid of the snake she approached him and observed him. She looked at his legs to find the snake bite. Then she identified the spot. The spot was already large and black. She turned to him and said something in her language. He did not understand her. She repeated her words and realized that he did not understand her. She leaned forward and reached closely to his face. He could see her slightly slanted eyes and her dirty face. She could see his swelled eye and the sweat drops all over his face. She knew his condition was critical. "She may be the last person I see in my life.", was the thought that crossed his mind. He never imagined that a little girl from Columbia would be the last person that he would see just before he died.

Then something unexpected happened. The little girl held his leg where it was bitten by the snake and put her little mouth on his wound. She then stuck her little teeth hard into his leg and he felt like he was screaming. Instead a sigh came out since he did not even have the power to scream. The little girl then started to do something. He could not clearly see what she was doing but could feel her efforts on his wound. He managed to make a half roll to the left and could see her sucking out the blood of his wound and then spitting it away. She was doing this repeatedly when all of a sudden something interrupted her. A man appeared. Boris recognized his as the third guy, the translator. He looked at the girl and then at Boris as his eyes got round.

"What happened?" He then asked in English. Boris wanted to answer him but could only make a weak sigh. Then the man turned into the little girl and asked her something in her language. She briefly answered him and continued sucking the blood out of Boris leg. The man franticly looked at her as he realized what had happened here a short time ago. He thought for a split second and then said something to the little girl who nodded. The man then turned toward him.

"You've been bitten by a very deadly snake Boris. We have to get you to a hospital immediately. This snake bite gives you no more than an hour before getting treatment. Otherwise you are going to die in great pain. I'll go get Rudolph. He will be able to carry you." Within seconds he disappeared into the bushes. Boris remained there with the little girl that was now leaning on a tree just in front of him. Amazingly he started to feel better.

"Thank you." he mumbled to her. He knew that what she did probably would save his life. He looked down to see his wound and noticed that it was not black anymore. It still looked like a bruise but not as black as it looked before. This must have been due to the fact that she had sucked the poison out of it. The little girl sat near him without saying a word. Her gaze was locked in a hidden spot in the air. Boris looked at her. She must be about seven or eight years old, he thought. Dirty cloths, filthy face, wild hair due, looks like she was not taken care of for ages. Yet, this little girl probably saved my life. Why?

Rudolph and the other guy stepped in. "Quickly boss, let's take you to a hospital." Rudolph urged him. The little girl said something quickly, like she understood him and the translator raised his hand.

"No, you should not move now. She sucked the majority of the poison out of your leg. Any move will not be good now. You have to wait for a while until you can move. Until then the poison will dissolve in your blood." The translator looked tense.

Rudolph was not convinced. "Let me take you, what does she know?" He approached Boris and leaned down to help him stand up.

"No, I believe her." Boris mumbled. "I trust her. She knew what to do."

"I agree." the translator added. "She knew what to do. She lives here. She is familiar with this scenario." Rudolph stood there and did not know what to do. He looked at the young girl and decided that they were probably right.

The girl observed Boris leg and said something. "The poison will not harm you anymore. In a little while you will be able to walk home", she said.

"Thank you . . ." Boris said quietly. He already felt better. "What type of nasty snake this is anyway?" The translator asked the little girl. She looked into the bushes, where it was seen for the last time and then answered.

"It is a very common type for this jungle. She had already seen many people of her village die from its bite." There was a quiet moment.

"Where are your parents or family?" Boris asked after a while. A disturbing thought penetrated into him. She looked aghast. "I hope that her family was not from the village." The girl pointed towards the path that came from the ruined village and Boris felt a finger of discomfort touch him inside. He had never felt anything like that before.

Then she started to talk, fast, in her language. The translator tried to keep up the pace. "Her parents were killed in the village down below this path. One day without any notice fire came from the skies. Machines that looked like big mosquitoes spit fire from the skies and killed everyone." Boris bit his lip quietly. He well knew what she was talking about.

"Only a few other children and I survived because we were playing in the jungle outside the village. When everything started we watched it all from our hidden place among the tall trees up the hill."

Boris watched her face that warped, showing a great internal pain. She stopped her story to regain control. "I killed her family." Boris felt a pain inside him, something that he had never felt before. They were just simple peasants who worked for me. Their lives were worth nothing anyway. He tried to convince himself. "Who cares about this type of people? Many like these died under my command. Why should I care about these?"

"I watched my mother and father burst into flames when the fire came from the flying machines." They must have been Napalm bombs. "My sister and brother were in the village. I could not see them but I clearly saw the fire and explosions of all of our homes. Quietly we watched our families die in flames as the flying machines were hovering above the village and killing all these people who tried to run away." She became quite for some time then continued. "We could not even cry. It happened so fast.

We were left to live alone in the jungle." Her look wandered from Boris to the translator and then to Rudolph who still stood there, erect like a soldier; an eternal soldier. Then she straightened her look into Boris eyes. Maybe because she had saved him or maybe because she felt that he was the authority. No one knew why she directed her speech to him from then on.

"We wandered in the jungle from that day on, trying to survive by ourselves. We were five children. One after another we got eaten by animals, bitten by snakes or died because of weakness. I believe that none of us wanted to live anymore. The last one, my best friend just died few days ago. She was sick for few days and I did not know how to help her. I tried to put cold leaves on her head, as I saw my mother doing but it did not seem to help. I think that maybe she been bitten by some insect and got sick. We went to sleep together at night and when I woke up in the morning I discovered that she had died in my arms while we were asleep. I buried her under a big pile of the flat leafs not that far from here." She lowered her eyes. "Since then I am alone."

Rudolph started to look bored. The translator looked shocked. Boris felt a strong pain inside himself. I am the one who caused all this to happen to her. I am the one who murdered her entire village, her parents, brother and sister and all the others. His soul felt tormented at a level that he never felt before. All of a sudden the excuses that he had typically used to himself did not seem to help.

She looked again at Boris. "When I saw you bitten by the snake I knew that you were going to die very quickly if the poison was not sucked out of your leg. I have seen my friends die from such bites. I have seen my father save my brother from the same kind of snake bite. I knew what to do."

As Boris struggled with the storm of emotions that flooded inside him, she added a sentenced that completely shook him. The fact that all of her words came from the translator added some strength to their meaning since when he looked at her, he could not understand a word.

"I saw that you were a good man." The paradox was so clear even to the translator that he had difficulties not showing his emotions but for Boris it was even clearer. "You are a good man."

"No, I am not." Boris had to respond in low voice. The translator translated his words back for the little girl.

She looked at him and could see his internal struggle. Somehow she could almost feel his internal emotions surfacing unexpectedly. She could feel his feelings floating and taking over. She watched his shaking lips, his face that got wrinkled in an effort to handle the realization, his eyes which uncontrollably filled with tears. She could watch his thoughts which tried to put some order to what he had been used to doing. Silently she witnessed his transformation into someone else. "Yes, you are a good man." She repeated. This time Boris did not have the power to respond. He was slowly accepting the true feelings that took him over. He breathed heavily and sweated all over his body.

The girl did not know why Boris claimed to be a bad man but she could feel the great burden that his soul suffered. By instinct she knew that what she was witnessing was a fight between good and evil. She was witnessing a person's very rare change.

She held Boris' hand. "That is why I decided to give my life to you."

Her words stopped Boris' thoughts. What she is talking about? Then he noticed something. Her lips were blue and slightly swelled. "What is happening?' he mumbled.

"This snake poison is very strong. If it is not washed from the mouth with lots of water immediately, it goes into the body through the mouth." She looked at him with calm eyes as she was still holding his hand. "I am going to die soon."

Boris' soul that was already completely shaken took another major hit with this knowledge as it was translated for him. "What?" it was hard for him to digest. "You gave your life for me?" A rage grew inside of him. His internal struggle turned into madness and extreme anger. "How could you do that?" he almost yelled at her. Then his voice changed into slow mumble, "I am not worth your life or anyone else's life . . ." He shook his head in great disbelief. She still insisted on holding his hand. All of a sudden he felt that she needed him. She tightened her grip as her lips started to shake. The snake's poison started to affect her nervous system. He sat and gently pulled her to him. He hugged her to him. She looked into his eyes and then cuddled in his arms. No one had loved her for long time.

Tears came into his eyes. "I killed your family. I am the one who killed your entire village." He told her. He had to tell her. He wanted to hear her response. He wanted her anger. He wanted her rage at him. He wanted her accusations, her blame, and even her curse. Instead she continued to hold him.

She looked at him and said calmly. "It was not you that did all of this."

"Yes, it was I who gave the order to destroy your village.", he insisted to her great disbelief.

"No, it was different person then." She held him in her both arms. He thought about this and the realization slowly enlightened him. He found the courage to look inside him. She was right, his conscious told him.

"You are a different human being now." The translator was rushing to paraphrase in order to convey the intensity of the epiphany.

Something hit him. Frantically he turned to the translator. "Do we have enough time to take her to a hospital?"

She could feel his desire to help her and slowly nodded. "No more time for me. The poison is already inside me." She looked at him. "Now it is your turn to be with me." He held her hand with both his. He knew that she had short time to live. He knew that she had chosen him to be with her in her last moments.

"Let's go back. You seem better." Rudolph suggested.

Boris felt a rage growing inside him. Then he remembered what type of person Rudolph was and he calmed down. He could take care of that business later. "Rudolph, this little girl saved my life sacrificing hers. I am going to be with her in her last moments. She seems to want me now." He tried to show his annoyance.

Rudolph raised one eyebrow. He was not used to this type of behavior from Boris. He figured that this was one of Boris' weak moments. The girl's lips turned even more blue and swelled so it was hard for her to talk. Her heart raced and she had difficulty breathing. She held onto Boris hand and he hugged her to his heart.

"I know what to expect. She whispered. "I've seen others die from this snake. I feel my body going numb. I like dying in the woods. I always liked the forest." She gave Boris a childish, innocent look. "Do not feel bad. I wanted to die. Without my family and friends there was no reason for me to live anyway." She reached with her shaky hand to his face and touched his cheek. He felt the warmth of her little hand and closed his eyes. It was hard for Boris to witness her suffer, the hardest thing in all his life. He opened his eyes and saw that she was giving him something. It was a piece of hair. She had reached into her little pocket and given him a small piece of hair. "It is my hair from when I was one year old. I always liked it so I stole it from my mother when we went into the woods that day. I wanted to give it back to her but she died. She never allowed me to play with it. I always liked it since it is so smooth and silky. It is yours now. You can feel its smoothness." Gently he took the little piece of hair from her. It was bright brown smooth piece of hair; a baby hair. He did not know what to say.

She looked into his eyes. "You are a good man. You are a different person. I know it." Those were her last words. Her body started to convulse. She held tighter to Boris' hand and buried her head in his chest. Boris closed his eyes and caressed her little head. He looked away so no one could see his tears. Within a few minutes her shaking slowed down but her hand still held his tightly.

Finally her body relaxed. A few seconds later her hand let go of Boris' hand. Her body became loose in his arms. He lay her on the ground and looked at her face. Her eyes were closed and she wore a calm expression on her face, like she was happy now. Boris gently caressed her sticky, filthy hair and arranged her body in a sleeping position.

"I do not even know her name." Boris mumbled. They stared at her for a while, each with his own thoughts. They covered her body with a big pile of those large leaves. Boris thought it would be the most appropriate burial for her. In the short time he knew her, he had learned that she really loved the woods. "Thank you young one, for saving my live." Boris said in a low voice. He could not think of anything. He did not recall their way back to the village.

When they arrived back at the village Armand asked him if he was satisfied with what he saw. Boris looked detached from reality. "Yes, yes, I am happy." He mumbled. He looked around him and saw the group of men and women who were preparing to go to the drug fields.

Then he looked at Armand who had a satisfied expression on his face and said, "We are maintaining this village with strong discipline and tight supervision. It works well; productive and loyal. No need to worry." He concluded.

"Yes, of course" Boris stood up "Thank you all for the presentation. I would like to leave now." They all looked at him in great surprise. This was not his normal behavior. Typically he concluded with some vulgar statement or a joke. He did not even ask for any young women like he normally did. This time he just announced his desire to be back home. Rudolph thought that this was probably due to the snake bite that he just experienced. He needed some rest. This was not the case. Boris could not find peace since he had come back from his trip. Something had changed inside him. After a few days he decided to take some time by himself. He flew to San Francisco and stayed at the top suite of a luxurious hotel from which he could see the ocean. He did not take anyone with him this time. There were no massage girls, no woman, no one. A change need to be made. He held the piece of hair that the little girl had given him just before she died.

"I built such a bad empire, an empire to make me millions. I created an empire that brings death and agony to many families but millions to me." He shook his head." How do I divert such a huge operation? How do I change its purpose? It will take time. It will take courage." All the guts he had used for many years to create crime he intended to divert to something else; something that he never thought he would do. He was well connected in the drug and crime world. He would have to find a way out. He'll have to find a way out and divert those multi-millions into good actions. He had many legal businesses he could use for donating funds. The more he thought about his plan the better he felt. He relaxed and allowed himself to enjoy the bright, warm sunshine. He would do good deeds. The little girl would not have died in vein. She would have been right. He was a good person now and he would prove it to her. That is how it was.

The next morning Armand received an order to clear the village. At the beginning he was confused by the instructions. He called to confirm and got his confirmation from Rudolph. The orders were clear. Clean the village of all drug operations. Destroy the underground plant. Burn the plants. Then use the village people to plant several types of vegetables. Rebuild the village. Make nicer homes for the people. Make the village self-sufficient within two weeks. Then leave it. Armand did not argue. Once he confirmed the authenticity of his orders he immediately moved into the execution phase. He figured that they needed to remove all evidence. Maybe Boris had gotten in trouble with the feds. He did not care much. As long as they get paid he did not care if they murdered or created heaven. As long as he got paid, he would do whatever Boris asked.

Boris closed all of his local drug activities. He got rid of his homes, cars and yachts. His colleagues assumed that he had been caught by the FBI or something similar. Others simply remained quiet. No-one questions when the largest drug cartel's owner goes under. At first the small drug dealers had difficulty providing drugs since Boris' operation used to supply almost the entire U.S. demand but they reduced their operations making less profit. After a while other drug dealers took over and with time they became the major drug suppliers in the continental US.

Boris moved to a distant country where he lived as a rich retiree. From there he conducted charitable activities for homeless children all over the world. Shortly thereafter, the entire North American region had completely forgotten Boris. It was like he had never been there.

*   *   *

Boris was standing on the balcony of his home in Rio De Janeiro, Brazil. It was a small house on top of a hill that faced the magnificent sea of Rio. From its location the entire city's scenery could be seen, including all the colorful neighborhoods and vivid colors of the local views. Just in front of his house an impressive statue called "Jesus the Redeemer" could be seen. The huge statue of Jesus that is considered the 5th largest Art Deco statue of Jesus in the world was just above his home opening it's his hands towards the small hill. On that sunny morning Boris looked at enormity of the Jesus statue. He had just completed his move and it was his first morning in his new home. He looked at the beautiful artwork as sun beams illuminated it gently with sparkle and shine, giving it a glorious look which nearly brought it to life. Boris was transfixed for a long while on the amazing vision as his soul rejoiced inside him. He had fulfilled his desire. He was a changed person. He quietly prayed for redemption. Not for nothing he chose his new place to live for the rest of his life. Standing in front of "Jesus the Redeemer" was something that he had wanted to do since he made his decision to change. He looked at the little plastic bag that he held in his hand. It was the little girl's hair, the little girl who had saved his life in the jungles of Columbia. Gently he took out the small piece of hair. The hair felt smooth and soft in his fingers. He closed his eyes and thought about that little girl whose name he did not even know. She had died to save him. He murdered her entire family and she saved him. She saved not only his life but his soul. Saving my soul is what I cherish the most. He thought.

He opened his eyes and prayed. He prayed for her, he prayed for her family who were murdered and he prayed for the entire village. So many people had died due to his commands. So many people had died directly on account of him. He would really have to earn his redemption if he were to be redeemed at all. He was ready. He was ready to dedicate the rest of his life to making up for his dark time. He was ready to give anything in order to help others. He had already established legal businesses in many countries in order to continue providing a constant income for his charities. He had already established a series of trust funds for children all around the world. From his home he would be involved in managing and ensuring that the money would be distributed where he had planned. As for himself, he would live the rest of his life in this small house in Rio. He would have a small car, a small home and a simple life. He did not need any conspicuous materialism in his life anymore. Every morning when he woke up he would pray for redemption. He hoped that his soul would be redeemed when the time came. All of a sudden he felt and heard something near him. The flap of small wings touched his shoulders. He opened his eyes and noticed a large, white dove standing on his shoulder. It was a magnificent bird. "It chooses to stand on me." He became happy. For many months he had not felt happiness. His soul was tormented by the realization of his past actions. He had a hard time sleeping and could not smile at all. This was the first time that a smile had come to him after so many dark months. This pure bird had chosen him. Was this a sign?

As he rejoiced in his thoughts, the pure white bird left his shoulder and hovered towards his hand. Like in slow motion he watched the bird grabbing the little girl's hair that lay in his hand. Like magic, the bird then stood on his hand with the hair in its beak. As he was speechless staring at the dove it flapped his long wings and flew away, taking the hair with it. Amazed, Boris watched her flying towards the Jesus statue like was approaching its open arms. To his astonishment the bird stood on one of its arms. It was a beautiful vision. It was a sign, no doubt. There was no other way. "I've been given a sign that what I have been doing is good." Boris smiled with tears in his eyes. Maybe, after many years of good deeds his soul would be forgiven. "I am sorry little one." his lips mumbled to the girl who saved him. "I hope you are with your family now."

The white dove looked at the large, blue sea below and gently flapped its wings. Then it dropped the hair that was in its beak. The silky hair spread out in thousands of individual small hairs and flew up in the light wind. The dove tilted its head and quietly observed the many hairs flying up in the sea breeze. The hair flew up, high into the skies above the giant statue that opened its arms towards them.

*   *   *

"Exception." the dark angel yawned. The light angel did not respond. Then he smiled quietly. The dark angel looked at him arrogantly. "Do not get your hopes up. There may be an actual physical explanation for this one. I suspect that his brain did not function properly. He was purely evil." He smiled widely. "There will be no more cases like this. Be sure."

"We'll see." the light angel took a thick piece of wood as a bright table was illuminated in the air. "Meanwhile, one check mark is mine." He marked the first check mark in the phosphorous table that glowed in the air.

A green lit check mark remained in the first column of the table and the dark angel looked at it in despise. "Enjoy your one and only check mark. There will be no others."

The light angel gave him a good look. "Good Prevails."

years. She saw something that used to scare her many years ago but not today. She saw something that she knew usually gets everything, the entire jackpot. People are typically disgusted by this characteristic but she was not. She learned to expect this feature to exist in humans. She even learned to take advantage of it. She put out her cigarette and observed Robert one more time. He simply sat there and smiled at her like he already knew her answer. She was not wrong. What she identified in him was pure, genuine evil.

She accepted his proposal and became Mrs. Boil.

Robert kept his promise. Within a short time he became connected with key figures in L.A. organized crime and made arrangements with them. They helped him get elected comptroller of the state tax department and he made sure that the right people would get tax breaks and even government subsidies for their businesses. The vast percentage of the budget which was supposed to be allocated toward noble purposes was significantly cut and the funds were redirected to less humane ones. Robert astutely navigated millions of tax dollars into the organized crime industry. Soon enough many other cartels and illegal businesses found their way to Robert and received pecuniary government benefits. Robert who held the highest position in the state treasury department used his position and talent to create artificial international deals and transactions for the benefit of those who secretly paid him many millions by way of deposits into a confidential account in the Cayman Islands. Robert was wise and careful and knew how to maintain the impression of a respectable government official yet had a bank account that would not have shamed an oil rich sheikh from Saudi Arabia.

His wife suspected that he was scheming on a large scale but as long as she had an unlimited credit card at, her disposal she was happy and quiet.

It seemed that everyone was very satisfied in the state treasury department especially big business owners, Robert and his wife.

*　　*　　*

In January Robert scheduled visits to a few metropolitan institutions for official reasons. The regulations required annual visits to hospitals and other publicly funded institutions in order to get feedback regarding their fiscal status and make budgetary assessments.

"This morning we will visit the metropolitan children's hospital.", announced Robert's secretary early one Monday.

Robert rolled his eyes quietly. He was not in the mood for a visit this morning. Actually, he was never in the mood to visit hospitals of any kind. It was more for the record as far as he was concerned but since he was the one who set the budget he knew that it was his duty.

"I'll be ready in fifteen minutes.", he said to his secretary and start collecting his papers. He never left any document on his desk when he was not going to be in the office. It was a precautionary measure that he had adopted over the years.

When he arrived at the hospital accompanied by his secretary, the manager welcomed them with an invitation to breakfast. They politely refused.

"We ate already on our way to here, thank you." Robert gave her one of his fake smiles.

"Okay", she responded, "then allow me to show you where we most need your help."

Robert nodded and gestured for her to lead the way.

She took them to the oncology department.

"Unfortunately we are worried about the increasing number of cancer cases in children.", the manager mentioned as she was leading them into the pediatric ward. "We have to put up to eight children in one room." They entered a room that looked dark. The window blinds were closed and the room stayed partially dark. As they entered they immediately noticed the large number of beds cluttering the small space. The beds were practically touching each other which left no room for visitors to interact with the children from the sides. The only access to the patients was through the end of the beds.

Medical instruments occupied the little space that was made behind each bed and the overall atmosphere was of a field or third world hospital.

The children were either sleeping or staring at them in gloomily. Robert stepped in without expression. He was already used to views like this. This was not his first trip to this hospital. There was a foul odor in the air.

"I apologize for the smell. We do not have the budget to hire more practical nurses to keep the children clean of feces so it is only done once per day." She pulled her shoulders "Obviously, it is not enough."

"Yes, it is an unpleasant situation." Robert mentioned, clearly losing his patience. "Where else you are going to take us?" He turned towards the manager with a demeaning look. "Make it quick, I have a busy schedule today."

The rest of the pediatric hospital was in worse condition but Robert was not moved. On their way out he put a fake smile on his face and promised the manager that he would definitely raise the hospital's grant this upcoming year. The manager was very happy to hear that. She seemed to forget the fact that every year she got this same promise from Robert.

"Fill out the hospital paperwork.", Robert mentioned to his secretary on their way to his car. "Put in the same budget as last year. I want it on my desk by tomorrow morning".

"But, Robert, you saw the condition they are in." The secretary was shocked to hear his decision. "Please review their situation before you make a rush decision. We have to help these kids."

"You heard me." Robert voice was cold as ice. He turned to her and gave her a chilling look. "I do not make a rush decisions but clear, logical ones. This hospital gets the same budget as last year, not a penny more."

He'd fix the report. He'd fix the numbers. The hospital was not important. His income was. The money had to be wired to the drug dealers with whom he was working. He knew all the necessary accounting wonders to make sure that the tax money of LA would be routed to the businesses under state treasury support programs. He was very good at this.

As for the sick children in the hospital, it was not his problem.

* * *

Robert was working quietly at his office on some funds transactions when his secretary knocked on the door. He looked through the glass door with obvious impatience. He did not like to be bothered while he was working on his duties. His specific instructions to his workers were not to bother him until his office door opened. Now, his secretary was knocking on the door and seemed to be quite upset.

"What?" the tone of his voice was cold as ice.

"Sorry to bother you but there is a situation that requires urgent response from you." She opened the door and apologized immediately.

He simply looked at her.

"The I.N.S. called us just now. They caught a large group of women smuggled on a container ship from Nigeria. The women tried to sneak into the country and find jobs as illegal workers. Since they lived inside a container for several weeks they are in bad medical condition."

Robert did not look impressed.

"The city of L.A. has a law requiring the coverage of their expenses. They asked us to pay immediately." She breathed heavily.

He took off his glasses and slowly cleaned the lenses with a dry cloth.

"The expenses are for their medical care, lodging and then teaching them English. Later they will be able to work legally in the U.S. An organization that is called 'Help for the illegal' is offering these services in order to help such women."

There was still, no response from Robert.

"Otherwise these women will be returned to their country and will be abused, used for the worse prostitution conditions or murdered. They have no mercy there."

Robert nodded. "How much?" His eyes sparkled without emotion.

"It should be really not too much for the city of L.A. They are asking for a couple million dollars." His secretary knew him and hoped that he will be in a good mood today and would approve this grant. She felt emotional about this group of women. She had heard horrific stories about the fate of women from Nigeria and hoped to help them.

Robert looked thoroughly at his secretary.

"She is an emotional, dumb and has no idea what a major profit potential this event can have".

"Sorry, as much as I would like to help, we simply do not have the budget for these types of things this year." He shook his head almost enjoying seeing his secretary's reaction. "You know very well that we are on a tight budget for dealing with illegal immigration."

"I know, but this is really a special case." She practically begged him. "You know what the fate of these poor women will be. We have to help them."

He squeezed his lips. "Sorry."

Her face showed anger now. She knew that he could help if only he just wanted. She had watched his actions for many months now. She knew that he was helping organized crime in hidden ways that no one could prove. He was probably the best accounting con artist of the modern world. Today she was on edge.

"Why you have to be such cruel?" Her face wrinkled in growing anger.

"This will be fun to watch", he thought. He watched her expressionless.

"I know very well that you can help if you only want to do so. The lives of many innocent women are at stake. You are condemning them to death or life in hell if you do not give the right order."

She was really upset this time He thought. "I wonder where she'll go from here".

"I am asking you to help them. Please . . ." She had tears in her eyes.

"My hands are tied. Sorry."

She was quiet for a few seconds before reacting to his comment. "I wish that your life would be at stake one day." She spit her poisoned words almost with hatred. "Then I hope that you'll feel what life is all about. It is not about money and material stuff. It is not about having everything and living carefree. It is not about superficiality. It is about helping others. It is about having mercy and consideration. Eventually it will bounce back to you. There is something called karma. What you bring to nature, nature brings back to you."

She was about to leave his office when he finally said something.

"I cannot help these women but I know someone who can."

She stopped and looked backward.

He cleaned his glasses again. "What are the ages of these women?"

"Early twenties. They are young and are suited to any type of labor. Why?"

"Well, I have a friend who deals with providing work for illegal immigrants. He treats them fairly and even provides them with benefits like medical and dental plans."

She looked at him and did not know whether to believe his words or not.

"He successfully created happy U.S. citizens out of many illegal immigrants who worked in his organization. I can give him a call. It will be much better then what you are talking about." All of a sudden he looked like a righteous person who sought the well being of others.

She had difficulty believing him. "And why you would do that? Why would you help these women?"

"For no particular reason." he answered honestly.

"As a matter of fact, I can take a break and talk with my friend now."

She hesitated. "Thanks . . ." She thought maybe she had been too harsh judging him. "Sorry for my . . ."

"Just forget about it." He signed with his hand. "I'll let you know what he says."

He did not wait long to make the call.

* * *

"Marcelo, I found you a good labor package." Robert talked slowly as he stresses his words. He wanted to make an impression.

"What do you have?" Marcelo talked without patience. He never had patience for long talks on the phone. He had a large network of prostitutes in the L.A. metro area and was always on the watch to enlarge his supply of woman workers. More workers meant more income for him.

"I have a large group of Nigerian women, fresh and young, just arrived."

"Young?" Marcelo spit his tobacco.

"In their early twenties." Robert talked to the point. "They are looking for someone to take charge of them. You can do it through your charity organization. I will recommend and even fund the beginning. You'll get them some medical attention and then they are all yours, ready to work." He could almost hear Marcelo's dollar sign sound. Marcelo was already calculating his profits.

"What do you want for this?" He cut straight to the business.

"The usual, fifty percent of the profit, monthly." Robert did not even blink. He had his answer ready. "What you are going to do with these women?"

"It will be the usual traffic in women. Some I'll use locally for work and others I'll sell. The most beautiful and young ones will be worth quite a bit."

"That's what I thought." Robert smiled as he thought about the additional fat income that would come his way. "I'll contact I.N.S. tomorrow and arrange all that is necessary."

"I should wire your bonus to the current account in the Caymans?"

"Please." Robert was polite as always.

"Consider it done." Marcelo hung up.

Robert looked at his office door for few minutes. He thought he handled it well. Soon enough his account in the Cayman Island would be enriched by a few more million far away from any official eyes. Practically he already had enough money to retire and live well for the rest of his life but he was not ready for retirement yet. There were still many more opportunities to make money. Through the glass of his door he saw his secretary passing by and a thought crossed his mind.

He called her on the intercom. "Please come to my office. I have good news" he smiled at her as she entered his office. "You will not think that I am a mean guy after all."

She raised an eyebrow.

"My friend is going to take care of these women refugees. Tomorrow I'll give him all the details about them. He'll provide them medical attention and job training, eventually making them proper U.S. citizens."

"Really?" She was surprised for the good.

"Absolutely." He replied and put on his happy smile.

"Well, this is good news." She smiled back at him. "I am proud of you." She paused and then added "for a change."

"Oh, I am not that bad" he pretended to be offended. "I just have to obey the state laws."

"Aha . . ." she teased him. Although she hated his guts she was infatuated with his personality; his slick moves, his ice cold logic when it came to make financial decisions and his way of dealing with the job's pressure. She did not know what he was really doing but was impressed with the way he ran operations in his office. Although they did not show any affection in public everyone in the office knew that they had more than just a working relationship. All the signs showed it. The fact that he was married and she had a long term boyfriend did not stop them from liking each other.

He threw his head backwards and gave her a meaningful look. "I believe I deserve some gratitude for my kindness in this case, what do you think?"

She closed the door behind her and pulled the blinds. "I can think of something." She gave him a naughty smile and approached him. She wore a short miniskirt that exposed long, provocative legs, exactly the way he liked it.

He had just returned from having lunch at home with his wife. They had also had sex on this occasion. Now he looked at his secretary getting close to him, taking her clothes off. A satisfied smile spread across his face.

"If she knew what help I am providing for these women . . . but then again, she is just a dumb broad. Now I am going to get rewarded for this help. Well, I already had lunch but there is always a room for desert."

*   *   *

"So what evil things did you do today darling?" Margaret teased her husband when he arrived home from work that evening.

Robert put his coat on the rack and sat near her on the couch in their gothic style living room. The living room was exotically decorated. Many wood sculptures were placed around the room. A large mahogany table occupied one side of it and a large, dark wood library stood on the other side of the room. Thick carpet covered the floor and there was a warm flame glowing in the red brick fireplace that gave the entire room an antique look. Margaret created a fancy, warm environment in their home, sparing no expense but he did not care. Her expenses were minor. He had plenty of money and gave her a free hand to do whatever she wanted.

She looked deeply into his eyes and knew that he was very satisfied with his daily work today. She already knew him and was sure that he succeeded in one of his scams. Although he never specifically told her about his deals he gave her all the necessary hints to understand that they had enough money for the rest of their lives. She knew that he had no mercy and that typically in each of his scam operations someone else had to suffer. She accepted the fact that she had made a covenant with a very bad person. He looked like a professional official but his actions were far from being good.

"I did my share for the day my beloved wife." he teased her back with a smile.

She looked at his ice cold eyes and felt that another evil deed had been performed. She released a long sigh. She knew that she would never be able to stop him from committing his smooth, well covered and planned frauds. She also knew that someone would have to pay for his actions one day. Someone would have to go to hell due to his evil actions and there was nothing that she could do about it.

"I am sure you did darling," she mumbled "I am sure you did."

*   *   *

A few days later Robert's cellular phone rang just when he was in the restroom.

"Bob, did I catch you in a bad time?"

Robert recognized his personal friend Martin. Martin had a wide variety of real estate properties and hotels throughout the city of L.A. His properties and hotels were located in key areas in the metro area and that was mainly due to Robert's assistance. Whenever Martin had the budget and urge to open a new attraction in the city he always contacted Robert for assistance. Robert made sure to assist Martin using all of his powers to ensure the utmost benefits for the new property. In exchange Martin rewarded Robert with fat bonuses directly from his profit. Both sides benefited.

"Actually you did. I am in the restroom going on number two. Is it urgent?" Robert answered with dry tone.

"Yes," martin answered bluntly. "I would like to meet you to talk with you about a great idea I have."

"Where and when?" Robert could always find the time for Martin because he knew that it probably meant money, lots of money.

"Today, early afternoon at the Sea Gardens retirement home."

"Why there?" Robert wondered. He knew the place very well. It was a beautiful retirement property on one of the most beautiful beaches in L.A. The city supported it with large grants in order to maintain it. The retirement home was populated by terminally ill people. Everyone knew that it was the most beautiful place to end one's life. Old people in terminal condition had to be put on a long waiting list to be accepted for residency there. Many of them did not make it but those who did enjoyed a magnificent sea view living for the rest of their lives. The property was on a long beach with full access to clean, white sand dunes in front of it.

"Just be there at one, I'll explain when we'll meet."

Robert arrived around noon. He parked his car in front of the large complex of apartments that belonged to the retirement complex. To its right he could see a long beach that was maintained daily for the benefit of the old people who enjoyed it. He decided to enjoy a walk on the beach until Martin arrived. He walked down the narrow path to the beach took his shoes off and walked slowly along the calm sea. The water was ice cold year around but it did not bother Robert. After walking for a while in the cold sea water he walked on the warm sand and sunk his feet deep into the white sand. He gulped the fresh sea air into his lungs and enjoyed his walk on this sunny day. Here and there he could see old people walking slowly or simply sitting on small beach chairs, enjoying the sunny day on the beach."

It is enchanted place to end one's life", he thought as he approached a beach umbrella with a few chairs underneath it. There were many scattered around the beach for the convenience of the elderly residents. He thought to relax for a while and noticed an old women sitting under the umbrella.

"May I sit here?" he politely asked the old woman.

"Of Course young man, be my guest." The old lady pointed to the chair near hers and smiled to him.

He sat near her and observed her. She looked very old. Her face was covered with age blemishes, and grooved by long, deep wrinkles. The white hair on her head was seriously thinning and not much was left. Her lips were narrow and looked like they had gotten so dry due to many days in the desert. Her eyes were the feature that was the most dominant. In a complete contradiction to her old appearance her eyes were full of life. They had a vivid blue color like the ocean and had a constant spark of joy in them. Her eyes gave the tone of her entire personality.

"So, are you visiting here someone?" she started with a smile.

"Oh, no I am just waiting to meet someone here." Robert wondered if he had made a bad decision when he sat near her.

"It is a lovely day." She beamed at him. "You picked a good day to meet here."

"Indeed." Robert gave her a brief look and then watched the calm ocean.

The old women sat still for a while but could not hold back her desire to talk with someone.

"I live here for almost a year and I must say that this is probably the most beautiful retirement home in the United States."

She continued without waiting for Robert's response. "Every day I spend many hours on the beach." She gave him a toothless smile. "The beach is just outside of my little apartment."

"That's nice"

"This place really enhances people's desire to live." She continued, happy that she found someone to talk to. "I have lung cancer, stage four. The doctors gave me few months to live."

Robert observed her silently.

"That was more than a year ago. Since I am here, my desire to live has overcome my illness. The beautiful beach that lies in front of me every day, the large white, beautiful seagulls that fly outside my window and the fresh sea air that makes me fall into a good night sleep, strengthen my desire to live longer. I want to have more of this. I want to live longer so I can enjoy this nature."

She paused for a while.

"There it is. Against all predictions, I am already living almost a year beyond what was predicted." Her eyes looked straight into Robert's eyes and wandered into his soul for a moment. "This place is a heaven for us; the terminal ill. To the majority of us it is an extension of life and for the others it is the best place in the world to end our lives."

Robert nodded silently. "It is amazing to hear that."

She shook her head silently and looked into the blue ocean. "Yes, this place is given to us from heaven." Then she looked at him.

Robert smiled at her but his eyes remained ice cold. She looked into his soul and for a second felt something. She always said what she thought or felt. She had always been a blunt type of a person and so she approached Robert with her sudden thought.

"But you do not really care about all this, do you?" Her eyes penetrated his all the way inside his soul.

He was surprised by her words and could not say anything. The fact that she was also right caused him to remain silent.

"Yes, that's what I thought." she mumbled. "What do you do for a living, may I ask?"

"I am comptroller of the L.A. treasury." He said in a low tone.

"Some sort of high accountant I presume."

"Something like that." He answered.

"But with power." She added seriously.

"Yes," Robert confirmed.

"So you are probably doing a lot of bad things as the chief accountant." The old woman said bluntly.

Robert was surprised to hear her judgment about him. "She is an old, senile old woman but has good senses", he thought.

"Sometimes I do." He spoke the truth.

She silently shook her head. "Well, you know we all do some evil at some point in our lives." Then she smiled to him "but we always have the opportunity to turn to the good side. Even if you did some bad stuff before, do not forget, you can always turn to the good. It is never too late to change your ways."

"Yes, well thank you for your inspiring words." Robert looked at his watch. It was almost one and he needed to meet Martin. "It was nice talking with you."

Suddenly she grabbed his hand and looked deep into his eyes. "You have goodness inside you, I can see it. You have to let the good in you come out." Then she released his arm and sat back in her chair. "You are a good man, do not forget that."

He looked at her for a split second and then straightened his pants and shirt, preparing to leave. "Have a good day Madam."

"Lady, you got your character judgment wrong." he mumbled as he started to walk towards the beach entrance. "What a crazy old woman."

He met Martin on time.

Martin was a short guy, skinny and always dressed meticulously. He always wore the most expensive clothing available to work and in his private life. His family came from France and he was raised with high standard of living. His father owned a respectable printing business and worked hard to provide the family with a comfortable life style. Martin and his brother attended good colleges and were raised on the principle of hard work. Although their father always preached decency and honesty the two brothers choose different paths as they grew up. Martin's brother became a famous doctor, opened his own clinic and became wealthy on his professional skills. Martin, on the other hand, became involved in the real estate arena and did not hesitate to go over the edge of honesty in order to do business. He was not as ethical as his brother and had no problem bribing, stepping on the weak or cheating. He quickly created an empire of business towers and fancy hotels in the L.A. metro area. From his point of view all means were justified to achieve a profitable target.

"Let's walk on the beach" Martin proposed and they started to go towards the south side of the beach. "Look around you, beautiful beach isn't it?"

"Yes,"

"Do you know that this property is sitting on almost two hundred acres, right here in front of the ocean?" Martin tried to impress him.

"It is a large property. No, I did not know that." Robert wondered where he was going.

"Guess what?" Martin stopped and looked at Robert like he was telling him a secret. "I have checked into the possibility of building a big hotel here, the biggest in L.A. Not only this, I want to build an entire resort here. Just think about it. A complete resort on the ocean. Great weather, fancy pools, restaurants, a small theme park and even an outdoor shopping center. This area can become the most popular resort and hotel on the west coast."

Robert looked at him puzzled. "Martin, this is a retirement home. How do you plan to build all that on this property?"

"That's exactly my point. What a waste of excellent commercial area don't you think?" Martin had a huge grin on his face.

"Here is my plan." He became serious. "You help me initiate relocation of the retirement home to another place and I get control on this area. You help me with everything and you can ten percent of the entire resort profit annually."

"Twenty five" Robert said without a blink.

"Now, don't rip me off buddy," Martin tried to reduce Robert's offer.

"I'll have to justify transplantation of the retirement home to another site. It is a long, tedious procedure including convincing or forcing many resisting organizations. Then I'll need to approve this area for private entrepreneurship and ensure that you get the bid." Robert already calculated everything in his head throughout the conversation. "Twenty Five percent or no deal. You'll never make it without me."

Martin stopped and looked at the old people who were walking on the beach without knowing what was heading their way. "Were do you plan to move these old people?"

Robert smiled. "I already have the exact place in mind."

*   *   *

Robert knew all the bureaucratic ways to execute their plan. He used his connections at governmental offices all around the city in order to assemble the puzzle to perfection. After few months everything was ready. There was serious resistance to execution of this plan from many organizations but Robert knew how take care of them in a way that left no room for argument or public activity. The media attacked the so called city plan with all of its might, showing images of sick elderly who lived in the retirement home. National T.V. channels interviewed many residents who cried in front of the entire country to cancel the decision to move their home. Robert knew how to take care of all these activities in a diplomatic manner. He made sure that the government officials would publish governmental support for these poor people. "We will do everything in our powers to prevent this act", they announced on T.V. and the country rejoiced. "We will protect our elderly and ensure a safe harbor for them", other officials promised the public, and the country cheered to hear that justice won. What they did not know was that this was Robert's way of silencing the resistance. As the country slowly forgot about the issue, he quietly moved forward in its execution. The new location for the retirement home was chosen. Unfortunately, it was in a very poor part of the city but for Robert it did not matter. They are sick old people and do not have long life expectations. He and Martin would make many millions of dollars and that was what all was about. No one really noticed when the Sea Garden retirement home closed down and moved into a poor area in downtown L.A., no one besides the old people who lived there.

It was Friday afternoon when Robert prepared to leave his office and go home for the weekend. He shut down his computer and looked outside his wide office window, observing the busy skyline of the large city. He had just checked his bank account in Cayman Island and was extremely satisfied. He was about to pass the hundred million dollar value. He could afford to retire at any time and live comfortably for the rest of his life. He predicted that in the next two years he would double this amount. He did well.

The phone rang. On the phone there was a woman from the retirement home, Sea Gardens. She claimed that someone there would like to see him as soon as possible. He could not recall knowing anyone there but decided to visit the place before going home.

When he arrived at the site he could not believe his eyes. He well remembered the previous location in front of the beach. The new location was completely depressing. The new home was now situated downtown between old buildings, among sex shops and drug dealing cafes. An old and deteriorating building was assigned as the new residence and its old apartments became the residents' rooms. There was filth and dirt everywhere. A small area in the back of the large building was prepared as a back yard and a small lawn was planted in it. A few old beach chairs were in it but no-one used them. After all, who likes to spend outdoor time in a filthy place where car smog and street dust permeate the air? He knew that the new place was old and poor but did not imagine that it would be that bad.

When he entered the building the receptionist welcomed him and took him to see an old woman.

"She is very sick and will probably die during the next week or so. When she was in the other site she was full of life but since we, moved here her health deteriorated rapidly. She requested to see you before she dies."

"I do not recall knowing anyone here." Robert still tried to remember whom he knew who resided here.

The receptionist led him into the woman's room. She lay on her bed and looked very pale. Her face expressed lifeless despair. Silently he stood for few minutes near her bed. She looked somewhat familiar but he could not remember where he'd seen her.

"Miss Brock, the man that you asked to see is here." The receptionist gently mentioned to the old woman.

She moved slightly and looked at Robert. "Yes, thank you.", she said slowly.

Robert felt his heart skip a beat. All of a sudden he recognized her. Her eyes reminded him who she was. This was the old woman he had met on the beach just before he met his friend Martin. This was the woman who sat under the beach umbrella. She looked ten times older now. Her eyes that had expressed vital life then were now dim and lifeless. Her entire expression was of despair.

"I am just an old woman and do not know much." she started all of a sudden. "But I saw you on TV. I met you then, on the beach. Even then I had a bad feeling that something unpleasant was about to happen after I saw you. I just kept telling myself that it was purely my imagination but apparently I was right."

Robert simply looked at her without saying anything. The receptionist left the room.

"I know that you were somehow connected to the fact that we lost our beach home and moved here to this horrific place." She talked very calmly but her eyes told him everything. Somehow this woman knew everything. Her senses were amazingly accurate. Of course, she would not be able to do any harm to him but her words were what hurt him. Every one of her words hit him like another arrow in the heart.

"I had a passion to live while we were living on the beach. I lost it all here. I am sure that you can see why. There, I used to be outside, on the beach at any free moment I had but here I sit at my small, filthy room all day long. I have no desire to be out in that little yard they made us. Here, I do not have the desire to breathe the black car smog and listen to the street sounds. This is not a place to live but a place to die and I know deep in my heart that you have something to do with this."

She paused due to a long cough then continued when it stopped. "Now please forgive me if I am completely wrong and you have nothing to do with the fact that we are all here, in this city dump." She looked at him for a while. "Can you tell me that you have nothing to do with this?"

Robert did not answer.

She looked at him for a while and shook her head. "That was what I thought." She continued. "I just wanted to tell you something before I die. For me it is already too late. I am not going to be here soon enough, thanks to you. I do not know why you did this. I can assume that it is probably because of money or profit of some sort. You probably got lots of money from our old home. I understand this. You are young and rootless when it comes to money and business. I met many people like you when I was young. But I wanted to ask you one thing before I die. Look into your heart. Really put everything aside and observe your soul inside. You will see what I see, I am sure. Down inside you have good, you just ignored it for so many years so it became almost obsolete. You are able to see what has been done here. You are able to see what this place does to its residence. You are capable of seeing that this place, here, in this location means death to every resident. As our old home meant life this place means death and this is a very wrong thing to do to us. There is one basic law in nature. This is the law of cosmic equilibrium. Some call it karma, some, nature or justice. What you are doing to others eventually will come back to hit you."

Robert moved in discomfort but still did not say a word.

"I see it in you. You can make the change inside you." She reached and held his hand. He looked at her old, wrinkly hand that held his now. "All you have to do is want." She gave him a final look and then lay back in her back. It seems like her words cost her great efforts.

"That's all what I wanted to say to you." She concluded. She looked very tired.

He looked at her face for a while knowing that she was right with every word she said. Then he turned to leave the room.

"Thank you for coming." She said with low tone.

Silently he left her room.

One week later he received a phone call from the receptionist. She informed him that the old woman died. She donated all of her little belonging but wanted to give him a small bag with sea shells. In a little note that she asked to be given to him with the sea shells, she described how she collected this bag of shells during a period of one year. These shells are for you, she wrote in the note, to keep and to enjoy. Remember, she added in the note, we are like the shells in a way, we keep our secrets inside us but our heart knows it all and we cannot lie to it. Sooner or later you will face your life conflict with yourself. You have to let the good in you to win. You have to believe in your true self. This is the only way that you can win over evil. Whenever you need some spiritual aid, I'll be with you.

He threw away her note but kept some of the pretty shells on his desk at his office. He simply loved their shapes or at least this was the explanation that he gave to himself.

*   *   *

Robert and his wife Margaret were about to embark in a special vacation. They were going to visit the majestic glaciers in Alaska. This was their annual summer adventure. As peculiar as it sounds Robert and Margaret had a wild side to them. They both liked exotic trips. They had already visited the jungles of the Amazon River, the deep forests in Thailand and this year they wanted to try dangerous glaciers in Alaska. They found a company that found large, tall glaciers in Alaska. They would be flown to the top of the glacier by a helicopter and would have to make their way down. They would be taken with full survival gear to the glacial peak. Some people chose to do this by themselves and others with partners. They went with a group of ten people who were to be spread over a few huge glaciers via the company helicopter. They were fully equipped with communication devices in case of emergency. The company's representatives would be waiting for them at a certain location where all the teams were to meet when they reached the bottom. The estimated time to complete the challenge was about one day. The pleasure, of course, cost a bundle but for Robert and Margaret that did not play any role in their decision. Typically their relationship was semi business oriented but with the years they found some common interests.

"It looks exciting." said Margaret as she was looking outside the helicopter window. The whole white image was spectacular.

Robert did not answer. He was focused on the endless iceberg view.

"This is going to be fun." She mumbled as the helicopter flew above gigantic glaciers and icebergs.

They were flown to their private glacier which had been picked especially for them.

"We would like to have a challenging mission", they announced to the company's representative when they ordered the trip. "We want it to be highly risky".

The company made sure to select of the largest glaciers in the desired territory. It was a huge iceberg that was located between many needle shaped icy poles that rose towards the skies like high towers. The iceberg itself rose to a height of at least one kilometer and had a flat peak. They already reviewed the map and the topographic details of their iceberg. The iceberg along with all other very high ice poles was located on an enormous glacier that slowly melted during the past few years. Still the glacier was one of the area's wonders and attracted many organized groups that came to see the wonder of many high poles that rose towards the skies like long fingers.

From their flight path Robert and Margaret could clearly view the icy, thin poles rising towards the skies. Some of them were extremely high and they wondered how they could be created.

"It must be the very low temperature and the unique seismic conditions of this region that created this sea of ice poles." Robert mentioned.

"Simply amazing to view." Margaret responded.

The helicopter made a sharp turn and headed towards the iceberg's peak. They felt the shake of the aircraft as it started to climb upwards towards the high pinnacle in the distance.

"Going up." Robert smiled. He felt the excitement slowly penetrating him. He liked this type of adventure.

All of a sudden, the helicopter trembled dramatically and then dropped sharply. After few seconds the aircraft stabilized and continued.

"What was that?" Robert screamed at the pilots. The Bell UH-1N Twin Huey helicopter was operated by two pilots who seemed to be very busy now with some problems. Robert and Margaret all of a sudden could hear all kind of buzzers from the cockpit as they noticed the pilots trying to control the aircraft. The helicopter engines started to make loud metallic cracking noises and they figured that something was wrong.

"We have some trouble with the engines." one of the pilots quickly turned towards them. "Hang on. We will try to land somewhere."

The helicopter then jolted sharply to the left and they could hear breaking noises and the engines seemed to stop their typical sound. The helicopter became steady for a second and Robert thought that it was actually a bad sign of what was coming.

"We lost the engine; I'll have to land somewhere using auto-rotation method." One of the pilots turned his head. They could hear the squeaking noise of the rotor that was still moving due to its kinetic energy.

The diminishing sound of the jet engine scared Margaret and she hugged Robert tightly.

He looked at her closely. They never had real love relationship and had not hugged each other for years. As a matter of fact they never hugged. He tended to see their connection as almost strictly business. She got everything she wanted and he could get all of his sexual whims fulfilled whenever he wanted. They rarely hugged or showed any type of affection besides at official parties or similar events. Now she was hugging him closely in fear.

Years of being together connect people, even if they are together due to a business relationship, he thought for a second. Then again, people develop feelings towards pets also. It is only natural. Then the aircraft hit one of the icy poles and the door near him broke. Freezing air burst into the helicopter and they held their belts. The helicopter completely lost control and started to spin. The pilots struggled with the aircraft controls as Robert and Margaret tried to remain inside it as it started to descend.

Margaret screamed as the out of control aircraft turned its nose down and fell while the rotor blades were still moving at high speed.

"This is it", Robert thought calmly. He was actually amazed that in such a moment he did not panic. He was in complete control and thought clearly. Margaret screamed in panic and he ignored her. He had to assess their situation. He looked though the big opening that was created due to the fact that they lost their door and could see that they were still at a very high altitude. As the aircraft increased the speed of its descent Robert analyzed their situation. It will fall faster and definitely crash into the ice killing all of us. Robert's brains worked faster as always at crucial moments. He was an analytical, calm, and purely logical person. He looked through the door opening and could see that they were approaching one of the ice poles. They would reach it within a few seconds. It was one of the short poles. Still its height was probably more than five hundred feet. At least they would be able to get out of the falling helicopter. If they were to stay in the helicopter they would surely die. No one would survive the crash. He blinked and then reached a decision. Now he needed to execute it.

"Margaret," he talked calmly but with loud voice, straight into her ear. "We are going to jump out of the helicopter when I tell you. We will jump out on top of one of those ice poles. You will have to grab to the top of the ice only, not onto me. I will also grab the ice pole. This is our only chance. If we stay in the helicopter we'll die. I have no doubt about it. Do you understand me?"

Margaret stared at him in panic and he could see that she is not coherent. She was in complete panic. He grabbed her hand and squeezed it hard so the pain would bring her out of her panic mode. Then she looked at him and he could tell that she was back in control.

"We are going to jump when I say."

She looked at him with realization that this may be their only chance to survive. His ice cold, blue eyes told her that he might just have the best plan to get them out of this trouble. She knew him and his logical ability to reach the best conclusion. She nodded without a word.

He turned to the window and saw the field of ice poles approaching quickly as the helicopter continued to fall. They quickly approached one of them.

"When I say now, we jump."

The aircraft started to spin slightly and he was not sure if they would get close enough to the pole but he knew that this was their only chance. The helicopter's blades shuddered and flew away. The aircraft now lost all chance of landing and nose dove down. Robert waited for the right time, grabbed Margaret's arm and screamed to her, "Now!" She obeyed blindly.

They jumped out of the falling helicopter just about a dozen feet from the ice pole that pointed towards the skies. They smashed into the flat surface of the pole with great power. Margaret instinctively held the surface with her both hands as Robert was sliding off. He stuck his fingers into the ice and managed to stop his sliding just before his body lost contact with the pole. They both held onto the ice with all of their power as they watched the smoking helicopter fall all the way to the bottom. The aircraft then hit the ice and burst into flames.

They both lay there, breathing heavily.

"We were lucky" said Robert after a while. "If the helicopter had hit the pole, we would be dead now." He peeked down. "I estimate the height of this pole is at least two hundred feet."

Margaret shook and still tried to relax from the jump. They pulled themselves near each other and lay at the center of the pole.

"What we are going to do now?" She asked, shivering.

He took a deep breath "Now we wait. I am sure that the pilots transmitted to the base that they were making a crash landing. There will be a rescue team soon." He was logical, as always.

"It took us about two hours to reach here. I am not sure that they'll find us." Margaret was skeptic. "We will not be able to survive for long time here, on the pole."

He looked at her and smiled ironically. "Then I guess we have some real quality time to spend here."

"Yah, right." she mumbled and turned her face away from him.

They both looked down at the smoking helicopter's remains.

"It does not look like anyone survived."

"I did not think so." Robert said with dry tone.

He looked around and down. "I hope you don't have fear of heights."

She did not answer. She was scared, cold and felt hopeless.

They laid there for a while without saying anything.

"The worst is happening," Robert said after a while. "Just as I thought but was not sure. Our weight is slowly disintegrating the ice that we are laying on. Our body heat is weakening the pole's structure." He looked at the skies. "I sure hope that the rescue team will be here shortly."

Margaret gave him a frightened look and cried quietly.

Robert ran all kinds of scenarios through his mind. They were about to die, he thought. Believe it or not, the time was getting closer. He had never thought that he would die in such a way; falling from an ice pole in Alaska."

Small pieces of the ice broke on Margaret's side and fell down. She scooted closer to Robert in fear. "The ice is breaking.", she mumbled quietly. She looked at him with realization. "We are about to die."

Robert searched the cloudy skies. "We need a rescue team."

Margaret released another scream to the air "More ice is chipped off the pole underneath me."

Indeed more ice broke and they squeezed together, lying on the pole.

We do not have much time before the whole pole will collapse." She said with a dry tone. She seemed to accept her fate. "This is it Robert."

She looked at him. "We are going to end our lives together. Now that is something I never imagined would happened to me."

He looked at her silently.

"We were not exactly a loving couple, were we Robert?"

"No, we were not"

More pieces of ice fell, this time on his side and he squeezed towards her.

Margaret looked down. "I never imagined dying like this Robert." She looked at him "I never imagined dying with you."

He nodded quietly.

"Ha," she laughed ironically. "I have a little confession to make. You know Robert although our marriage was not what you call, marriage of love, I developed feelings towards you over the years."

She extended her shaky hand and touched his face. "I woke up with you every day. I went to sleep with you at night. We went on vacations and we spent quite some time together. I prepared your clothes in the morning and cooked you breakfast. I was functioning as a loving wife, wasn't I Robert?

"Yes, you were Margaret."

She silently looked at him for a while.

"You know, Robert, I believe that I do love you." She said softly.

She released another short scream when large part of the ice broke underneath her and fell. She had to climb on top of his legs in order to stay on the remains of the pole.

Robert smiled "You really love me Margaret?"

"Yes, I do Robert. Beside your quirks and business approach to life, we like the same things, enjoy doing many things together and come to think about it, had a fun life." She paused "Yes, I do not agree with your heartless business decisions. I do not approve that you are willing to sell your own mother for money, but this is between you and the lord. You will have to explain your actions later. As for me, I love you Robert."

"Only a prostitute can love me." He mentioned quietly. "No one else would."

He was still for a while observing their condition. "I believe that the pole will not hold both our bodies' weight for much longer Margaret."

They both looked down.

He removed his glasses. "I have an idea."

"If one of us will not be on the pole, the other one probably will be able to stay safely until the rescue team arrives. The pole can safely hold only one person."

She continued looking at him, grasping the meaning.

"I am truly sorry if I hurt you during our life together." Robert held her hand. "I now realize. You became part of me, unconsciously. I guess I never thought that someone would be able to love me so I bought everything, including your love, or at least that's what I tried to do." He looked straight into her eyes. "I love you Margaret. I am sorry to leave you but I really think that you are the one who should live between the two of us. You will be able to lay here until the rescue team arrives."

She could not talk for a while. Here was Robert, the husband who paid her to marry him. The man who made sure that she had everything she wanted as long she provided him with anything that he wanted. This man was now declaring his love to her. Furthermore, he was willing to give up his life for her.

"No Robert." She smiled faintly and squeezed his hand. "Thank you for your love and willingness to let me live but I do not accept it."

He looked at her puzzled.

"I grew up with a mother who was a prostitute all her life. I was raised that way from the age of fourteen." She looked at the ice around her. "When I reached the age of sixteen I already had enough to buy a house and a fancy sports car. But all this took a toll on my soul. I always felt like the scum of the earth. I was willing to do whatever they asked me to do. Anything goes for the right price. Mentally I ignored everything. It was just a body, a tool to survive and a means to make money, nothing else. But my soul inside felt dirty, my soul inside felt worthless. There was no meaning to my inner self. I was expendable. I felt like this throughout my life Robert. You, on the other hand, did horrible things. I watched you take money from children's institutions and re-route it to criminals. I watched you cut budgets from senior citizens and give it to drug cartels. You did very bad things. No, your hands did not get dirty with blood like murderers but you are responsible for the death and suffering of many children and older people, even if it is indirectly. It happened on account of your heartlessness, greed and desire for fortune."

He listened silently. *She was right in every word.*

"I am not the one to be spared here." She looked straight into his eyes. "You should. You know why? Because you have the power to fix things. You have the power to make things better. Only you know the way to revert money back to the right channels. Only you know how to work the system so this time the poor children and the poor elderly will get relief. I am ready to die anyway. My soul is striving for light." She smiled faintly "You brought me some light over the past few years." Then she became serious again. "As a matter of fact you brought me great light just now. Knowing that you love me, believe it or not, it is the biggest light I ever had."

"You have a mission Robert. You have a purpose for the rest of your life. You have to make things better. You have to correct your ways. Now the mighty lord has given you a chance to observe how precious life is. You can redeem your soul."

She took a deep breath and looked around her. "I enjoyed life with you Robert more than I ever had before."

"Anything," his voice broke, "I can do?"

She turned to him. "Say a prayer for me the morning after."

His eyes filled with tears in the split second it took for him to understand her words. Reality hit him with great force and he began to shake wildly. "What have I done?", he asked himself. For so many years sinning had been an integral part of his life; a natural part of his regular behavior. The memories flashed in front of his eyes. The children's hospital; how many children died because of him? He closed his eyes in pain. The senior citizen home; how many lost their will to live and died there? What about all the money that he had cleverly diverted to drug cartels and crime organizations? He did not care. All he cared about were his millions that were nicely accumulated in the Cayman Islands. As long as his fortune was growing, he was happy and nothing else mattered. His dark soul did not care at all.

He never really had a relationship. It was all business. Everyone he worked with, including women had functioned on his behalf. It was even true of Margaret. For many years he simply paid for her services until he eventually decided to make her a business offer, not a marriage proposal like it should have been done but a financial offer. He paid for her company with money. There was simply a stipulation that everything was included. No wonder she preferred death.

He looked at her with the realization of how he had treated her.

"I am really sorry for what I have done to you Margaret." he whispered.

She looked at his eyes and could see that he has been hit by his conscience. Now, when he was facing death he realized what he had done. She felt happy inside. She was about to die but she had brought light to someone's soul. She had shown the light to a dark soul. It is something that does not happen every day. Maybe she would be forgiven for the sinful life she had lived.

She held his hand firmly and smiled at him. "You are going to do the right thing Robert. You are a good man inside, I know it."

"But, I do not want you to die Margaret." he turned into a child. He did not realize it but Margaret was a mother for him also. She took care of him and he knew it. Tears welled up in his eyes and he lowered his face.

Margaret cried quietly. "I love you Robert. I always did and I always will." She gave him a last look and then closed her eyes. She gently pushed away from his body. He squeezed in fear and then it was all over. With one push of her arm she slipped off the ice pole.

As he felt her falling he raised his eyes and stretched out his hand but it was already too late. Her body fell backwards silently while she looked straight at him. She gave him her best brave smile and he never forgot it. Within seconds she vanished from his eyes as cold clouds surrounded the pole.

He continued staring at the last place that he saw her. He was in shock. She did it. She really did it. She had sacrificed her life for his.

In great disbelief he looked down. He could still see her in his mind, falling backwards with her hands opened towards him, her eyes on his. In his mind he could still see the despair in them. He had watched her fall. It was surreal, not of this world. His soul refused to believe what he had seen. This was not happening. He could not see her face. She was too far down. Her body had slammed into the ice and did not move anymore.

He closed his eyes. He could also let go and fall but that was not what Margaret had wished for. She wanted him to fix things. Only he had the knowledge to revert his own actions. *"I have to find the will to carry on. The show must go on the right way this time, otherwise she died in vain"*, he told himself.

He was exhausted and laid his head on the ice. The cold ice made his cheek numb but he did not care. He closed his eyes hoping to fall asleep when he heard a noise far away. He raised his head and listened again. Yes, he was not mistaken. He could hear a noise. It was a very familiar noise. It was the sound of a rotor that was chopping the air. It was a helicopter.

"Thank you Margaret. You'll always be with me".

*   *   *

Robert sat on his large desk and stared at the picture of their wedding. Their wedding picture ad been on his desk from the day they returned from their honeymoon. Yes, at the time it was just for show. He wanted to make sure that everyone knew that he had married a beautiful woman. At the time he did not really care about her. She gave herself to him for money. It was a business marriage and nothing else. But then' just before she died, she had told him that she loved him. She actually loved him, Robert Boil, the rootless and heartless person. That was when he realized that he loved her too. She was the only person that he had loved throughout his life. She gave up her life for his. It was a life for a life but she did it for a reason. She asked him to fix his ways. Furthermore, she asked him to reverse all that he had done.

They both look very happy in their wedding picture, like they really loved each other.

"Maybe we did then and were not aware of the fact?"

"I love you Margaret," he whispered and wiped a tear.

He took a deep breath. He arranged the picture nicely on his desk. Then he stretched his hands and turned to his computer. From the large window he could see the top of a beautiful church whose large, shiny cross was sparkling in the morning sun. Margaret was a believer. She always tried to convince him to go to church on Sundays. He found all kinds of excuses not to go.

He'd go to church starting next Sunday.

He'd say a prayer for her every Sunday. *Now, it was time to do some work, good work for a change.*

He turned on the computer. Soon enough the screen filled with numbers and details. He smiled as a plan formed in his mind.

"It's show time", he told himself.

Within few weeks an order arrived to move the retirement home to the Monterey area. A large anonymous donation had arrived from overseas especially for the purpose of relocating the retirement home to a much better place, a place by the sea. The children hospital received a large grant from the city, purchased advanced equipment and renovated the entire facility. Homeless shelters in the city received grants and donations from all over the world to increase their capacity to meet local needs. Public schools were furnished with brand new computers, a gift from twin cities in Europe. The city seems to be booming with extra funding that arrived from around the U.S. and abroad. Robert was invited a few times each week to cheerful ceremonies in schools, hospitals and retirement homes which wanted to express their gratitude to the municipal authorities. He knew the channels through which to divert funds to where they were needed. As for the crime organizations, he simply blamed the new federal rules and regulations. There was nothing he could do anymore. They tightened the system and his hands were tied. He would keep his eyes open, he told them. It was worth it for the organized crime principals. They trusted Robert. He had worked with them for years. Yes, now they had to pay more taxes and he encouraged them to donate money to public institutions and such, but it was all worth it, Robert promised them. They would see the benefits in the future. So they funded schools, hospitals, shelters and so forth, according to Robert's recommendations.

Robert did not forget his personal funds either. He put almost all of his savings into a charity organization to help children world-wide. He closely monitored the organization's transactions to make sure that the funds reached their intended destination.

As for himself, Robert sold his large home and purchased a small one in one of the nicest suburbs of L.A. where he quietly continued his work to make the world a better place. He vowed to do so for the rest of his life and he kept his promise.

*   *   *

"Circumstances", the dark angel said as he observed his finger nails with extra attention. "It would never have happened if his wife would did not die."

"There is a reason in every case. The reality is that good was always inside him.", the light angel calmly responded.

"I Disagree." The dark angel gave him a skeptical look. "This case is completely circumstantial."

The light angel did not answer. He turned towards the phosphorous table and inscribed a second green check on it. A green lit mark showed in the second column. The dark angel looked at it with discomfort. He did not like the fact that there were two green check marks and no red marks at all.

He was determined to put more effort into the next case. He must win red check marks at any cost.

Chapter III

IT IS NEVER TOO LATE

*   *   *

Tony Crew was hot. His motorcycle had had stopped in the middle of the road in the Death Valley, the Mojave Desert. The temperature was high, he estimated about hundred and twenty five degrees at least. It was almost noon and the sun was almost mid sky.

"I am in big trouble", he thought.

The highway was empty. No cars were seen in the horizon. Tony licked his lips. He was thirsty. The fact that he had gotten drunk last night did not help. He still had a serious hang over and that made him even thirstier. He looked at his silent bike. Everything seemed to be working well but the engine suddenly stopped. He checked the gasoline gage, the oil level and even the electrical system. All seemed to be working well. He had no idea why the motorcycle stopped.

"You stupid, dumb bike." Tony was mad and kicked the motorcycle repeatedly.

Then he got tired and sat on the ground. He knew that he was seriously at risk. If no one passed soon through the highway he would likely die of dehydration.

Tony was a big guy in his mid fifties. He was the son of an Italian father and an American mother who had lived in New York City for many years. His father worked as a fright crane operator at the port in New York City and was hardly ever at home. He had to put in many hours in order to support the family. His mother was a waitress in a local restaurant so he quickly learned to manage by himself. He did not like school and by twelve years old was already roaming free in his neighborhood. His parents were Catholic and tried to embed values and tradition in him without much success. Tony was a sweet child but fairly early they detected a major problem with his behavior. Tony had a hot temper. At first, his parents tried to help him in the typical ways that parents do. They punished him, they explained to him for hours why having a temper is not a good thing in our world. They even sent him to a therapist for many sessions but without much success. When he was eight years old he got suspended from school in account of the fact that he broke one of his classmate's teeth during an argument. In another case he lost his temper and broke a chair on another student's head. The child was hospitalized for few weeks and needed surgery in order to restore some of the damage that Tony had caused.

By the age of ten the school counselor advised his parents that Tony might be a sociopath. Furthermore, he recommended seeking professional help for Tony. "Otherwise, the situation could escalate", he warned them. "It can get really bad", he told them. His parents did not realize the potential for trouble with their son. They were busy with daily survival and focused on their work and home.

On his fourteenth birthday, his parents threw him a party. Since he had practically no friends at school, they did the party at home. They decorated their living room and his mother baked him a large chocolate cake. They even bought him a new bicycle. Tony asked them for money. When they asked him why he needed the money for, he answered that he wanted to travel to the big city and find a prostitute. He said that was what he wanted for his birthday. His mother almost passed out and his father got very upset with him. He thought for a short time and decided that he was ready to leave home. He asked for his parents for some money and when they refused he simply pulled out his gun and killed them both. They did not even know that he had a gun for few months already. He had purchased it from a good friend. He took all the money that he found in their home and just to be on the safe side, torched it. Then he left for Chicago. He heard that this city was a good place for young people interested in adventures. When he arrived in Chicago he celebrated his birthday with two prostitutes. It was his first taste of the big city. When they asked him for money he killed them also.

He found Chicago a very nourishing place. The city had millions of people and it was easy to get lost. This also gave him all the opportunities that he sought. He could do whatever he wanted with a very slim chance of getting caught. He settled in the city for many years. Tony was street smart and knew how to manage in life. He was not ambitious and wanted to fulfill his needs when he felt like it. He never worked, never had a house or an apartment and never earned his money with dignity. He also was never a beggar. He never begged for money. When he needed money he took it by force from people. He robbed neighborhood convenience stores, small kiosks and grocery stores. Whenever he found an easy target he robbed it. He had sharp survival instincts like a rat. He knew how to commit his crimes without getting caught. Those who sensed his personality feared him and stayed away. Those who did not identify his character were apt to be murdered by him. Killing was casual for him. The police never succeeded in locking him up. Whenever the police bumped into him they simply considered him a drunk, harmless homeless person. Tony Crew was like a shadow. He came from nowhere and went anywhere.

After forty-eight empty years in Chicago Tony decided that he needed a change in his life. He heard about California and decided to change his view, even if it would be for only a few years. Another benefit, he thought, would be to vanish off the radar screens so his presence and crimes would slowly fade away in the Chicago area. So he got on his bike and left for the west coast.

He was sweating heavily in the hot sun. He lay near his motorcycle and almost fell asleep when he heard the noise. He was wondering if it was the heat of the sun that caused him to imagine sounds but then he could hear it loud and clear. It was the noise of an upcoming car. Just when he had almost lost hope and was about to let himself fall asleep in the dry heat, an old car was approaching.

"Hallelujah." he mumbled and tried to stand up.

The mission was not easy. He had already been in the sun for almost two hours without any water and felt dizzy. In the heat of the Death Valley two hours was a significant amount of time.

"Wow, now that's not an easy mission here." he mumbled and tried to stand steady. He put his hand above his eyes and tried to see in the distance. Instinctively his other hand felt his gun. His gun became his second nature. He had to know it was there. He actually felt naked without his gun, concealed in his clothes.

"Who is this bastard coming my way?" he grinned. He had no problem killing people and taking their belongings.

An old, rusty blue pickup truck arrived. He raised his hands to the air. He was weak and could hardly keep his hands in the air. His throat was dry and a terrible headache clouded him. The car's driver noticed him and slowly pulled over. A large cloud of smoke surrounded him as the car stopped near him.

"What is this shit?" he coughed "Do you want to kill me with this smoker?" Tony had difficulty breathing due to the thick smoke.

The car's door opened slowly with a scratching sound. From within the smoke cloud he could see an old lady holding a huge steering wheel like she wanted to chock it. She wore a flowery old dress and had large glasses on her nose.

He waved with his hands trying to clear the smoke as he sat on the front seat of the truck, near her and closed the car's door.

"Are you trying to kill me woman?" he spit as his face are turning red. "What the hell is this smoke coming from this piece of junk?"

"I am truly sorry for the smoke." The old lady smiled to him with shaky voice. "I need to take the car in. It has been doing this for quite some time now."

He gave her a look and contemplated if to kill her now or later.

"Just an old crazy lady, he thought."

"My bike just died here in the middle of the desert and I have a fucking terrible headache. Can you believe it?" he said to her and held the door's handle. He felt a breeze of air conditioning in the car and that helped him.

"Here, have some water. You must be thirsty." The old lady handed him a bottle of water.

He grabbed the water bottle, opened it and started to gulp the water, he was making loud sucking sounds.

The old women looked at him with a smile.

"I see you are feeling better. I am Elsie; I am pleased to meet you."

He drank the whole bottle of water before answering her. Then he wiped his face and released a loud burp into the air. Then he turned to look at her like she was some kind of disgusting creature. "Fucking bike broke right here, in the middle of nowhere and now I have to travel with you to the nearest town."

"Now that is not polite young man." The old woman gave him a serious look. "I just stopped for you and saved you from the killer sun out there. Now be courteous so as to thank me."

He gave her a look and then laughed loudly. "You should thank me that you are still alive." He looked at her with amusement and then nodded and added with sarcasm "Elsie."

He then pulled out his large gun and observed its cleanliness. "Elsie, where are coming from and where are you heading?"

"So you are prime evil type of guy." Elsie looked at him with a smile. "That doesn't impress me."

She put the car into first gear and with plenty of jumps and shakes navigated the old car back onto the highway.

Tony held his seat in great surprise. "Is this a bad luck day or what?" he shook his head. "Getting rescued by a crazy lady in this motorized garbage . . ."

"I am coming from my little ranch about one hour south." Elsie smiled at Tony like she completely forgotten how he was talking to her just few minutes ago. "I deliver fresh milk to Venice Cafe which is about seventy miles away from here. They like my milk and not the commercial one. They appreciate the milk from my farm. No hormones, no pesticides. It is all natural." She smiled a toothless smile at him.

"Damn, this is my worst luck ever. You are practically dead already Elsie. Is this fucking air condition on maximum? I am melting here." Without asking her he tried to turn some knobs and buttons but nothing seemed to work.

"Fucking car, old as you Elsie, worth nothing." He gave up on the air conditioning.

"Do you mind watching your language young man, I really don't like it."

He looked at her like she went out of her mind and then laughed loudly. "You crazy bitch, just continue driving while I'll try to take a nap. Lucky you that I need a driver otherwise I would have killed you and thrown you out."

"I don't believe that we were properly introduced. What is your name young man?" She asked nicely, again, like he had never talked rudely to her before.

"The name is Tony, Elsie and now please shut your fucking big hole in your face and continue driving. I want to sleep. I was on the road for many hours."

"It is my pleasure to meet you Tony." she gave him a gentle smile.

"Fucking unbelievable." he mumbled to himself.

They continued quietly for quite awhile.

"So, Tony, what are you doing for a living?" Elsie asked in a friendly tone.

"Nothing."

"Well, that's not much." She seemed to have a sense of humor.

"You must do something for a living. Otherwise, how do you pay your mortgage or rent and buy your food?", she continued.

"When I need money I rob someone or something and I do not own any home or apartment. I live wherever I want.", came his laconic answer.

"Really," she sounded almost like a parent. "I am sure your mother would not have approved of your behavior Tony."

He had not heard anything like this for years. He gave her a brief look and then burst into loud laughter. "Now, that is something I didn't hear for years." He was amused. "Granny Elsie how about you shut your toothless mouth and concentrate on driving us to a place with humans. I am sick of this desert around us and you are driving me nuts."

"Still, I am sure that you mother would not be happy to see you like this." she did not give up.

"Well, my mother is dead."

"Oh, I am truly sorry." Elsie seemed to feel sorry for him. "I am sure that it was probably very hard on you. Did she die when you were a child?"

"Actually yes," Tony gave her an amused look. He was entertained by where the conversation was going.

"I am so sorry for you my dear. It must have been a traumatic event for you. No wonder why you turned to be who you are."

"Not really," he smiled widely "I was not sorry at all. As a matter of fact I killed her."

"Oh." She flinched on her seat.

He enjoyed watching her reaction.

"What about your father?"

"Killed him too. I torched the house on both of them. See, I am an orphan. I deserve mercy." He burst into a loud laugh from his own humor. "I can be funny too."

Elsie was not amused by his sense of humor. Instead she remained quiet. After a while he looked at her. To his surprise she did not look shocked as he expected. She even had a tiny smile on her face.

"So you were up to no good Tony." She concluded "why?"

He looked through the car's window. He was caught by surprise. No one had asked him this type of question before. "I really do not know why but that's the way I am. That's the way I was for all my life. Other humans' lives or property meant nothing to me. Whenever I wanted something, I just took it. It did not matter to me if it was people, property, or life."

He gave her a long look, wondering what she would say but she did not respond at all. She continued looking at the empty road.

He sank into thoughts. "Maybe people are born in such way that they just don't care about others. I heard once my school counselor telling my mother that I was a sociopath, whatever that means."

"What brings you to this part of the country?"

"Nothing in particular," he was about to swear but remember that she did not like it and stopped himself. He was wondering why he did so. "I wanted a change in my life."

They were quite for a while.

"What about you Elsie? What is your story?" he asked her after a while.

The air conditioner in the old car made all sorts of noise in great effort to cool the air. Yet, the air became hotter as they progressed into the desert.

"Oh, I have a very interesting story of my own, I just don't tell it people . . ." she looked at him through her glasses with a teasing smile.

"You are funny, crazy old woman." Tony shook his head. He did not bother to ask her for her story. He thought that she was probably senile or too old to be coherent. "I can't believe that you actually stopped for a stranger on the road in these times".

"You probably assaulted and murdered many people." She concluded.

"Yes, I did Elsie. Yes, I did. I did not count them but the number is high up there."

"Were you violent as a child or teen?"

He thought for a while. "My violent nature burst out when I was about eleven years old. Somehow, and I do not know why, I had to solve everything with physical power. I was big boy and quickly discovered that I could get just about anything that I wanted by force. I started to hit. I started to scare other kids. I wonder why?"

"Probably what you saw at home." she suggested "Did your parents fight and argue?"

"Not that I remember." He answered and sank into thoughts "They were hard working people and spent most of their time at work. I was their only one child and stayed at home alone a lot. No, they were not violent at all."

"Then it is all you."

"I guess it is . . ." he mumbled.

"Anyway, what is this nonsense talk? When will we arrive to our destination?"

"We have about two hours. We are going to a place called Venice Cafe. It is a small gas station on the road. They also have small restaurant. They like my farm fresh milk. Every week I travel there to deliver milk." She pointed to the back seat. See, these are cooled tanks."

"Well, this is a waste of life" then he observed her again "but then again, you don't have much life left anyway."

"This is not nice to talk to me, Tony." She talked to him like he was a child.

"Ah, if only you were a young, hot chick, things were different. Ha Elsie.", he winked at her with humor. "Then we could probably have had some fun during this drive."

She smiled. "Who said I would choose you?"

"Who said I would ask you?" he answered and laughed loudly. "Oh Elsie, when will you understand that you are lucky to be still living. Typically, I would already have killed you and thrown you out of your car." He scratched his head. "Maybe I should have done it earlier."

"And the fact that I helped you and saved you from the hot desert does not mean anything to you?" She added and gave him a serious look.

He did not answer.

"See, you do have some kindness inside of you." She was happy with her little victory.

"Nonsense," he waived with his hand.

He looked around the cabin. "I am thirsty, do you have more water?"

"Well, I have only this homemade juice that I keep for myself. You can have it if you would like. It is in the back seat. Please leave some for me too, in case I get thirsty." She smiled a tiny, hidden smile.

He found a plastic bottle with some light blue juice in it. Without asking for her permission he gulped the entire bottle and then threw it through the window. "That was actually not bad. What did you say was it?"

"My home made juice." she smiled with happiness. "I always make me one for the road."

"Well, you will make yourself another one next time. This one is gone." He seemed to enjoy talking rudely to her.

Again she did not answer.

"It is hot and your damn air condition is not good, woman", he almost screamed at her.

"This is a very old car. You should be happy if we just make it safely to the cafe. They have good air conditioning there."

They came to a bumpy section on the road that gently shook them for a while.

"This road makes me sleepy." Tony mumbled. "I want to sleep."

He fell in and out of sleep a few times. "You know Elsie," he started to talk in a slow tone as he woke up from a short nap. "When I was a child I had this weird dream all the time."

She looked at him, puzzled.

"I had this dream when I slept at night. The Lord comes to me and takes me with him. Then he takes me to the edge of the skies, at the end of the desert, to his special garden." Tony got excited when he told her his dream. "The Lord's garden is beautiful. Beautiful, wild flowers are blooming everywhere. They are huge and have vivid colors. There is this sweet smell in the air and I breathe it deep into my lungs. There are tall green trees everywhere and narrow fresh creeks flowing in between rocks. Birds are chirping and the skies are blue. Everywhere there are green meadows and I can see chipmunks and rabbits running everywhere. It is the most magnificent garden that I ever saw. And the lord is taking me and showing me his garden and I am amazed."

Tony looked like he was in a trance. He had a dazed look on his face when he told Elsie about his dream.

"Then the lord explains to me about the flowers in the garden. 'These flowers are forbidden to pick', he tells me. 'This is my garden and here are my creations and here I watch over them. I am here all the time to watch so no harm is done to them and to protect my flowers."

Elsie was fascinated hearing his story.

Tony continued in his state between sleeping and waking. "So I don't say anything and the Lord asks me all of a sudden "Are you careful with my creations Tony?" and then great fear falls on me. I do not know even why or maybe I do know? I have no answer for the Lord. And he is asking me again "Are you hurting my garden Tony?"

Tony covered his eyes. "What have I done Lord? I have done terrible things to your garden. I've destroyed many of your creations." Tony started to cry.

Elsie pulled over and stopped the car.

Tony that felt the change looked at her "What happened?"

Elsie straightened her position in the seat and turned to him. "I will tell you about my life Tony."

He looked at her puzzled. He was fully awake now but somehow felt very tired.

"Must be the heat", He thought.

She arranged her hair with very feminine movements. "I live in my little farm more than fifty years now." Elsie started and stricken him with penetrating look. "My husband, Bernie and I lived here forever." A smile spread on her face. "Ah, nostalgia about me and my hubby Bernie. He never knew me, or at least not as he thought he did."

Tony looked at her like she was crazy.

"We were married for forty eight years before he died in tragic circumstances . . ." she gave him an aerie look.

Tony started to fill discomfort.

"One stormy night he went to the old barn. I told him that I heard some noises coming from there. Poor him, the door got locked and then lightening struck. Bernie got locked inside and burned to death. I can still hear his screams even today."

She released a sigh. "But he deserved to die in such a horrific way. He was not nice to me." She raised her eyes to Toni's and he felt the chills. Her eyes were cold as ice.

"What kind of woman is she?" thought Tony.

"I will not talk about it. Let's just say that I made sure that he received his punishment."

Then she continued with a tone that caused Tony to freeze in actual fear.

"I discovered a real rush, Tony, something like you probably had." She took off her glasses. "The rush of a kill. The rush of terminating a human life. It is better than ice cream." She laughed loudly.

Tony didn't laugh at all. As a matter of fact, he got scared. For the first time in his life he felt real fear.

"Ridicules, that he should fear an old, crazy woman? So she killed her husband. It is still not a reason to fear her".

"Then I started to travel the roads. Lucky for me Venice Café wanted to buy my milk, a great excuse for being on the road. I am on the road for thirty five years. You'd be amazed what can be done in thirty five years." She put her glasses on and straightened her no longer innocent look at him.

It was his turn to flinch.

"Do you know how many people disappear here every year Tony?" she asked in quite tone.

He swallowed his saliva.

"Do you know how many people are buried in barrels in my back yard Tony?"

Again, he did not answer.

"Many, Tony, many . . ."

He shook his head. He felt dizzy and tried to clear the clouds that filled his head.

"No one suspect a crazy old woman." She talked casually "no one. So I started to travel here and take people with me. I stopped my old car for many young boys and girls that ran away from home and I stopped for many old beggars that got lost in life. The result was the same. They all ended in my back yard. So many, I stopped counting after few years."

She gave him a friendly look. "You know, I believe that I could easily get into the Guinness book of records for the number of people that I buried. Some were still alive."

Now he really feared for his life but felt paralyzed. He thought that he froze from fear but Elsie reassured him that this was not the reason.

"You wanted to drink my home made juice, remember?" she said like an old granny that gives a wise advice. "It is such a shame that you finished it all and nothing left for me." She laughed gently. "I would not drink it anyway. Well, young man what you drank is the poison that I have been making for years. It always works in the same way. First you will be paralyzed for a while, with almost no capability to move". She looked at her nails with great focus.

"Then I will be able to do to you whatever I want." She looked at him again. "Do you feel paralyzed Tony?" she asked in calm tone.

"Yes, I am, you crazy bitch." he sweat heavily.

"Good, this is the first stage. Second will be the numbness of the limbs and third is probably the most not nice one . . . But I'll not scare you anymore."

He looked at her with hatred.

"Hey, now that I am thinking about this, I definitely beat Charles Manson."

"How long do I have?" he almost spit his words.

"Let's see, you drank the poison about one hour ago, I would say maybe one more hour before you lose conscious."

He laid his head on the seat.

"We shared our life events together Tony, I like you." She told him and then remembered to preach to him "Although you treated me not nice at the beginning of our relationship, but I forgive you. I'll be with you all the way to the end. I like you. I promise not to bury you alive."

"Thanks . . ." he mumbled.

They sat there, in the car where the air conditioner sound and the engine were the only noises.

"You never know how you are going to end your life." she commented after a while.

He nodded. "Yes," he agreed. "I feel that this is the right thing though. I do not deserve to live really. Quite frankly, I should have died years ago. I destroyed so many lives. I am wondering why now my time has arrived?" he straightened his look at her. "Why now? Why not many years ago?"

"I don't know Tony. The miraculous wonders of life."

He laughed ironically "It is the irony of life. I have another one hour and I am here discussing the philosophy of life with my murderer. I tried along the years to imagine my death but nothing like this came to me even in my wildest dreams."

She looked shocked when he mentioned that she was his murderer. He noticed that fact.

"What's the matter Elsie?" he stressed her name on purpose "You did not like to hear that you are a murderer? I guess you knew it all throughout the years but never discussed it with the person you killed." He nodded slowly "I assume that they all died before you had a chance to discuss life with them. Didn't they Elsie?"

She lowered her eyes. "Yes, I never talked with none of my victims."

"How does it feel?" he asked her calmly "How does it feel to talk with the person who is about to die within one hour because of you? I am not afraid of dying. I know that if there is heaven and hell, I'll definitely go to hell. I deserve it. What about you Elsie?"

She lost her calmness and now looked disturbed. He continued.

"What about your soul Elsie? What will you say when your day will come?" he grinned "I mean, damn, you did much more than anyone can ever imagine. Hey, and I thought that I was cruel."

"Yes, I did . . ." she mumbled.

"Are you prepared for the time?"

She raised her eyes to him. He saw something that he did not see before. He was with her for no more than few hours but felt like they have lots in common. In a very bizarre way he felt close to this woman.

"What have I done to the garden?" she looked scared.

"Yes, what have you done?"

"The Lord is watching his garden. It is forbidden to pick his flowers."

Realization penetrated into her.

"The Lord is there and sees everything. 'At the edge of the skies. At the end of the desert'." She continued.

"My dream . . ." he smiled "The garden flowers are forbidden to pick. The flowers should not be destroyed."

Then she turned desperate. "I can't save you Tony, even if I want; the poison is already in your system." She shook her head "There is not enough time to even get you to a hospital."

He smiled calmly then he reached for her hand. Slowly she have him her shaky hand and he held it.

He took a deep breath. He didn't feel his limbs anymore and knew that he did not have much time.

"You know, the most important thing is that you have remorse for what you have done. I deserve to die anyway. My soul is darker then the darkness itself. My mother told me when I was a child that when the angels are crying in a different world then in our world we are sadder." Her eyes sparkled. "I always asked her 'Why do they cry, Mom?' She just said that it was because it is not easy to be an angel in our world". I wanted to cry with them but my tears wouldn't come out." he added in a low voice.

His body started to shake and she held his hand tightly. Her eyes told him everything. This is the time of separation.

"I am sorry Tony." she whispered "I am very sorry that I killed you. I am sorry I killed so many others. I am so sorry."

He smiled. "I am sorry that I was rude to you Elsie."

She laughed shortly with sarcasm. "Good thing you still have sense of humor."

"Tony," she looked at him with sad eyes "I do not want to scare you but bad death is approaching. You will soon not feel your limbs and then . . ."

"I already don't feel them." He cut her.

"Then we don't have much time. The next stage is even worse. Shakes are coming follow with convulsions. After that horrible death by lack of oxygen."

He took a deep breath. "I do not want to die this way Elsie."

She held his hand. "I'll do whatever you want."

He sank into thoughts.

"This death caught me by surprise."

"I never imagined that I'd die like this, under pressure of time. I guess I hoped I'd have some period in life in which I would be able to do things right, to live a decent life and contribute some good to the world. I'll never have that chance. Death caught me early. I'll die as a bad person; I'll die as a murderer."

She could read his thoughts. "Tony, you will not die as an evil man. You helped me. You made me realize what I have done. You gave me a reason to change my ways."

He looked at her with some amusement. "At your age it does not matter anymore. How many years do you still have to fix your ways?"

His words penetrated her heart like a sphere.

"There is always a chance to change, even if it is at the last minute of your life."

He did not answer but shook his head instead. "I have a gun in my coat." He raised his look to her. His shakes level increased.

Without a word she pulled out his gun.

"It is loaded", he mentioned. I have just . . ." his voice broke.

"What? Anything you want."

He looked into her eyes and all of a sudden she could see him as a little boy. A little boy that was very scared to die.

"Could you please hold my hand?" he closed his eyes "I am scared."

She took his hand in hers. "Do you want me to contact anyone for you? Do you have any . . . ?"

"Nobody. I have nobody. As a matter of fact the only person I talked for so long for my entire life is probably you. During the few hours we have been together I talked with you the longest time I ever talked to anyone."

She wept quietly.

"You, the one who killed me, were the closest person to me." He laughed with irony "and will hold my hand when I die."

"Yes, I'll be at your side to help you through this . . ." she added, wiping her tears "I know it is an awkward situation but all I can say is what my true heart feels. I wish I could die instead of you; I would do it in a heartbeat. I am so sorry I caused you to die."

He could see the regret in her eyes.

Then he told her something that he did not remember saying to anyone before.

"Thank you Elsie."

He was sweating profusely.

He took her hand with the gun and aimed it at his face. His eyes were transfixed on hers. He held her other hand with his.

Her hand was shaking slightly. She looked at him without knowing what to say.

"Goodbye Elsie." he mumbled.

She saw him close his eyes. She closed hers and pulled the trigger.

*   *   *

It was another boring hot day in the Sheriff's office in Needles, California. The population of the city of Needles was about five thousand people and the Sherriff's office was contracted to the larger city of San Bernardino. The small office was fairly empty and included an old desk, three chairs and an empty water machine.

The Sheriff for this week, Don Logan was bored out of his mind. There were no law enforcement incidents in this town for months at a time. It was his third day this week and he already finished three cups of coffee and was wondering what he a very famous Sheriff.

He heard a car approaching and looked through the wide window. He could see an old truck arriving at the parking lot and slowly stop. The car brought with it a large cloud of blue smoke.

"Now, there's some work for me. A hefty ticket for emission violation." he mumbled to himself. "That's something that will fill my whole day." he grinned to himself.

He never expected what happened next.

An old woman, in flowery dress walked slowly out of the car. The woman was quite old, at least at her eighties, he estimated. With slow steps she climbed the few stares to his office and opened the door. Then she entered and approached him.

"Are you the Sheriff in this town?" She asked with low voice.

"Indeed madam," he took his hat off. He kept his manners since childhood. "What can I do for you on this lovely day?"

She straightened her look into his eyes. "My name is Elsie Roman and I have a dead man in my car." she said in a shaky voice.

"What?" he scratched his head and did not know if to believe her.

"I have a dead man in my car." She seemed to control herself now and spoke in a steadier voice. "I killed him this morning."

The Sheriff was stunned. The old woman looked like the type of ladies who come to ask for help for a cat that needs to be rescued from a tree top and not one to make a murder confession.

"That is not all Sheriff." she continued in a loud tone. "I need you to come and dig out all of the people I poisoned over the years. They are all buried in my back yard."

Then she presented her hands. "I am ready."

The entire continental United States and the whole world were shocked to hear about the case when it was published about two months later. The gruesome findings in an old woman's back yard caused chills even among the most experienced police officers. One hundred and twenty-eight victims were recovered from her back yard in a great digging effort that lasted more than a month. The old woman was brought to a trial in the city of Los Angeles and after a long trial received the death penalty. There were many opinions in the U.S. regarding this punishment. Many human rights activists claimed that she was obviously mentally ill and did not deserve the death penalty. Others were happy about the sentence and claimed that this was living proof of a good, effective justice system. Soon a nick name was attached to Elsie, "The Butcher Granny".

The old woman started her waiting period on death row. Due to her old age many wondered about the effectiveness of the waiting period. The old woman gave many interviews to the T.V. networks in which she clearly stated that she accepted society's verdict and that she believed that it was the proper punishment. She was ready to pay for her crimes and her only wish was to preach in favor of good deeds during the upcoming years. She wanted to pass on to others that evil actions should never be considered since eventually they would come back to haunt the person who committed them. She wrote a book about sins and punishments. Her book sold millions of copies in the U.S. and around the world. The Butcher Granny became symbolic of remorse and many people had difficulty not liking her. Watching the old woman on T.V. was similar to watching a good grandmother and people had a hard time believing that she was probably the most horrific mass murderer known in history.

Furthermore, many groups organized and claimed that her trial and evidence were a government conspiracy and she was an innocent old grandmother. People started to like her and demand that her life be spared. She was very old and due to her recent remorse they insisted she be allowed to live. But the state attorney refused to cancel the verdict at any cost.

Elsie also refused to have her sentence commuted. In the periodical interviews that she conducted she consistently announced that she would live until her execution date arrived. "I committed a hideous crime and I deserve this punishment. I do not want to be spared. I wish I could turn back the wheel of time and not commit these crimes. At least I can try in the next few years that I have to convince others to refrain from similar crimes. Then there would be a reason for keeping me alive.", she claimed and the people loved her.

After the waiting period her execution night arrived. Thousands of people gathered in front of the prison, protesting for a change in the verdict at the last minute. Elsie asked to sleep for few hours before her execution. Her last meal was brought to her at exactly eleven P.M. She had simply requested cream of wheat and a donut.

At eleven forty-five the pastor arrived at her cell.

She accepted him with happiness and held his hands.

"I am so happy to see you father.", she smiled at him.

"I am here for you my child." The pastor was a tall man in his late thirties and had a serious look on his face.

"Oh, stop being so serious father, I am good to go." She looked at him for a while. "We all know that this is the right thing to do. 'An eye for an eye.', isn't it?" she released a sigh. "I just hope that my last few years discouraged others from similar crimes. After all, that was the main purpose of my continued living."

The pastor nodded. He simply listened. That was his purpose on these occasions. "Is there any prayer that you'd like to say?"

She lowered her face. "No thank you, father. On this journey I pray alone, not with anyone else around me."

"Is there any prayer you would like me to say for you?"

She smiled to him "No, thank you father."

He nodded quietly.

Two people arrived. One of them held a camera. A prison guard escorted them.

"We are from . . ."

"I know who you are." She raised her hand to stop him. "I'll give you two minutes for the final interview."

They arranged their equipment quickly and she started to talk directly to the camera.

"In about ten minutes I'll be executed by lethal injection for my crimes. I committed horrible crimes and I deserve this punishment. I have a request to all of you who wanted my pardon. Do not make me holy. Do not light candles tonight. Do not make me a martyr because I am not. I took many lives. This is against the Ten Commandments. This is against humanity. That is why I am here. Soon I'll have to face judgment. I alone. Honestly, that is what I fear the most. Not this execution, this is nothing. What comes after that is my real fear." She took a deep breath. Small sweat drops could be seen on her forehead. "I hope that my efforts during the last few years will prevent horrors similar to those I caused."

She became silent.

The two men left and another three prison guards arrived. "It is time." Said one of them.

She stood up and straightened her orange inmate dress.

They took her to the chamber where she was laid on a table and shackled. A medical team arrived quietly and started the procedure. All the people who were with her performed their duties silently. An intravenous tube was inserted into her arm.

Suddenly she was scared. She got scared from the process itself and from what she'll have to face after it will be done.

She looked outside the chamber window. No one attended the execution. The small attendee's room was empty. All of a sudden she saw something. Was it her imagination or could she see one man enter the room and sit in the front row? She raised her head to see better. Who could this man can be? She concentrated on the man's face and could not believe her eyes.

Was it really him or as it a figment of her imagination? It was Tony. Tony, the guy to whom she gave the last ride. The man she killed last. What is he doing here? He was already dead. The circumstances were causing her to imagine things.

Tony was smiling at her and this brought tears to her eyes. It was him. He came to be with her, as she was with him in his last moments. She wanted to wave to him but her arms were tight. Then it was like he read her mind and raised his arm and gently waved to her. He was with her. He would be with her throughout the process and maybe even after.

All of a sudden she was not scared anymore. She took a deep breath and lay there, looking at Tony.

The clock reached midnight. The executioner pulled the lever.

The first injection flew through the thin pipe. The first one would put her to sleep. The rest of the injections would deliver the lethal poison.

Quietly the witnesses watched the fluid moving in the pipe to Elsie.

Her gaze was stuck on Tony who sat there, assuring her.

Just do not leave me now, she thought.

He did not leave. He stayed there until she started to feel tired. It was a deep tiredness, she thought, the type of tiredness you never wake up from. He was still there, looking at her, with her.

She gazed at him for the last time. Then the blessed darkness took over and took her away.

There was no one in the attendee's room.

*   *   *

"Well done Elsie." The light angel was quite pleased.

"Ah, this case is not clear." the dark angel interjected. "She was on my side for many years, too many years to relinquish my hold on her." He raised his eye-brows.

"Look what she has done for the past seven years." The light angel pointed towards the air where dim images showed. The images flashed rapidly but they could easily see people watching Elsie preaching in favor of good deeds. They could see many who gave up the idea of doing evil after listening to her. It was obvious that she convinced many to abandon their bad ways.

"Then again, do not forget this", the dark angel pointed at his side and vivid, shocking images of Elsie burying victims in her back yard appeared. "She was on my side for many years." The dark angel had a wide smile on his thin lips.

"It looks like we need some help here." the light angel looked upwards.

A wide light beam appeared above them and illuminated them in a bright light.

"First there was evil.", came a loud voice from above "and the evil was very bad."

The dark angel's smile broadened.

"Then there was regret." The voice continued, "Then there was a turning point. Then the good appeared. And the good took over."

"But . . .", started the dark angel. His eye-brows curled and his eyes glowed bright red. He was mad.

"There are no buts here. There is no doubt about actions and intentions. There is no middle way. It is either good or evil. There is nothing in between." The voice continued, "This case is clear. It turned toward the light."

Another green check mark appeared on the table suspended mid-air. This time it was not marked by the light angel.

Chapter IV

THE GOOD OF THE MANY

*   *   *

Little Angela watched the dark clouds slowly covering the blue skies. It was the end of the day on Monday and she knew that her mother would come to take her home soon. For a five year old she was quite developed and knew how to identify events and occasions. She figured out that after lunch and play time, there would be a short movie, then play time outside and then shortly after that her mother would pick her up. That's how it was in her kindergarten.

She also knew what the dark clouds meant. They came from the big factory near their small town. This factory made all kinds of glue and adhesives and was in general very good for their small town. After all, it brought many jobs to the people. She heard her father say it to her mother one night. Then again the fact was that the plant produced serious air pollution caused severe lung disease especially in children. That was her mother's claim. They needed to move out of there, she mentioned to her father almost every evening. Then she would hear her parents argue about the topic. Her father would claim that he worked in the factory and it was their bread and butter. Her mother continued preaching about leaving the area before they were stricken by serious illness.

The clouds spread now and covered almost the entire sky. The warm afternoon sun could not penetrate the clouds and the skies turned dim. She released a sigh. She really loved the sun and was really happy to play outside. Now it would soon become chilly and the teacher will force them to go in. That is unfair, she thought.

She also knew what was going to follow later that night. Her mother told her everything. Most likely the cloud would take over the skies choking the sun beams and the wind. Within few hours a bad, acidic smell would spread all over their little town. Many of the children in this town who were already sick with asthma and emphysema would have to be locked in their homes. In addition, many of them would have to connect to an inhalation machine in order to be able to breathe clearly. She also had to watch her breathing. She well knew that in case of severe pollution she would have to take few sessions of medical inhalation. Last summer she encountered severe breathing difficulties and her parents had to take her to the emergency room. Later, they purchased an inhalation machine so they would be able to take care of her at home.

"Hi sweetie, did you miss me today?" her mother arrived and hugged her to her heart.

"Yes mommy. Look Mommy the cloud is here.", she pointed towards the cloudy skies.

Her mother looked at the skies and her happiness was gone. Now she looked worried. "Let's go home quickly, love, the bad cloud is here again." She shook her head. "I can't believe it. It is the fourth time this week. It can't continue like that."

Little Angela looked up. The cloud was large and seemed to come down quickly on the little town. "Oh no, this is no good" she hung her eyes at her mother who looked very worried.

*   *   *

Angela's mother rushed home. There was something wrong. The clouds that fell on the little town seemed larger than ever. The skies got hazy and the air became hard to breathe. The air had a strong acidic smell and burned the lungs. She was very worried for Angela. She was already suffering from severe asthma and had to be put on the inhalation machine whenever the air pollution worsened.

They had clear instructions to call the environmental health department to complain immediately when hazardous conditions appeared. The chemical plant in their town was constantly emitting chemical clouds into the air. They had already complained dozens of times but with no real change. The people in town formed a society to fight the plant but without much success. They even hired a lawyer and filed a law suit against the plant but then again, the plant owner who was a wealthy man hired his own attorney who was very experienced in legal battles. He knew how to handle cases like this and always came out the winner.

The end result was continuous pollution and many people with breathing ailments.

Today there was very severe pollution.

As they were driving Angela started to have breathing difficulties. Her mother immediately turned on the car air condition but it did not seem to help much.

"Hang on sweetie. We are almost home. We'll put you on the inhalation machine immediately." Her mother drove as fast as she could.

She called her husband on her way. "Angela is having a severe asthma attack. Please come home."

When they arrived home Angela breathing difficulties became even more severe and her face turned red in her great effort to breathe. It seemed like her lungs were shutting down. Her mother put her on a larger dosage of inhalation medicine and held her to her heart in an effort to comfort her and make her feel better. Angela tried to fight her lung difficulties but it seemed like the inhalation procedure did not help this time. Her lungs seemed to be closing.

"Matt, I am taking her to the emergency room." her mother called her husband who was already on his way home. "She is turning blue."

She rushed her to the emergency room. The E.R. was already full of people who had lung disease and breathing difficulties. Angela lost consciousness and a team of five doctors started working to revive her. Her mother waited outside crying quietly. Her husband entered the waiting room and rushed to hug her.

"How is she?" he asked as sweat drops are forming on his forehead.

His wife did not answer at first, though her eyes rested on him. "Not good. Her lungs seem to be shutting down. Accumulated damage over time, they say." She shook her head and covered her mouth in great agony.

He hugged her tightly. "I am sure that the doctors are doing their best honey. It will be okay."

The treatment room door opened and a young woman stepped out. She removed her face mask and approached the husband and wife and held their hands. Her eyes said everything.

The mother screamed in great despair.

*   *   *

"A young girl died last night." The attorney threw the morning paper on Gilbert Denner's desk.

Gilbert took a long sip from his cup of coffee and looked at the paper. The headlines screamed everything. "Another young girl died due to lung failure. Parents claim that it is because of the severe air pollution. This is the fifth case of child death due to lung disease this year."

He threw the paper. "It is unfortunate but many people die every year from all kind of illnesses."

The attorney gave him a long look. "This is the fifth case of child death this year. The entire town is mad on you. They are sure that this is a result of the air pollution from your plant."

Gilbert put a piece of bubblegum in his mouth. "It is not from my plant. These people always blame the plant."

"Well," the lawyer talked in a very cold tone "that's not what the expert that they hired said."

Gilbert raised his eyes and the lawyer continued "They hired an expert who took air samples. He claims that the air is extremely dangerous. He has strong evidence to prove his claims."

Gilbert's tone became business oriented. "We did the best we can. The plant emits pollution according to the standard criteria. We installed detectors and filters to clean whatever we can. That is it. I am not putting even one more penny into it."

"Your plant made more than three hundred million dollars net profit last year." The lawyer lit a cigarette. "You should put more into filtering the air. After all, the plant does pollute the air. We both know the truth."

Gilbert ignored his comment.

"People are dying Gilbert. This is more than just money." The attorney's tone turned serious.

"That is why I pay you the big bucks." Gilbert gave him a meaningful look. "Your salary just doubled." Gilbert sat backwards in his large armchair "As a matter of fact, your salary has just tripped. Get us out of this legal mess. I do not care about the cost."

A wide grin spread on the lawyer's face. "Well, this changes everything. Let me take care of this matter and now please excuse me. I have plenty of work to do."

Gilbert saluted in a gesture of politeness and the lawyer left the room.

Gilbert turned towards the large window in his office. He could see the high snowy mountains in the distance. This business had been in his family for generations and always succeeded. He never forgot his father's last words on his death bad. "Do not let this empire fall. Do whatever it takes to continue its glory and success. The end justifies the means." His father's words penetrated deep into his heart and right there and then he decided to do everything in his power in order to preserve his family's empire which they had created over years. Whatever it would take!

*   *   *

Gilbert parked his brand new Mercedes Benz 600 in his garage and took the glass elevator up to the main room. He owned a villa on a hundred acres including an Olympic size pool, tennis court and thirty rooms, most of them without any use. His wife worked as a teacher in the local school and found quiet satisfaction in her work. They had two children. Renee, the oldest daughter was fourteen years old and a typical teenage girl. She spent most of her time in her own teen world. Ned, the younger son was only ten and enjoyed what life gave him. As young child he already grasped his parent's wealth and even joked about it. One evening, as they were watching T.V., Ned said "Hey Dad today I figured it out." When Gilbert asked him for the meaning of his words he replied with a serious look on his face.

"Father is a banker by nature. Right?" He burst into loud laughter as Gilbert remained astonished by this declaration.

Gilbert's wife, Jillian, was not impressed by his achievements in the business world. She seemed to focus on her students and work as a teacher and on many occasions expressed her unhappiness about his actions. She was not a business oriented person, he thought about her.

He entered the large living room and saw his wife drinking tea and watching the news.

"How was your day honey?" He smiled to her on his way to grab a cold beer from the fridge.

His wife gave him a cold look. "I assume that you already heard about the poor little girl who died yesterday."

He opened his beer and sat on the white leather coach. "Yes, I heard about her. Very unfortunate case."

"She died from lung disease and complications." His wife hardened the hidden accusations.

"So I heard. I feel sorry for her parents." he continued in a serious tone.

She observed him carefully. "No you don't." she said in a dry tone. "I know you. I bet your attorney is already working to build a case against the suit her parents are bringing against you."

He gave her an innocent look.

"I guess I did not fool her again."

"Indeed.", he continued. "Although her death does not concern our plant I know that her parents will probably sue whomever they think is responsible. I have to protect myself." He gave her a long look. "I have to protect my family."

With anger showing she approached him. "You know damn well that she died because of our plant's pollution. You know well that she suffered, like many others in that town from a severe lung condition and this is due to the poison gas that our plant emits into the air." She looked at his face from a very close distance "If you had a conscience you would pay her parents something to compensate for their daughter's death."

She paused for a while and then continued.

"There is no price for a child life but at least we can show some sympathy."

"Not my problem dear." he said quietly. "This is not the first and not the last person to die because of lung disease. I will not pay for all of them."

"You know that this is because of the poison that our plant releases into the air. You know it." She took a deep breath as she was excited. "You know it and you don't do anything about it."

"O.K., I am going to play golf." He smiled at her impishly. "There are still a few good sunny hours and I want to catch them."

She shook her head in great disbelief "You such a heartless bastard. I hope you'll be punished one day for all you are doing."

His anger exploded inside him. He jumped from his spot and with a red face stood one inch from her and almost spit his words "Look my dear, you should be on my side. I know that people are getting poisoned by the plant but we also have to make a living, don't we? You want to have nice things for you, for the kids? You want to go on fancy vacations every year? You want to buy a nice car? Well, all of this costs money and lots of it."

"I do not want any of these if it comes with the price of children's life." She cried "As I already told you many times before."

She cried quietly. "Why can't we simply shut the plant, clean the land and retire? We have enough money for many years to come. Can we Gilbert? Please. It will make all of us so happy to know that this demonic plant is gone."

"No," he yelled "This plant was my family's life for generations. I'll not shut it down just because children die." His face warped in anger. "I will not be the weak link in my family. This plant existed for many years before you and I were born. I will not shut it down."

She wiped her tears. "Fine, then at least install filters and systems to clean the poisoning pollution it releases to the air. We are killing people here."

"I already did. This should be enough. The plant does not need any further cleaning systems. It cost a fortune and will not provide any significant improvement." He took a deep breath "I am going to play golf."

She lowered her eyes in sadness. "You know Gilbert, one day you will have to provide some answers in front of someone. Now you are strong because of your wealth but money isn't everything." She raised her red eyes to his. "You will have to face some questions and honestly, I fear for you. I fear that you won't have any answers."

She approached him and touched his face. "I love you Gilbert but there is a greater power then us in nature. You will have to stand trial one day in front of it. What will you do then?"

"Nonsense," he moved away from her. "There is no such thing. Everyone is alone in this world. Everyone is for himself. There is no greater power in the universe. People have to push their way forward if they want to succeed. Even after they succeed, if they do not continue fighting they will lose everything. Others will take everything away from them. People are not here to help each other. They here to fight and to win, even at the price of stepping on others. This is a price that every good business man must pay. Otherwise he will not be in business. He'll become other's stool to step on. He'll become worthless. It is cruel world Jillian. It is either that you are the eater or you are eaten. That's all there is to it." He lowered his tone "And sometimes we have to pay the price. The price may be that other people suffer. Nothing we can do about it."

They looked at each other for few quiet moments. They had this discussion many times over the past few years. No results were achieved. He continued with his claims and she tried to convince him differently, without any success.

"I'll be back later.", he announced and left her with her thoughts.

She stood there for a while. Then she went to the large window/wall that overlooked the huge golf course. She looked at the beautiful trimmed grass and the little artificial pond in the distance. She could see magnificent white swans swimming quietly in the clear water. The swans visited them every season for few months. Then they flew to warmer countries but they would be back the next year.

"Where is justice?", she thought. "A little girl is dead and we live here in such a fancy unreal world." Could she live like most people, in a small house or apartment but with morals and principals? She was sure she could and she would happily do it if she knew it would save lives. She had even considered divorcing Gilbert for the past few years but did not want to shake up the family and hurt the kids.

"Where is nature's involvement? How come such situations exist?", she asked the world quietly.

She did not get any answer.

* * *

"There is a protest near the plant. I estimate a few thousand people are there. They demand answers." The lawyer talked laconically.

Gilbert listened quietly. "I'll go to talk with them. I have an idea."

The lawyer raised his eye-brows. He was not sure about Gilbert's intentions.

Within fifteen minutes Gilbert stood on a small wooden stage that the protesters had built.

"Tomorrow I'll start the installation of new air filtration system." He started and the crowd cheered.

"Tomorrow I'll sign an order to check the chimneys on a daily basis to ensure no position gas is released into the air. Although you are safe today, starting tomorrow you and your children will be much safer."

The next day Gilbert met his lawyer at the office.

"I heard that the protest was successful." the attorney smiled at him.

Gilbert smiled "Yes, I could say that it went rather well."

He took a long sip of his coffee and then continued "Please prepare the contract with the two corporations from Korea. We will have to double the shifts."

"But wait," the attorney's forehead wrinkled in surprise. "This means that we will manufacture more of the warm glue. The government forbids it. It is extremely poisonous. I am talking really bad air for people to breath."

"No one needs to know about this production line." Gilbert dunked a small biscuit into his coffee. "We'll hide the production line among others, the legal ones."

The attorney was shocked. "But Gilbert, the US government did not authorize us to use these materials within fifty miles of populated areas. We are breaking a serious law. Also there is a reason for this law. This production involves severe pollution, especially dangerous for children. All the documentation proves it."

"You are thinking about the wrong thing here." Gilbert beamed at him. "This is a fifty million dollar contract. We manufacture the warm glue quietly for a one year period and then we are done. We get the money, shut down the production line and no one knows about it. Everyone is happy."

"What about your promise to the town's people yesterday? This new, hidden production line will increase the poison level in the air hundreds of times more." He wiped some sweat from his forehead. "This is serious matters Gilbert."

"Sometimes, you have to take some risks in life." Gilbert smiled to him briefly.

"Yes, but this one is coming at the price of human life."

"That is a price that I am willing to pay." Gilbert was determined.

Within forty eight hours a new production line was created in the chemical plant. Twenty four hours later this production line started to manufacture warm glue. The plant's chimney smoke color did not change. There was no sign to show that a new product was being manufactured in the plant. There was no new smell, no out of the ordinary smoke and worst of all there was no odor at all. The poisonous gas that was emitted into the air was completely odorless.

No one had any knowledge of it.

*   *   *

"You have a visitor." Gilbert's secretary entered his office.

Gilbert looked at his watch "Anyone important? There is nothing scheduled for this time."

"It is a priest." The secretary gave him a meaningful look.

Gilbert released a sigh. "Send him in."

A tall skinny priest entered the room with a serious look on his face.

"It is my pleasure to see you in my office father." Gilbert extended his hand but the priest remained with his hands behind his back.

"Mr. Denner," he started without any polite introductions. "With your permission, I would like to take you to visit someplace."

Gilbert remained silent and then apologized. "Well, under normal circumstances I'd love to do so but I have some meetings to attend in thirty minutes."

"Your meetings can wait", the priest cut in. "This is something of greater importance. Believe me."

Gilbert did not know how to respond to this peculiar request.

The priest looked straight into his eyes and repeated his words. "Believe me, this visit is worth your time. It's worth everyone's time."

Amazed to see the priest's persistence Gilbert agreed to join him.

"With your permission, I'll drive." he suggested.

The priest was quiet throughout their drive. He navigated the car to a daycare facility in town. The daycare center was about ten miles away from the plant and still, a heavy smell of chemicals was in the air. Gilbert had difficulty breathing the horrendous smell that was all over the facility.

"Why the hell do they place a daycare facility in such close proximity to the plant?" Gilbert mumbled.

The priest heard him. "This is not in close proximity at all. We are at least ten miles or more from your plant. Hard to breath, isn't it?" He looked straight into Gilbert's eyes. "This daycare facility has existed here for many years. I want you to see it."

When they entered the large play-room they could see the teacher who was playing with the children. When she noticed them she stood up and walked over to welcome them on their visit.

"This is Mrs. Carmen, the teacher of this daycare facility." The priest introduced her. "This is Mr. Denner, the chemical plant owner."

Her smile disappeared as she observed Gilbert's face. He was glued to his view of the playing children. All of them, without any exception, were coughing every few minutes. They played and laughed and giggled like every child would do but there was something different about them. There was something different in the entire scene. Gilbert could not point to what it was. He continued to observe the daycare facility, the teacher and the children. The atmosphere seemed to be that of a normal child oriented facility and then he noticed.

All children were bald. No one had hair. Not even the girls. The realization stunned him. He observed the children running playfully and happily. Children have an amazing mental mechanism that protects them from life's bad events. They seemed to be occupied with their toys and games, ignoring the fact that they were sick.

"Yes, it is the miraculous way of nature." The teacher talked in a sad tone. She seemed to read Gilbert's thoughts. "It does not matter how sick they are. Their desire to play and explore the world is taking over and they laugh, play and continue conducting their activities. For us adults, it is typically much harder. We have our basic, deeply embedded fear of disease and sickness. For us fear and sadness does not fade away like in children."

She gave them a gloomy look. "We are afraid to be sick. We are afraid of death. They are not. The power of life is stronger in children. That is their advantage over us adults." Tears glistened in her eyes. "See, they do not know and therefore they are not afraid." She wiped her tears. "What is unknown is not scary for them. They simply ignore it and move along with their games and toys. I wish I could be like them."

The lull was disturbed by the noise of the paying children.

"We lose at least two to four children every year in this day care center." She continued as if without any feeling now "We lose them to the deadly chimneys that poison the air around us. Although we are fairly far away from the plant, when we arrive at the day care center in the morning, many times we have to scrape the thin coating that accumulates during the night from our windows. This material hardens everywhere and we breathe it in during the day. It hardens in our lungs and enters our bodies." She looked straight into Gilbert's eyes.

"This material causes deadly cancer in every person who breathes it."

"Well, you can see the results. Almost all our children are in radiation therapy twice a week. They all have cancer in one way or another. Those who don't have cancer suffer from severe asthma or emphysema, clearly severe lungs diseases. You see them at their best now. Many times each day they vomit. They hardly eat anything and typically they are tired." She faintly smiled at them. "Your visit is at a good time. The sweethearts are simply playing now. At other times the scene is not pleasant at all."

Gilbert stood there as his body started to shake. His hands sweat and his heart raced. He could not believe what he saw. It was all because of him. It was all because of the deadly plant that emitted chemicals into the air. They breathe these chemicals and get sick. This is only one daycare facility. This town has many. What about the residents' homes? Fear fell on him, horror struck inside him.

How many children and people had he killed?

He looked at the priest. The priest looked deeply into his eyes, penetrating into his soul. He held his both hands as his were shaking.

"I have done wrong father." Gilbert mumbled.

All of a sudden he noticed something he had not noticed before. He thoroughly observed the priest who was standing in front of him. He looked familiar. He got closer to him. His face changed right in front of him. His heart skipped a beat.

The priest looked like his father who had died a few years ago.

"What is going on?"

He squeezed his eyes and blinked a few times but the vision did not change.

"Dad?"

The priest took a deep breath. "Yes, Gilbert, it is I."

"But . . ." Gilbert's voice faded in disbelief.

"I am here to show you something son." His father continued in a calm tone. "You need to see beyond success and materialism. You need to see the damage you are causing to your surroundings; the children, the people in your environment. There is more to life than just success. As a matter of fact your life is not measured by your success but by your contribution to the world. What you have given to life is what matters."

Gilbert stood quietly in front of his father.

"You have not done right until now son. You must correct your ways."

Gilbert took a deep breath.

"How many times have people told me to correct my ways? My wife, my friends, even my blood sucking lawyer; People tried to tell me this for many years but I never listened to them. I was blinded by success. I was blinded by foolishness. I was blinded by evil."

His father put his hands on his shoulders. "Unfortunately, I raised you this way. It is my fault that you grew up this way and I feel responsible. I am very sorry for embedding these ideas in your head then. I am truly sorry son. It is never too late to make the change. It is never too late to bring the light into your soul and others."

Gil looked down at the playing children. One striking little girl caught his attention. She was playing with a small doll and sang to her. All of a sudden she vomited and started to cry. The teacher immediately rushed to help her and he was shocked by the scene.

"You have to change your ways." His father nodded. "You have to do it now."

Gil closed his eyes.

There was a bright light. He smelled sterilization solvents. He smelled hospital odor. Gil opened his eyes to bright white neon lights.

"What?" he mumbled. He was disoriented. He did not know where he was.

"Do not make fast moves dear. You are still under anesthesia. Just rest for a while."

He looked and saw his wife standing near him. Beside her were his children, smiling slightly at him, worried about him.

"The disorientation will be gone soon." A doctor in white told them. "We will only know the results in the next few days."

He felt weak. But more than that he felt confused.

"Father . . ." he started to say but his wife looked at him with love.

"What about your father?"

He stared at her and realized that it was all in his dream. Maybe?

"Nothing . . ."

He lay there and thought about his experience. What a long, vivid vision he had. He tried to remember how he got into the hospital but nothing came to mind. He could not remember what he was doing there.

"What happened to me?" he asked his wife.

She looked at him with worried eyes. "You had a brain surgery today. You suffered a stroke two nights ago. Don't you remember?"

He couldn't remember anything. But he clearly remembered the priest. He remembered his father and the advice that he gave him. Nothing else. A bright lightning struck inside him and he grabbed his wife's hand.

"You have to help me."

"Of Course dear, what would you like me to do for you?"

"The plant . . ."

Her face showed annoyance. "Do not worry about the plant now. You have to be better before you back to work."

"No, this is not about work. It is about something else." he mumbled to her.

He started to shake "My father . . . he told me . . . I saw the children . . ."

His wife did not know what was with him but he continued obsessively.

"We have to fix this . . ."

"What do we have to fix?" his wife looked to see if there is a doctor or a nurse in the room. She started to think that he was going through some episode. "Should I call the doctor?"

He looked at her. "No, No, a doctor is not necessary." He understood her train of thoughts and breathed deeply to calm down.

"I have done very badly with the plant Jillian." he told her.

She stared at him without understanding.

He looked straight into her eyes. "I have caused terrible suffering." He shook his head and looked through the large windows. The sun was bright and warm. It was a lovely day.

But not for the many people whom he had made sick. Not for the many people who had died because of his plant. Not for the many children who contracted horrible diseases because of him.

He took a deep breath and told his story to his wife.

"For many years now I was motivated by greed and by the endless desire to succeed. 'The end justified the means', I thought and that's how I acted. I did not care about the impact on people, the impact of my chemical plant." He looked straight into her eyes. "I did not care. I didn't care about other people's health. I did not care about their lives. I did not care about their loved ones."

Jillian looked at him with astonishment. After so many years that she had repeatedly told him to consider others, suddenly he did. What happened to him?

He read her thoughts. "I saw them." He swallowed his saliva. "My father showed me." His voice started to shake. "He showed me the sick kids. The dark daycare with coughing children everywhere. The children coughing because of what they breathe. Their heads were hairless." His eyes filled with tears. "They all had cancer because of me, because of my plant . . . ."

Gilean hugged him to her heart with tears. She could see his sorrow.

"I never realized what I had done." he whispered to her. "I never saw it at close range." He stared at the floor. "Until today, when my father showed me . . ."

She silently wept with him.

"I am so sorry." He held her hand, clinging to her for a while.

"Here is what I would like you to do for me" he implored her quietly.

"Talk with the attorney. Tell him to buy and install all the necessary chimney filters to make sure that the plant does not poison the air. Tell him whatever the price is, I approve it. Fix it so it will be completely safe. This is the first priority."

His wife shook her head in great disbelief. That is what she wanted to see from her husband for a long time now. What dream did he have? Was it due to his brain surgery? It did not matter. She liked what she heard.

He continued. It seemed like he was on some kind of mission that he wanted to complete.

"Look at the area within a fifty miles radius of the plant. At every daycare facility or school, and I repeat, every daycare center or school, check for sick children. Make sure that any of them who are sick with any type of sickness, get the best doctors and treatments, at any cost. Use the millions that we have accumulated, all of it if need be".

She stared him without believing what she just heard. "All of our savings?"

"Yes, you heard me correctly. All of our savings. Keep a minimum for our family. All the rest goes to help the sick; children or adults."

He then continued "All adults in a fifty miles radius from the plant who are sick from chemical emissions should have their medical expenses covered. Get them the best treatments and doctors. Spare no expense."

He lay back on his bed. He seemed much calmer now. The emotional outburst was spent. "It is important to keep the plant fully working though. There are many people who are making a living at these jobs. Especially now a days, people need their jobs. Your job will be to make sure that we pay for all that is necessary to make it safe and not poisonous. People should not die from it but see it as their healthy source of income and pride."

"I will." she responded in a quite tone.

"Make sure that everyone who was hurt in any way due to the plant's poison gets help. If it financial help, if it is emotional help or anything else they need, make sure they receive it." He raised his glance back to her eyes. "We have to help all these poor people who were hurt because of it. We have to try to make things better. I am aware that in many cases it may be too late but at least I would like to ease the suffering and agony of these people. Let us do everything that we can do for them."

He lowered his eyes. "I wish that I would have seen things clearly many years ago." He looked defeated and broken.

"I am very proud of you Gilbert." Jillian whispered with tears in her eyes.

"I do not know what happened but you are doing a marvelous thing here. Helping these people, making the plant healthy and clean, these are good deeds Gilbert. These are righteous acts."

"Well," he said bitterly "I wish I had done this years ago. I wish I had listened to you from the beginning." He shook his head. "I do not know why I didn't do so in the past. Maybe it was my ambition that blinded me or maybe it was my greed. All together I've done very wrong and I hope to fix at least some of it."

Jillian caressed his hand gently. "I love you and amazed by you." She gave him a lovely smile. "This is the man I met many years ago. You do have a good sense of business but you have proven that you also have a good heart. Everyone makes mistakes. To admit and correct your ways requires courage and integrity. Not everyone has it."

He looked at her with sad eyes. "I hope . . ."

"What do you mean you hope?" she pretended to be mad at him. "Now, we will have a great life. The plant will be safe, people will have jobs and we will be a happy family." She smiled and wiped a tear. "Like I always wanted."

He looked at her and gave her a little smile. Then he lowered his eyes and held her hand. "I guess when I was in surgery I had this vision with my father visiting me as a priest and showing me all these ill children."

She nodded silently and he continued.

"Just before I woke up he told me one more thing." He tried to make this as sound easy as could be. "He told me that I have one last chance to correct my ways but only if I really feel that this is coming from my soul. It cannot be done for any other reason. Then I looked inside myself and felt the horrors that I have caused. I am truly sorry and I want to help as much as I can try to fix things and help people I've hurt."

She felt that there is some more coming so she remained focus, waiting for the message.

Then he looked deeply into her eyes. "But that does not mean that I can escape my destiny."

"What?" she mumbled quietly.

"I've been given a last chance to try to fix things, to help improve the future." He paused for few seconds. "My dear wife, I will not continue on with you."

"Why? What do you mean? You just had a successful brain operation."

"I know how it all seems." He talked calmly and with confidence, "but I know it. I got my opportunity to talk with you and express my sorrow. I got the chance to express remorse. This is why I am still here."

"But, but . . . . How do you know it?" She refused to acknowledge his idea. "You are in good shape and . . ." She gave him a shaky smile.

"I know, loved one, I know.", he smiled at her. "Let's not talk anymore. Can you please lay with me in my bed now?"

He made room for her and she cuddled with him. She laid her head on his chest and he hugged her gently.

"I love you with all my heart. I always did. You know that?", he told her as he caressed her hair.

"I love you too, sweetie but stop it. You are making me cry." She cried, "Why do you have to say these things? You are doing so well."

"I just know it, love; I know it and you have to remember that this is a good thing. I earned my last chance to correct my ways. I hope that there is still a lot that can be done. You have to promise me to do all that I asked you."

"I promise." her voice was shaky.

Their children who had left the room returned.

"Come here kids. I would like to give you a hug.", he declared in joy.

He hugged them to his heart. They were happy to see him well after the surgery.

"But why are you crying, Mom?" his daughter asked.

"I don't know, sweetie. I don't know."

"I want you to know that I love you both very much." Gilbert held their hands.

"We love you too, Dad," the children smiled.

"Always remember to do good deeds."

His children did not understand why he gave them this life lecture just at this moment but cooperated with the process and promised they would become good grown-ups.

Gilbert seemed to be satisfied with their response.

Jillian seemed not to accept Gilbert's premonition. The doctor visited again and seemed to be very pleased from Gilbert's condition.

"He looks great. His vital signs are very good. I think he'll be out of here at no time." He grinned at them and left.

"See, what nonsense all that you are telling me is." Jillian was encouraged. "You'll be out of here within few days."

Yet Gilbert silently stuck to his mysterious claim.

They enjoyed an entire family day in the hospital where they talked about their precious past moments. Gilbert loved their vacations in Europe, especially France where they had rented an entire fancy house in the country. He loved the endless green fields and the tasty cheeses and wines. Jillian loved their Mediterranean moments, particularly their cruise to Italy, Greece and Sicily. She loved the sun-shine and waking up to seagulls chirping in the mornings. Their children loved everything else; the swimming pools, theme parks and of course the beautiful beaches.

Night arrived.

They sent their children home with Jillian's mother.

"I don't want this to be hard on the kids.", he told Jillian "Could you please stay with me tonight?"

"I'll stay with you" Jillian smiled to him. It will all pass in the morning, she thought.

Gilbert held Jillian tight to his body. "Thank you for trying to show me the way, all these years. I wish I had listened to you."

"What's matter is that you have changed. You will do good from now on." Jillian kissed him gently. "And now you need to go to sleep. You still need to rest and we want to take you home as soon as possible." She was very tired from the entire day.

"One more minute please.", he asked with the charming boyish smile that she loved so much.

"I'll always love you . . ." he told her but she already fell asleep.

It was about midnight when she woke up to the loud beeping sound of the monitoring machine. The nurses and doctor were already there. She looked at her husband who laid calmly on the bed. His eyes were closed but he had a big smile on his face. As the medical team was preparing for revival procedures he seemed very peaceful in his sleep.

Jillian put her hand on her open mouth in utter disbelief. Tears came to her eyes. "He was right, he was right after all. He just got a last chance to make it right".

*   *   *

The light angel silently marked another green checkmark on the table. It was the forth checkmark.

"Weakness." The dark angel looked at the glowing checkmarks. "Weakness and nothing else. Fools listen to their parents, even when they are dead."

"Parents have the right to help their children even after death.", the white angel spoke calmly. "It is their natural right."

"Well, do not forget." The dark angel gave him an evil smile as his eye-brows curled to stress the sassiness. "The same parent caused him to behave like that. The same parent made him an emotionless, selfish, greedy person."

"The same parent also gave him his last chance for remorse, which he wisely exercised.", the light angel enunciated his words precisely.

"Ha," The dark angel had run out of words. He looked at the air. "Still, weakness is inherited. Weak parents produce weak children. 'The fathers have eaten sour grapes and the children's teeth are set on edge'."

The light angel quoted back: "'Honor thy father and thy mother that thy days may be long upon the land which the LORD thy God giveth thee'. The door to light is always open."

Chapter V

DELIGHT

*　　*　　*

Tahir Sabach did not like to see people happy. On the contrary, he liked to see them sad, miserable and ultimately suffering. He was born to a simple Turkish family in Istanbul. His father owned a produce stand in the Istanbul market and he helped him from a young age. His father was dominant and violent. Since he was very young he frequently witnessed his father beating his mother for no reason. One evening when he and his father returned from their work day at the market, he saw his father beating his mother without any reason. Noticing his son watching his rage against the poor mother, he sat him on his lap and explained his wisdom to his son.

"You see son, women were designed for a few things only; to cook, clean, serve their husbands and raise children. Men, on the other hand, are the center of the universe. They go to work. They work hard and they bring food to the family. Therefore men are much more important than women."

When he quietly asked his father "But father, if women do all these things, why do you beat mother so hard? She did not do anything wrong."

"Ah, that is another story, my boy. Women are like animals. You have to keep them tame otherwise they get wild. They may runaway one day and leave you all alone. Therefore a man must beat his wife at least once per day so she continues to be afraid of him and obeys all his commands." Then he gave him a puff from his nargila and while he was trying to breathe through the choking clouds he heard his father continue his lecture "See, my father", he told him with an expression of importance on his face "told me something very wise. 'When you come home from work every day', he told me many years ago, 'beat your wife very hard. Even if you do not know why, she will.'"

He looked at his father and tried to understand the meaning of the entire conversation without much success. He was six years old then and the events left an impression in him. His mother died when he was in his teens due to his father's exceptional abuse of her on one particular day. Deep inside he hated his father and a few years later he put poison in his dates. So his father died and he was left alone. But he already knew how to run the produce stand and continued the family business for many years by himself.

Tahir was well connected in the Istanbul marketplace. He knew all the stand owners and their families. The owners respected Tahir but more likely were afraid of him. His violent nature and ruthlessness were well known. The Sultan himself sent his guards to consult with him whenever he needed to catch thieves or other criminals. In most cases Tahir provided vital information about the criminals and also attended the public hanging ceremonies. He became rich from the gold and silver bonuses that he received on almost a weekly basis from the Sultan. Tahir also developed two faces. From one side when criminals were asked for his help, he offered them food and a hiding place for a fee. The next day he disclosed their location to the Sultan and received another fat payment.

Tahir never hesitated to take advantage of weak or poor people. Whenever he saw an opportunity to steal or rob others he took it. He kept up good relations with the Sultan's guards by bribing them with his merchandise or gold so even if someone complained about him, he was all set ahead of time. His stand made him good money and silver and gold continued to pour in. Whenever he saw an opportunity he took it by force or by stealth. In essence he did whatever he wanted to do and got away with it.

For Tahir life was good.

It was another sunny day in Istanbul's marketplace. Shouts of the stand's sellers were heard from long distances. People arrived from all over Istanbul and its vicinity to buy dried fruit, spices, herbs and many other delicacies. Bare-foot children ran all over the place asking if anyone had jobs for them to do. They were willing to work for a few apples or a juicy watermelon. The smell of spices was everywhere. The cinnamon, mint and other strong spices were dominant. New merchandise was constantly flowing from the port and people inland who came to sell their products in the market. People with large baskets were seen everywhere as they poured the contents of their baskets onto blankets, trying to sell their wares. Every once in a while the Sultan's guard patrol was seen as they maintained order in the market. No vandalism or riots were allowed and the punishment was severe if anyone dared challenge the rules. Stealing and cheating were serious crimes and severe punishment was meted out against the criminals. Dust clouds could be seen in the air from donkeys marching on the dry earth. It was the middle of the summer in Istanbul and it would be a very hot day.

Tahir walked slowly from his home to his stand. He was not In a rush at all. As he did every day, on his way to the stand he was observing his surroundings searching for quick and easy opportunities. Once he traded for a sack of saffron with a child who stood at the side of the road. The child was easy prey for him to cheat. He gave him three apples for one of the most expensive and rare spices in the market. Another time he noticed a little girl playing with a little lamb. When he noticed that there were not many people around, he told her that her mother had sent him to take the lamb back home. With smiles and smooth talk he convinced her to give him her lamb that she loved so much. The lamb became an excellent dinner that day.

Today seemed to be boring without any quick schemes, he thought as he noticed an old man standing on a side road. The man stood quietly near a blanket. On the blanket Tahir noticed shiny sparkling objects. He approached the old man. The man had a long white beard and was obviously poor as could be seen by his simple clothes. He wore dusty sandals and looked filthy as if he had come from far away.

"And what do you have here?" Tahir asked him smoothly, giving him a wide fake smile. "What are you selling?"

"Good day to you and Allah's blessings my good man," the old man smiled at him. "These are copper pots and pans that my family collected over the years."

"Good, let me look at them." Tahir checked the pots and pans. Some of them were decorated with amber and silver.

"This was fine artwork." He thought and shook his head.

"So what brings you here?" He asked the old man as he observed his merchandise.

"My family was murdered by criminals who stole all their work. These are all I have left. Now I need some money to buy food, so I thought to sell them here, in the Istanbul marketplace." He gave him a toothless smile. "Here, we have the Sultan's guards. No one can kill us for money."

"Indeed." Tahir nodded.

"Are you interested in buying any of these?" the old man offered.

"I may, I just may." Tahir played with his beard. "I am thinking about it."

He quickly observed the old man and their surroundings. They were alone on the street corner. The man had built a small tent beside his blanket. He probably lived there. The old man looked skinny and weak. Greed took over Tahir. He really wanted these fancy decorated pots and pans.

"Today is your lucky day my good man," he proclaimed happily. "I would like to buy all of what you have.", he declared with a big smile and patted the old man on his back.

"Many Thanks to you and may the blessing of Allah be with you." The old man said, happy to hear his wares would be sold. "See, I am very weak and cannot work. Now I will be able to buy some food and survive."

"*Doubly worthless*", Tahir thought as he made a plan. "Let's step into your tent here to discuss the details."

"Of Course, I'll collect all the pots and pans and put them into my bag and bring them in. I can even tell you when each one of them was made. They are all family treasures." He put his merchandise into a big bag that looked like was made of a blanket and they stepped into his tent.

The tent was almost empty. There was one blanket on the ground and a few dirty dishes near it. It looked like the old man had basically nothing.

"*The fact that he had no family or friends was an added benefit*", Tahir thought. "*He would not be missed by anyone.*"

As they entered the small tent he grabbed the old man by his arm and firmly sat him in the far corner.

The old man felt what was coming begged for his life. "Ah, do not kill me please. I beg you, in the name of Allah. Have mercy on my life." He cried hot tears.

Tahir did not even answer. He took a long rope from his side bag. He prepared to strangle the old man. "Quick, no mess and efficient", he thought.

"No please, take all of my pots and pans." cried the old man "I am the last of my family. They were all killed by robbers. Please, I am an old man and don't have many years to live anyway. Let me see the sun shining for few more years." The old man had seen Tahir pulling out his rope and tried with all of his powers to convince him to spare his life.

Tahir did not even blink. "You will bring no good to anyone anyway. No one will even notice your absence . . ."

"Allah will," the old man said. "He sees everything."

Tahir grabbed him with force and wrapped the rope around his wrinkled neck. "Allah doesn't care; otherwise he would do something to stop this, wouldn't he?"

His eyes met those of the old man.

"He is here and he sees everything." The old man seemed to have come to peace with what was going to happen. "Don't do it." he took a deep breath. "I will be killed but your soul will become dark. I will die but you will be punished."

Tahir stopped. He could not believe what he heard. The old man was now threatening him?

"You are worthless on this earth anyway", he claimed. "Why would I be punished for killing someone like you? You are less than a cockroach."

"Every human life is a secret", the old man continued "Even the lives of worthless old people like me. Besides, life was not given by you and you do not have the right to take it away. No. No."

Tahir looked at him for the last time.

"Crazy old man. I hope he won't scream."

"Ah", the old man raised his hand, knowing his end was coming. "Don't do it, please. Now I am asking for your soul."

Tahir stopped. "You know something, maybe you are right." he said.

The old man's face illuminated. "I may earn my life", he thought with joy as Tahir without any warning tightened the rope around his neck. Caught by surprise the old man tried to say something but gasped for air instead. His eyes bulged out of their sockets, staring straight at Tahir's eyes but it did not bother Tahir. He held his tight grip until the old man's body became loose and his eyes closed. Then he threw his body on the filthy blanket that he had used for a bed. After that he turned to the shiny copper pots and pans and laughed loudly.

"Now this is a nice reward for a day", he said into the air and played with his little treasure. Then he looked at the old man's body "And you old fool, just had bad luck; the bad luck to meet me this morning."

Later that day two of the Sultan's guards stopped at his stand.

"We found the body of an old man on the street corner.", one of them said quietly. They were familiar with him and knew that if a new body was found, most likely it was he who had committed the crime. They also knew that if it was him he'd reward them with something. As a matter of fact, for them it was like he was admitting to the crime.

"Really, I did not see anything this morning." Tahir proclaimed but as the two guards continued staring at him quietly, he pulled out two gold coins. "But since you are already here, here is a little gift from me." He tossed each one a golden coin and smiles spread across their faces. Now they knew for sure that he killed the old man but they did not care. They got their gold coins and that was all that mattered.

"Have a good day." they wished him and rode away on their fancy horses.

He released a short laugh. "Problem solved."

He never sold the old man's pots.

Autumn arrived and the skies turned gray. Winds from the black sea started to blow and occasional rain showers soaked the ground. Tahir hated the autumn and the winter. He did not like the wind or the rain. It caused him to have bad mood swings.

One day at noon time, Tahir sat on his chair near his stand. The skies were gray and every once in a while there was a short rain shower. His merchandise was covered with a large cover against the rain. There was hardly any customer traffic due to the weather. Here and there a person showed up to buy a specific item that was needed. It was an empty day in the market. Tahir scratched his head, obviously bored. He debated what to do. It seems like there were almost no customers that day. "Well", he thought, "It is natural. It is the fault of the weather. What can I do? I could visit the house of women. That is fun." He enjoyed one woman who entertained him wildly every time. He paid her generously and got his reward. But then he had visited her just few days ago. He yawned. He could search for someone weak and poor to rob. But recently there were no new people around due to the weather of course. He could smoke one of those nargila mixtures that he bought from his friend, a crook who stole the mixtures from another poor guy who brought them from the east. These new mixtures got him really high. They were not the regular type of hashish that he typically smoked but some stronger blend with some type of drug and scent in it. He did not care what was in this mixture. All he cared about was the relaxed feeling he had while smoking it. It had a sweet taste to it also.

He decided that this was a good idea and started to prepare his long tubed nargila for smoking when some noise caught his attention. He stopped and listened. He could hear the noise again. It came from his stand. He listened carefully again and now identified the source and nature of it. Someone was crawling under his merchandise cover. Without making any sudden moves he moved towards the source of the noise. As he got closer to the point he could clearly see a little moving bump under the large cover. An evil smile spread under his mustache.

"Someone is trying to steal from me? This guy must be new to the area. No one steals from me. Everyone local already knows it." Slowly he got closer to the moving bump. He observed it for a short while and with a quick move removed the cover. The dirty face of a young child appeared. Tahir grabbed the child's arm before he had a chance to make any move.

"And what do we have here?" Tahir said in a threatening tone.

The child had a red apple in his hand and Tahir took it. He gave a close look at the child. He was definitely new here. All children already knew not to mess with him otherwise their hands would be cut or they would at least be severely beaten for stealing. Everyone knew about Tahir's evil nature and took extra precautions with him. *Everyone knew except this child.*

"You were stealing one of my apples, weren't you?" Tahir screamed at him in a loud voice.

The child started to shake from fear. "I am very sorry, I was very hungry. I did not eat for days . . ." cried the young one. He was about ten years old. According to his torn cloths and look probably was one of these abandoned children who had to survive on their own. It also might have been that his parents were killed somehow and he was left to live in the streets.

"Where are your parents?" Tahir asked the terrified child.

"My father died and my mother and I arrived today to the market. We are selling spices that my mother makes from plants." The child looked at him with great fear.

Tahir thought about what to do with the child. He had a few children who tried to steal from him in the past. When he caught them the punishment was according to the ancient law, chopping off their hand with an ax. He had no mercy on young or old. All children in the market place already knew him and never got close to his stand. Obviously this child was new. Well, it sounded like his family was new here also. Maybe it was worth seeing the mother. Who knows what kind of adventure this could bring. Today was a boring day anyway and these events brought some action in Tahir's life.

"Take me to your mother." He spoke to the child as his eye-brows curled in anger.

The child took him to a small distant tent that at a far section of the marketplace. Typically new traders and sellers pitched their tents here and presented their products for sale. Only after long survival in the new seller's area were they allowed to move into the main marketplace.

He entered the tent firmly holding the child by his arm. Inside the tent he saw a woman sitting in front of a collection of spices. When she saw her son she stood up in fear.

"Allah, what happened? Umar, what did you do?" She ran towards her son but Tahir kept him away from her.

"Your child tried to steal from me." Tahir told her in a vicious tone.

The terrified mother covered her mouth in great horror. She knew what the right of the owner was.

"Umar, why? Why?", she cried. Then she turned to Tahir.

"Please do not harm him. He is my only son. His father died a year ago and he has no other father figure at home. I have to work all day and do not have much time for him. Please do not harm my child." She burst into tears. "I'll give you anything you want."

Tahir observed the situation. As always, he liked to be in power. It gave him a feeling of superiority. He looked at her thoroughly. The mother was young and pretty. She could be useful. They did not have any unique merchandise that he needed. Obviously they were very poor. Only few homemade spices were on the floor. There was slight chance that anyone would buy them. He looked around. They had nothing else. No wonder that the child stole. He was probably constantly hungry.

"Not my problem. I need to benefit from this case".

He looked at the mother. She was still young and in good shape. It could be some free entertainment.

"I'll spare your child's hand in exchange for having you." he said and nodded towards her.

She looked like a frightened animal when she grasped his intentions. But she knew that this was her only chance to save her child's hand.

"Umar, wait outside until I call you." She told her son with a shaky voice.

The son went out and she closed the tent's entrance.

After Tahir had his way with her he went out. When he saw the boy he grabbed his arm and dragged him with him.

"And you need to be punished."

The mother ran after him crying and begging for mercy but Tahir's ears did not hear anything.

He dragged the crying boy to his stand and put his hand on a large piece of wood. The mother tried to stop him and he hit her away. She fell to the side as a few people gathered to see what was it all about.

"This child stole from my stand today." Tahir declared in a loud voice "He will be punished now so no one else will dare to do the same."

The child screamed for mercy. His mother passed out. The people looked without intervening. They already knew Tahir's nature and did not want to aggravate him further.

Tahir gave a last look at the boy. He shook all over his body and his eyes expressed horrific fear.

"Please," he whispered with tears "I returned the apple. I'll never do it again."

Tahir felt a tiny, unexpected spark inside him.

"Should I spare him?"

As quickly as it rose, it went away. His face turned red and unforgiving. The boy closed his eyes.

Tahir raised his ax.

A flock of crows flew off the trees.

*   *   *

Tahir yawned with boredom. It was another day of the week and he had nothing to look forward to. As every day, he woke up early in the morning without any target or goal in his life. He had a full schedule in front of him but he was not really enthusiastic about starting it. He stared at the sunny skies and breathed in the early morning fresh air.

First, he'd dress, wash his face and then make very strong coffee. Then he'd sit for a while and drink his coffee before going to the market. These moments were typically empty for him. No thoughts, no memories, no future plans, just zoning out with his coffee. Then he'd eat goat cheese, pita bread and olive oil. With his food he'd drink fresh squeezed orange juice that he'd make by himself. Dessert, ah, he never finished a meal without a delicious dessert. He had one planned for the beginning of every day. A Turkish delight, Rahat Lokum in strawberry flavor. Turkish delight or Lokum was a family of confections based on a gel of starch and sugar. Premium varieties consist largely of chopped dates, pistachios and hazelnuts or walnuts bound by the gel; the cheapest are mostly gel, generally flavored with rosewater, mastic, or lemon. The confection is packaged and eaten in small cubes dusted with powdered sugar or cream of Tartar to prevent clinging. This was his favorite way to start the day, with the Rahat Lokum in his hand he'd walk to his stand in the marketplace. That had been his morning ritual for many years now.

"Yes, it is all nice but still, there is nothing to look forward into. No surprise, no excitement."

But, it has to be done, he thought and forced himself to stand up and start the day. There was always a chance that he'd find some-one interesting to rob or mug on his way to his stand.

Then he had a disappointment. He wanted to make coffee and noticed that he had run out of wood. He needs the wood to heat the coffee pot. He released a long sigh. He'd have to cut some of his logs that were outside his tent. Without any real passion to go out into the chill morning air he grabbed his ax and stepped outside to his yard. At the far end there was a pile of dried logs that he typically cut for fire purposes.

"It is chilly today."

He picked a large log and looked at it. It looked dry enough for fire although the morning dew made it wet. It would dry with the fire he decided and cut a few grooves to mark his chopping points. The first hit fell on the log with amazingly accuracy and a small piece detached. Tahir was impressed by his work.

"Good work old man. You still have it."

Then he picked another groove and raised the ax in the air. All of a sudden, due to the morning humidity, the ax slipped out of his hand. With surprise on his face he slowly watched the ax fly through the air. Instinctively he sent his hands to catch it and that was when the ax hit his open hand, ripping his palm, cutting a huge whole right through the center of his hand. The ax's weight contributed to the size and strength of the impact. Tahir continued watching as a large gush of blood streamed from his badly injured hand. At the beginning, he was too surprised to scream so he simply looked at his torn hand. Then he felt the excruciating pain and screamed at the top of his lungs. He held the base of his hand with the other hand as his body rapidly went into shock. Large amounts of blood flew from the injured hand. He saw the blood flowing out of his hand and this scared him. He felt weak. The world spun around and he fell on the ground. Then came the blessed darkness.

He woke up as he felt his head pounding. Why was he sticky? Slowly he remembered what had happened to him. He looked at his hand and it looked dark, covered with dried blood. He felt his hand throbbing with pain. He was alone.

"*I have to stand up and take care of myself*", he thought. "*No-one comes to my place. I'll have to take care of myself.*"

Slowly he stood up and walked to his well. With the other hand he raised some water and washed his injured hand. The cold water washed the darkened blood and he could observe the wound. It was serious. The falling ax cut his hand in the middle, ripping veins and tendons. The wound looked ugly.

"*I had better cover it with some cloth*", he thought.

He washed it more and then wrapped it with some cloth. The pain was excruciating. Tahir did not have any medical knowledge and could not know that the filthy cloth would make the wound worse. The pain had reduced after a few hours and he could function at his booth but on the second day he got a high fever. The wound in his hand became even more painful and he sought the help of his friend who lived near him.

His friend, a stand owner named Salim with similar nature to his, looked at the wound and whistled to show he was impressed.

"This is a serious cut Tahir," he scratched his head. "It also does not look good. I think you'll need to sink it in salty water every day." He gave his advice. But Tahir was not even willing to hear about it.

"Are you crazy? That will burn like hell." he became angry. "I will not sink my hand in salt. Do you have any other idea?"

Salim was already afraid of Tahir. He knew that he could get mad and hit him. It happened before and therefore gave up his advising.

"I do not know what to say Tahir. I do not have much knowledge of injuries." he apologized in a low tone.

"Oh, you are useless friend;" Tahir was mad "I'll go home and wash it with water again."

But the water wash did not help and after a week Tahir's entire arm hurt badly. He had high fever and could not go to his stand in the morning. Salim came to visit him on a daily basis and helped him with food and water. After few more days, Tahir's condition worsened.

"Your hand smells bad", Salim told him one evening when he put a wet cloth on Tahir's forehead. He had high fever every day now and could hardly concentrate on his words. "We need to find serious help Tahir. Otherwise I think you could die from this."

Tahir turned his head and looked at Salim. He knew that Salim was right. He also smelled his hand for the past week. It stunk badly. He had to turn his head away from it so he did not get nauseous. He did not feel well at all and knew that without serious help he had a good chance of dying.

"My son knows a very wise man who has great knowledge of medicine.", Salim said quietly. "He lives far from Istanbul but I think this man can really help you. I already talked with my son about you. He recommends that we seek his help." Salim wiped Tahir's face. Tahir was mumbling unclear words in his high fever. This condition persisted for a week or so. In the morning Tahir could focus on eating or being somewhat coherent but at night his fever went up high and he could not even respond.

"I'll talk with my son and leave in the morning to bring this man." Salim wet a few cloths and put them in Tahir's warm hand. "Here, use these for the night. I'll leave early in the morning."

Tahir did not even hear him. He sank into a fitful sleep.

*   *   *

Salim returned late the next day. With him arrived two men and a woman. They arrived in the dark. Salim led them into Tahir's tent. On a large fur mat on the ground laid Tahir. He was calm and sound asleep. He had a rough day and at last fell asleep in his hallucinations. He woke up when Salim and the people entered into his tent.

"Salim, is that you?" he asked in a weak voice. There was only one lantern in the tent that gave out very poor light. He could hardly see them.

"Yes, it is me.", Salim answered quietly. "I brought with me the wise man. His whole family arrived with him. They are all helping people with illnesses and injuries. They are wise healers."

Tahir turned his head to the side. He was too weak to respond. "Do what you need to do.", he mumbled.

The tall man approached Tahir and checked his hand.

"Quick, I need better light", he announced.

The woman lengthened the little lantern's wick which then produced brighter light.

"His hand smells very bad." The tall man gently removed the filthy cloths on Tahir's hand. He observed the black colored wound silently. "Just as I thought." He turned to Salim. "Your friend's hand is rotten."

Salim looked at him without understanding. "Can you cure him?"

"We'll have to take a better look at it in the morning." the tall man said. "I suspect that his hand is in a very advanced stage of gangrene. If this is the case, the only way to try to help him is to amputate his hand."

Salim covered his mouth. "What? Do you mean cut his hand off?"

"Indeed," the tall man stood. "That would be the only way to save his life. Otherwise the infection could poison his entire body and then he'd die."

He turned to the other man who arrived with them. "What do you think Hakim?"

Hakim observed Tahir's hand. "Yes, by the smell and the look it looks like progressed state of gangrene." he stood up. "I agree with you."

The women stood there quietly. "We'll have to take a look at his hand in the morning." She said in a delicate voice.

"Please come to my tent, I have plenty of room for you to sleep." Salim offered.

"No, thank you" the woman answered. "We need to prepare some clean cloth to help your friend pass the night. We'll sleep here, with him."

She took some clean cloth from her bag as the other man went to get clean water. They prepared for a long night. They were determined to fight for Tahir's life. They could not even imagine the surprise that dawn would bring.

*   *   *

It was early morning when Tahir turned his head. The women that were keeping wet cloths on his forehead had a chance to take a look at his face for the first time.

"Wait.", said one of the women, His face looked familiar. Then with an expression of a great surprise she screamed.

Her family rushed to her.

She covered her mouth in disbelief and an angry expression appeared on her face. "I can't believe it. It is him!"

The tall man who stood near her looked at Tahir's face. When he recognized him his face turned angry as well. The other man stood there quietly without any expression on his face. It seemed that he did not know Tahir.

The woman pushed away the bowl with wet cloths and it splashed on the ground. "He does not deserve our help." She went outside.

The tall man stood and looked at Tahir's face. They looked calm. It seemed that morning was a good time for him. He took a deep breath.

"Hakim," he turned to him. "Take a look at this man we are helping today."

Hakim looked at him and at Tahir without understanding what was going on.

"Today, you will see the great wisdom of Allah, Hakim. You will witness nature's ways but most of all you will see that we have to overcome hatred and evil feelings. We have to find our kindness and mercy." He paused and then added, "even if it is regarding people who harmed us in the past."

"I do not understand Umar." Hakim whispered.

"Hakim," Umar smiled calmly to him. "Your name means wise man. One of Allah's ninety-nine qualities. Today you'll understand."

Tahir opened his eyes. "Who are you people?" he whispered in a low voice. He was very weak.

Salim entered the tent. "Tahir my friend." He was happy to see that Tahir was capable of talking. "I brought these wise people last night. They are experts in medicine. They will help you." he beamed from happiness. He was sure that things would be better from then on.

The woman entered the tent. Her eyes looked cold and emotionless. An expression of despise was on her face. She approached Tahir. "Do you remember us?" She hissed her words like a poisonous snake.

Tahir looked at her face with great concentration. Her face was familiar but he could not remember where he saw her. "I do not remember.", he started to say as the memory struck him. His entire being shook and his mouth became dry. "No, what are you doing here?", he mumbled. Cold sweat of sweat showed on his forehead and his heart raced.

"What is happening?" Although Salim was witnessing the entire scene he could not grasp the chain of events.

Umar turned to him. "We all know Tahir your friend." He said in a loud and clear voice. "We met him many years ago. Actually I met him when I was ten years old and my mother here met him at the same time."

Salim was astonished. Tahir calmed down and listened to Umar's speech.

"I was ten years old and we had no money to buy food so I stole an apple from Tahir's stand." Umar's look turned towards Tahir. "Tahir wanted to exercise his right to remove my hand as a punishment. My mother begged for mercy." His eyes flashed with anger as he talked "Tahir demand my mother's dignity in exchange to my hand."

Salim knew Tahir's nature and remained quiet, lowering his eyes to the ground.

"After he had his way with my mother, Tahir did not keep his word and chopped off my hand." Umar raised his amputated arm to show that he had no hand. "Now, he wants us to help him with his hand?" He paused for a while and then added "Karma exists in nature and sooner or later it plays out."

Tahir started to shake when the facts were thrown at his face. He shook his head in great disbelief. "No, No."

Umar looked at Tahir and slowly calmed down. "Sorry, this was our initial response. Tahir was very mean to us and I am sure to many others as well but we will overcome our feelings of hatred and desire for revenge. Hate, anger and evil thoughts are not good for the human soul. We do not believe in them and we do not give ourselves up to them." He lowered his eyes to Tahir. "We will help you today Tahir though I must say that Allah sent you an appropriate punishment, as you punished me many years ago."

Tahir stared at him in great fear.

"If you want to live Tahir, we will have to remove your hand. It is rotten; gangrenous in a very advanced stage. That is why it has such a bad smell. If we will not remove it the rot will spread to your entire body and you will die."

Tahir silently heard Umar's words.

"We will help you today." The woman talked calmly. After their initial anger had passed the entire family was determined to save Tahir's life. "Although you disgraced me and cut off my son's hands many years ago, we humans should not punish others. Allah sees all and punishes those who deserve to be punished."

Then she added, "We will do our best to save your life. I think that you have a great chance to survive if we cut off your hand."

"Who are you?" Tahir nodded towards a young man beside Hakim. Now that he knew who the woman and Umar were he was wondering who the third man was. He looked younger then Umar. He also had a wise expression on his face.

"Miraculous are nature's ways." The woman spoke and a slight smile spread on her pretty face. "Hakim is my second son.

He, like my first son Umar, brought light and joy into my life. He is wise and kind. He is considerate of others. He cares about others. He helps the weak and the poor. He is like an angel."

She looked straight into Tahir's eyes. "He is the complete opposite of his father." Her eyes glazed when she looked outside. "His father who raped me many years ago did not have mercy on his brother's hand."

Tahir closed his eyes for a while and then opened them looking at Hakim.

"This man is my son. He is the son of a violent crime I committed."

Tahir tried to focus on his typical behaviors.

"You did not do anything wrong", he told himself. *"You were the strong one so you took what was yours anyway. The thieving child had to be punished. Those are the rules."*

"I suffered great trauma after you cut my son's hand off", the woman continued. "I could not sleep at night. I was with him day and night, watching, caring and loving. I did not know if he'd survive the wound. Many people die after a hand is removed. I worried about his future life. What would he be able to do without one hand? How would he work for his living?" Then she smiled at Umar. "But he survived and so did I. From our humiliation and agony came strength. We became stronger. Umar was very curious about what happened to his hand and started to learn about the human body. After I helped Umar heal I found the world of medicine and healing amazing. We studied, learned and excelled in this area and today we are a known medicine family. We help people."

"It gives us a good feeling that we help people. We save lives." Umar continued.

Tahir listened quietly.

"There was another result of your disgraceful actions against us". The woman spoke. "I got pregnant. At the beginning I thought it was be the worst day of my life but Umar encouraged me not to lose hope. 'Children are innocent, Mother' he told me and I believed him. Furthermore, I believed in him. And he was right. Hakim was born and brought us both only light and happiness." She looked at Tahir with mercy. "See, we were not the people who actually got punished. We got blessed. It was your soul that got punished and you did not even know about it."

"Miraculous are the ways of nature, governed by Allah'." Umar continued. "Here we are today, trying to help you and I hope that we will be able to do so." He looked at his brother Hakim "For Hakim's sake. After all, you are his father."

"I heard only bits and pieces along the years." This was the first time that Hakim talked. "Mother and Umar never told the whole story. I guess they wanted to save me the agony and sorrow. But I figured it out from details that they shared with me here and there." He approached Tahir and knelt beside him. "I am sorry to hear of bad things that you have done my father. Still I am glad that I got the opportunity to find you. Deep in my heart I know that you have good in your soul. I hope you'll find the strength to let it out."

Tahir's heart was in great struggle. He refused to recognize that he did wrong in the past, very wrong. Yet, very deep inside him, a small, tiny voice told him that he was wrong all throughout his life. He turned his head not to see Hakim and the others.

"Better die now and save myself the pain.", He thought.

Then he heard Hakim mumbling "I hope we are not too late to save you." He then added, "in both ways; your life and your soul."

Without a word Umar and the mother started to prepare for the operation. They washed Tahir's entire arm thoroughly and wrapped his arm with a clean cloth.

According to their request Salim brought wine and they let Tahir drink a significant amount of it.

"You will probably pass out from the pain but we will be here when you wake up." Umar told him as he instructed Hakim and Salim to hold him tight.

Tahir felt very drunk but he knew that serious pain was coming. "Wait." he called just before they started. "I would like to say something." For a moment he wondered if this was happening because he was drunk. All of a sudden the small seed of light grew stronger inside him and he felt he had to tell them something, just in case something happened and he did not wake up. He felt a desperate need to ask for their forgiveness. Something came from his soul but he could not get it out. Instead he looked at them with glazed eyes lacking the power to express his words clearly. "I wanted to tell you . . . Ah . . . Ah . . ."

Hakim put his hand on Tahir's head. "You do not need to say anything, Father. I already knew." He smiled to Tahir that looked at him with great astonishment. "You do not need to say anything."

Umar looked at them and signaled to his mother. It was the right moment. He raised the ax on Tahir's hand, exactly as Tahir did to him more than fifteen years ago.

*   *   *

Tahir survived the amputation procedure. The entire family took care of him until his complete recovery. Then a miracle happened. Something that no-one would ever have imagined. Immediately upon Tahir's recovery he asked Umar's mother to marry him. After few days of debate she agreed and a big wedding ceremony was conducted in one of the most beautiful parts of the marketplace.

Tahir became a new person. He never apologized to Umar and his mother for what he has done to them. Instead of using words he changed as a person and proved to himself by the person he became. He started to help people, especially the poor and the hungry. He made sure that he found someone to help every day. The people who knew him for years in the marketplace could not believe the change that befell him. Everyone knew that if they needed any type of help, all they had to do was ask Tahir. He took care of everyone who came to see him with any problem.

Salim, his best friend claimed that Tahir was re-born. He had become a completely different person; good and kind to everyone. No one could imagine that this was the Tahir they had known for many years.

Umar explained to Tahir that his name, Tahir, meant pure, clean and modest. Tahir answered that he wondered what had happened to him in the past. He could not even believe that he had done such evil. He was determined to earn his dignity back by doing good deeds. Tahir vowed to help his family to help others and save lives. He adopted Umar as his son and the entire family lived righteousness lives ever after.

*   *   *

"Coincidence," whispered the dark angel, "Coincidence and incoherency. That's what caused this one to move away from my side." He was very frustrated. He felt that with this one he had been very close to turning him permanently to the evil side. He had already lost on five occasions. Now he wanted to win only one. One incident in which evil prevails would mean that good lost the battle. It would only take one such case.

"The final result counts." The light angel nodded and illuminated another green checkmark. "A thimbleful of light can make a whole world of difference."

Chapter VI

CHILDREN OF LIFE

*   *   *

Isabel screamed in surprise.

"I found my mother!", she thought with astonishment. *"I found my mother after almost forty* years. *What are the odds? I am going to see her in two days. I can't believe it."*

Her phone rang, interrupting her thoughts and she answered it without passion.

"What?"

She listened for a while. It was bad news.

"Damn," she scratched her head with obvious irritation. "These girls were worth millions. Oh well, make sure that anything connecting us to this shipment will be disappeared."

She sat in her large, fancy office and looked through the large windows. Down below there was the big city of Chicago where she lived all her life. She had definitely risen high since she was a young prostitute, she thought as she was pouring a glass of bourbon. She was born to a poor family and her father died when she was young. Her mother worked a few shifts in order to support them until she got sick and could not work anymore. As their financial situation had gotten worse, at the age of sixteen her mother brought her a man as her first client. She was beautiful and men were willing to pay hefty sums to be with her. For many years she thought about that episode and could not make a judgment. Was her mother right in what she did? Many would say no, of course, but the reality was that she supported both of them in dignity until the state discovered the case and took her away from her mother. She was transferred to a distant foster family and never saw her mother again.

A large bird flew near her window and she wondered where it was flying. She drank another shot of bourbon and felt the familiar warmth start spreading inside her. She runaway from her foster family after the foster father tried to have sex with her. She was almost eighteen then and determined to make it big in this world. With her beauty and passion to become rich she became an exclusive call girl and charged a few thousand dollars per night. Her customers typically wanted an entire evening girlfriend, not just a quick adventure, and she gave them the entire show. With her sharp mind she figured that rich men would pay a significant amount of money for a pretty young girl and soon enough she was rich enough to think about other ways to make big bucks. One of her high class customers introduced her to human trafficking business.

Importation of young humans from China, Thailand and Africa was a serious industry. Humans were smuggled in large container ships into the United States. There was an entire system in tact starting with finding the people, preparing them for shipment and passage to pickup, a procedure that was typically conducted late at night. The mechanism was working smoothly like a fully lubricated machine and the money reached six or even seven figures a year.

She learned Karate and how to use weapons and became a sharp warrior in the streets of Chicago. Big men learned to respect her and she even earned a nickname in the crime land, Iron Beauty. She discovered that a human's life was worthless for her. She simply did not care about people; adults or children. Something was numb inside her and she conducted her business calmly and without any emotion.

She had just been informed that a shipment of young females from Thailand was caught in mid-sea. The sailors found them after they made noise inside the container. Unfortunately, told her assistant the sailors were extremely bored and when they discovered the young girls they tried to have fun with them. One of the girls resisted and pushed a man who fell, hit his head and died. Scared that their involvement would be found out by their business partner, the shipping company, they put all the girls on one of their life saving boats with some food and water and deserted them in the middle of the ocean knowing their chance of survival was minimal. Even her assistant mentioned to her that these girls probably died a horrible death of thirst and hunger. She did not feel anything about the girls' fate but a deep sorrow about the lost of her investment. These girls would bring her few good millions of dollars and it was a shame that they were discovered. She knew that this was not the first and would not be the last difficult case at sea. At one time another shipment never arrived at its destination. The sailors claimed that they did not know anything. Of course, anything could happen and no one could file a complaint. But the majority of the human shipment arrived on time and the payment was generous. When there was a large shipment of people like they brought last month from Guatemala, they had a special person escorting the container on board. She had devised this initiative and enforced it without any compromise. Overall, beside rare glitches here and there, business went well and she was looking to new horizons to expand her income.

Everything goes. That was her motto and she kept it successfully.

Her thoughts went again to those girls who were abounded mid-sea. Adolescent girls were abandoned in the middle of the ocean with little food or water. She pulled her shoulders, "Oh well", that was not her problem. Life is not something that required her interference. Some make it and some don't. It's all a matter of luck. Luck came from where you were born, how you grew up and what events that happened to you.

"This day was not a good day.", she thought in bitterness. *"Not for me and definitely not for these poor girls."*

The next day was not good either. Early in the morning she got a phone call with more bad news. Her large group of imported workers who labored in one of the underground sweat shops was badly injured when a fire burst out in the warehouse. All hundred and eighty people were suffering from serious burns and smoke inhalation. There were basically two options. One option was to get them medical attention, including hospitalization. That would cause her and her organization to be exposed and the direct result would be a clash with the law. The second option was to try to provide the injured black market medical attention. From initial reports it seemed like this would not do much since almost everyone who got hurt in the fire needed hospital amenities.

"Bad luck", she mumbled.

Then her assistant mentioned a third option. "There is a third option that Rich suggested. Rich was her other type of assistant. Sometimes when gruesome tasks needed to be done, he was the guy to call. Rich had suggested taking that shipment of females out to mid sea and exposing them all. He would make sure that this group would also be taken far into the sea so no bodies would reach shore. It may cost some money to execute this operation but still much less than all other options. Even her assistant hesitated about this idea. After all, he said, there were fourteen year old boys and girls in this group.

She didn't even flinch. Dispose of them all, she gave the order, and make sure that there will be no traces that lead to us.

Her assistant sounded hesitance "Isabel, there are children there."

"Just do as I said." she concluded and lighted a cigarette. "We do not have too much time here."

She could feel his response from the other side. He remained quiet. That told her everything. He had worked with her for many years and although she liked him she always thought that he had soft side.

"Ramon," she softened her tone "Just think about this, we can't afford anyone to survive. Any evidence left behind can lead to us and our arrest. We will get many prison years."

"What kind of women are you Isabel?", he did not hesitate to ask her bluntly. "You are supposed to bear children one day. These are not just objects. These are human beings. They are all burnt and need medical help. Taking them to mid sea and killing them all?"

He may not fit his job anymore, she thought quietly. I have to replace him.

"You know something, you may be right." Isabel said in a softer tone. "Let me consult with Rich directly."

"Good decision Isabel," she could hear the relief in his voice. "I started to think that I am working here with an inhuman person." he grinned.

"No worry, we'll take care of everything." she reassured him.

She looked at her smoked cigarette for only half a second. Then she called Rich.

"I have a small mission for you." She told him in dry tone.

"At your service, as always my dear." he was always smooth with her. They had more than just working relations. He admired her beauty and did not hesitate to ask her for sexual favors occasionally which she provided with no hesitation. She needed him for dirty work and it was simply worth it.

"I need you to take care of the accident that I had in my warehouse." She said without any introductions. "Everyone needs to quietly disappear. You already suggested a good solution. Execute it."

She could almost see Rich smiling on the other side of the phone line. "Sure, I'll take care of this."

"ASAP." she added shortly. "I want to close this incident and put it behind us."

"I'll take care of it first thing tomorrow morning." Rich answered in a low but confident tone. "When can I see you?"

She paused. She knew why he wanted to see her. "Tomorrow night with a full report about the cleanup."

"May I take you to your favorite place my dear?"

She smiled. He knew her very well. She considered him a kind of boyfriend over the years. She had never had a relationship and he was the only person who was ever close to her. Although most people disliked Rich due to his aggressive nature she found him quite attractive.

"Yes, let's go to my favorite place. I am craving a good Italian dinner and few large margaritas."

"The treat is on me." he concluded.

"Oh, and one more thing." She added in a soft voice.

"Up to half the kingdom for you."

"Get rid of Ramon."

"Ramon?" he was surprised. Ramon was her personal, dedicated assistant for the past few years.

"Yes, he became too weenie. I need stronger person then him." She responded dryly.

"Will do."

"Call me tomorrow." She hung up the phone with a slow movement.

She did not need Ramon. In the past few crises he had shown too much humanity. She saw it as a weakness. She'd have to replace him with someone who was not affected by human death. Then she thought about Rich. He was always there and she somehow missed him. He was an emotionless sociopath. He would fit her perfectly. She'd just have to make him an offer that he could not refuse.

She met Rich the next day. He picked her up and drove to the Italian place that was located downtown.

"Everything is done, exactly as you wanted." He raised a toast of Champagne.

She raised her glass and took a small sip from it. "Ramon?"

"It has all been done." He answered with a smile.

"You know, I must say that Ramon had one question before he died." Rich gave her an arrogant smile. Then he continued. "He knew that he was about to die. When I was putting the silencer on my gun he simply threw his question at me."

She looked at him with curiosity.

"'Isabel is still a woman', he said." Rich started and she laughed. "'Does the women factor mean nothing to her? She is supposed to bear children one day'."

"Yes, he told me this cliché also", Isabel smiled at him. "That is why I don't need him. He was too weak, sentimental, and merciful. I do not need nuns in here. I need people who have strong stomachs. I need people who will know how to handle operations like you executed today." She raised her glass again. "You are a perfect fit for the job. I need you to take his place." She shot her demand without a blink. "Will you do it Rich? Will you do it for me?"

She knew that Rich typically was involved with other businesses. He made lots of money from drug dealing and she knew that she had to match a good salary for him.

"Wow, Isabel, you know that I have other jobs . . .", he started.

"I'll double your monthly income to run my businesses." She poured him more Champagne. "I want you all to myself, nothing else."

He smiled widely. "Well, my dear, in this case, I am all yours."

"I didn't think differently." She gave him a naughty smile.

"With one condition," he added suddenly. She didn't even let him complete his sentence.

"You got it."

*   *   *

The next day she flew to see her mother. She lived in Columbus Ohio, which was fairly close to her. She had hired a private investigator to locate her mother and it was not an easy task. She had not kept any records of her and had to rely on what was left in her memory. But the private investigator conducted thorough research that took months and finally found her in a very near state. The meeting was set at a local restaurant.

Isabel met the investigator on time at the restaurant. They ordered coffee. The private investigator's name was Jim. He was a short chubby guy, in his mid forties and looked constantly happy. With his red cheeks, sparkling eyes and permanent grin on his face, Isabel thought that he looked like a figure from children's story. Yet he was considered one of the best in this field and that is why she hired him. Apparently, she thought, as she was observing him, he did a good job. After many months he had traced her mother all the way to here, Columbus Ohio and now, here she was, expecting to meet her after almost forty years.

"How was your flight?" Jim sipped from his coffee.

"Smooth, thanks." she answered with courtesy.

"Stop with this constant stupid smile on your face!", she thought.

"Good, mine was a bit bumpy but considering the fact that I am arriving from Buffalo, New York it went fairly well. Typically this time of the year, there is a lot of turbulence when we cross the Adirondack Mountains." he looked at her thoroughly. "So, are you ready for the big moment?"

"Oh, Yes I am.", she replied with a large fake smile. Honestly, she did not know what to feel. Inside she had mixed feelings about her mother since she was a child.

"Many years have passed. This is the part of my job that I like best." Jim seemed extra happy now. "Reuniting together. This is something I would not miss when I solve a case. I've seen so many people reunite with their families and loved ones. It is simply heartwarming."

"Very touching. What is with this ugly purple tie?"

He read her mind.

"I told her that I'll be wearing a purple tie" Jim like read her mind "I keep this tie for identification purposes only." He laughed briefly and she nodded with hidden impatience.

Two women entered the restaurant. One looked like she was in her late fifties and the other one younger, in her twenties. The older one looked around and headed towards Isabel and Jim's table. The younger women followed her. When they approached the table the older women extended her hand towards Jim.

"Jim, I presume?"

"Indeed mam and you are Miss Morgan?" Jim stood up and moved towards the women in an almost exaggerated, theatrical move. "And who is this lovely lady accompanying you?"

"This is my Daughter, Kai-Lan." the older lady sat quietly in front of Isabel and Kai-Lan sat near her.

The older lady's eyes were transfixed on Isabel. Jim had already told her on the phone who she was coming to see today. Her eyes scanned Isabel's thoroughly trying to identify familiar features that she remembered.

"Many years have passed . . ." she mumbled. "But I remember your eyes."

Isabel looked at her mother. She identified her immediately. She'd never forget her look which basically remained the same, just a much older version of it. The same eyes, the same structure with high cheek bones, the nose . . . everything fits. This was her mother. She did not know how to feel. Her mother was the one who, many years ago, put her on the track she was on that day. After being introduced to prostitution she was taken by the wheels of fate to where she was now. Yes, she excelled and became very rich but inside her she had mixed feelings. "Is this what a mother should have done? Yes, they were in a very poor financial state then but still . . . And who is this other daughter she brought with her, Kai-Lan? Asian of some sort . . ."

Many questions went through her mind as she was looking at her mother.

"Hello Mother", Isabel said in a scratchy voice.

"Hello Isabel", her mother's tone was cold as ice.

Kai-Lan looked down.

"What is going on here?", thought Isabel.

"OK, this is not the welcome that I've seen in similar occasions." Jim tried to break the ice. He never saw such a cold meeting between mother and daughter, especially after so many years they had not seen each other. "Maybe you are both overwhelmed. It is understandable . . ."

"No, this is not the case." the mother interrupted him. "Then she turned to Isabel. "It is you Isabel."

Isabel moved discomfortably in her seat. "It is me."

The mother sent shaky hand towards her face. "Years I have dreamt of touching you again. Years I have dreamt of hugging you again, years . . ." Tears were in her eyes.

Isabel extended a hesitant hand towards her mother. Then just before they touched her mother quickly pulled her hand back. Her eye-brows curled in anger. "No, I've heard that you are on the side of evil."

Isabel was surprised. Jim remained speechless. He decided that it was better for him to remain quiet.

"This woman", she held Kai-Lan's hand, "brought me the evidence. Then I checked about you. It is all correct isn't it Isabel?"

Isabel shook her head. "What are you talking about?"

"Tell me that you are not bringing innocent girls from China and Thailand to be sold as prostitutes?"

"Ah, ladies, could we please return to our family reunion here?" Jim tried to stop the negative direction but the two women completely ignored him.

"Tell me that these women are not abused, raped and murdered and you know about that?"

Isabel remained silent.

"Tell that you have nothing to do with this inhumanity?" Her mother stopped and was breathing heavily. She was very upset. "I found Kai-Lan when I was driving home one night. She was thrown on the side road near my home. I picked her up and brought her home. What I discovered was shocking." She paused to gather the power to continue.

"She had escaped from one of the most horrific places that I've ever seen or heard about; a whore house of the worse kind.

A whore house where they keep young girls like her, fifteen years old girl who were kidnapped from China and smuggled into the United States. She and many other girls were kept in distant locations and used as prostitutes. Kai-Lan was brave. She escaped but the others are probably still in that hell if not murdered."

Isabel was in shock. She never expected this to happen.

"I would never imagine that you would be involved with this type of occupation." She said the word 'occupation' with great distain on her face. "But Kai-Lan was smart enough to steal some documents from the place before she escaped. She wanted to disclose the information to the police so those bastards would be put in prison for the rest of their lives. I looked at the papers and I was shocked to find your name there. Some not too smart guy wrote contact numbers on a piece of paper. He was probably was not allowed to do so but obviously was not bright."

Her eyes sparkled with anger towards Isabel. "I called your number and hung up. It was you in Chicago and I was ashamed to discover that you were actually managing these types of operations."

She hugged Kai-Lan who started to cry. "I called the police and gave them all the information that night. Besides handing over the note with your information on it, I never told this to anyone, not even to Kai-Lan, my legally adopted daughter." She wiped a tear and continued, encouraged by her own voice. "Today she is a social worker, helping girls who have lost their way in life. She is saving the lives of young girls who have lost the light in their lives and are at the bottom of life. I ran a check about a woman named Isabel Grant and got all the necessary information about you. You are the one who brought those girls from overseas and sold them here like cattle. You are still doing it."

She shook her head in great agony. "I know life pushed you into dark corners and I even had major part in it but you excelled in a very wrong direction." She looked straight into Isabel's eyes "Other than prisoners we all have the right and responsibility in life to make our own choices and we all have choices to make. You made yours and it is not a good one."

Jim stared at the scene. He did not know what to say but his senses told him to stay quiet for his own wellbeing.

Isabel did not move. Her mother's words penetrated into her like knives. After a while she answered her in a steady tone. "Well, yes it was me on that paper that you found. Yes, it is me who own this operation and many others. Somehow," she made a noticeable pause to stress her next word "Mother, I learned that life belongs to those who are strong, not to the weak but to the strong. Only the strong survive." Then she added with great irony "You are the one who pushed me into this world, remember?"

"Yes, I remember and I truly regret doing so. I should have sent you to work in the local grocery store to make a living but I didn't. Still, to reach your level of large scale operations is not justified. This is taking innocent human lives and trashing them without any mercy. And you continue doing it. Day after day, more innocent girls and boys are condemned to hell because of you."

She stood up, holding Kai-Lan's hand and threw a little note on the table. "I saved one poor soul, Kai-Lan but how many souls are entering into hell, right this moment because of you?" She took a deep breath and concluded before they left. "As far as I am concern, you are not my daughter anymore."

They both left the restaurant. Isabel sat there for a little while and then looked at the note that her mother left behind. In a sloppy hand writing her name was there, along with her cellular phone number. It was screaming evidence of her crime that someone left behind.

*   *   *

Isabel returned to Chicago the same day. She called Rich.

"Hey, how about dinner tonight, this time at your favorite place."

Rich was surprised. She never allowed him to pick a place for dinner. "With a pleasure my dear. I'll pick you up at 9:00 tonight." Right on time, he thought. "I missed her."

Then he thought for a moment. *"What is going on with me? I thought that I just miss having sex with these women. She is rootless like me. No emotions are involved in here."*

"Really?" He scratched his head, wondering.

He picked the fanciest place in Chicago. The restaurant was located on the roof of a very high tower a hundred stories high. It cost him a grand just to reserve a table.

"You look wonderful tonight my dear." He flattered her. He thought that she seemed distant that night.

She gave him one of her glamorous smiles and thought that this is quite sad that she actually wanted his company tonight. She observed him; a handsome guy, in his late thirties, wealthy and artificially nice. She also knew that he was rootless and capable of committing horrible acts.

"Is this the part of him that I am attracted to?"

"No, not necessarily", she concluded. *"So what? What do I see in him? Why is it that tonight I need him with me? I know that he'll want sex later but this is somehow making us closer even without him noticing it. Oh, my, am I in love with this guy?"*

"What's on your mind tonight dear?" he raised a toast. "And how was your trip to Ohio?"

"Oh, just a boring trip."

"I have good news for you." he moved closer to her. "I saved you today from a sticky situation. We caught few women who were planning to escape."

She wanted to say something and then stopped. "And?"

"I used one of the girls as an example punishment. Now the others will never even think about running away." He laughed like he told a good joke and she knew what this meant.

Her eyes lowered. "Poor girl" she said, and thought,

"What is happening to me?"

"Not tonight" she added quietly.

He realized that she does not want to hear anything about work tonight.

She raised her glass towards him "For tonight." The night air flattered her in her gown and exposed her beautiful legs for a split second.

He could not restrain his eyes from her beauty and smiled widely. "She is truly beautiful", he thought and raised his glass. "For us tonight."

*   *   *

"I have a good news and bad news", her doctor told her with a large smile a month later.

"What?" she did not have much patience for her doctor? Although she admired his medical skills he was like a chatter box sometimes.

He looked at her like she won the lottery. "The bad news is that you'll continue feel badly for the next few months."

"So what is the good news?" She got mad. "I can't imagine good news with such bad news."

"Well, the good news is actually connected to the bad news."

"Oh, why does he have to be so annoying?" she thought.

"You are going to be a mother soon."

She had to sit down.

"I am pregnant. I can't believe it!"

*   *   *

"I can't believe it!"

That was all what she could think about.

"How has this happened to me? I don't want this! I don't have time for it."

She woke up and did not get out of bed. She already had severe morning sicknesses and was vomiting most mornings recently. She was in a mild depression. Her doctor told her that it can happen especially for new mothers but she could not comprehend it. The father was Rich, of course. She did not tell him yet and wondered what he would say. Probably he'll tell her to get rid of it. Maybe she should?

She did not know why she even kept the baby until now. Somehow her brain did not tell her to go to the doctor's office and get rid of the baby. What a joke nature had played on her. She was the one who vowed as a young woman not to have children simply because she saw what her childhood was, and now she was pregnant. She should have been more careful.

Yet nature has its ways and with every day she actually found herself somewhat enjoying the idea of having a baby. She still had many thoughts about her fitness to be a mother. She did not appreciate life, how could she be a mother?

The wheel of life continued to turn and with the third visit to the doctor he showed her the fetus on the ultrasound machine. Watching the little life growing inside her caused her something that she never felt before. Something moved inside her. A spark of light was created in her soul. A spark towards her baby.

It is still too early to know the baby's sex." Her doctor smiled at her. "We will probably be able to see it on our next appointment.

"Yes." She was fascinated by what she saw. She put out her hand and touched the little baby image on the black and white monitor.

"It is absolutely beautiful." She whispered.

The doctor was encouraged by what he saw. He had tried to convince her for the past few meetings not to have an abortion but she refused to listen to him. He was happy to see a change in her state of mind.

"Yes, it is. That's how life is created." he smiled at her. "I'll schedule you for another appointment next month."

He looked at her and stopped smiling. She did not look well. "What happened?"

She did not answer. Her world started to spin. The doctor laid her on the bed and then her world became dark.

*   *   *

At first she heard noises. Then she opened her eyes slightly and saw lights. Slowly the blur faded and she could see people in white. She is in a hospital.

A nurse approached her with a smile. "I see you woke up, and how are we today?" She measured her pulse and seemed to be satisfied with the results. "I see you are in fairly good shape."

"I feel good, what happened?" she asked as she sat straight on her bed.

"It appears that you passed out but you are better now. The doctor will talk with you and explain everything." She smiled with reassurance.

The nurse left and she remained there wondering what happened. She felt well but knew that something was wrong.

"Hey you." her doctor sat near her with a large smile on his face. "How do you feel?"

"Great, what is going on Pat?" She asked him directly.

He became serious. "Well, here is the deal Isabel, you have a rare condition of pregnancy. We do not know yet what the cause is but it seems like the pregnancy is poisoning your body. Now this is not something that we haven't seen before but typically it is more manageable." He opened his hands in frustration. "In your case we are still trying to figure this thing out." Then he looked at her for a long while.

"There is a slight chance that we will recommend terminating the pregnancy."

"No." came her immediate response.

"Why?" She was in shock.

"Well, only if we think that the risk to you is serious." He mentioned.

She sank into her own thoughts. A few weeks ago this news would not be that bad but now she felt differently about her baby. Now, she wanted her baby. Now she wanted to fight for her baby's life.

"Is there anything that we can do? Medicine, something?" She asked in a low voice.

"We are still checking into it." he apologized with a shy smile "but for now it looks like it is metabolic, that means that your body is having difficulty with the fetus, serious difficulty." He stressed. "After you'll go home, you will have to really watch it. That means stick to your house. No extra activities. This is serious. You will have to be under a constant monitoring."

She nodded silently.

"Does the father know about the baby?" Her doctor knew that she was not married.

"Not yet."

"I would let him know. Also I would let him know about the current situation. We need his help. You and the baby need his help."

She slowly leaned backwards. She was not sure about Rich's reaction to the news.

Rich's reaction turned to be quite surprising. At the beginning he disappeared for few days and Isabel thought that she'd never see him again. When he showed at her house he was a completely different person. He was caring and affectionate in a way that she never saw before. They became closer until one day he told her that she was the only women that he ever loved. She discovered new emotions inside her. Emotions she did not even know existed. She was confined to her house in an effort to maintain a stable pregnancy. Things seemed to be going fine until one day just about three months before the baby was due.

Rich found her bleeding heavily in the shower and took her to the hospital. The doctors were determined that the pregnancy be terminated. Isabel did not want to hear about it.

"Isabel, your life is at risk every minute that you do not terminate the pregnancy." Rich tried to talk with her. His heart was broken from the thought that the pregnancy had to be terminated. He wanted this baby so much but Isabel's life was at stake and according to the medical team, they did not have much time. Her body's systems could collapse any day if the pregnancy were not terminated.

Isabel wanted to maintain the pregnancy at least until the thirtieth week since then the baby would have a good chance of survival in an incubator. In the meantime Isabel's condition worsened. She did not feel well at all but refused to let go of the pregnancy.

"I can hold it a couple more weeks Rich I can do it and then the baby will be okay." she whispered. She felt very weak. Her feet swelled to an enormous size and she felt hot flashes constantly. Inside her she was not sure that she would be able to hold two more weeks but somehow her will told her differently. She wanted to give life to her baby at almost any cost.

*   *   *

It was almost midnight when Rich woke up. He had shared Isabel's bed for the past few weeks and now she woke him up. He looked at her and was immediately worried. She was heavily sweating and felt very warm.

"I am going to call the doctor honey." Rich was about to get up.

"Wait, before you do that I have a request please." She held his hand.

He wiped her forehead with a towel. "We have to stop this honey. This is not good for you." Rich protested.

"I know, but I think I am ready to deliver the baby now." Isabel said her words with effort. "Maybe tomorrow."

Rich did not know what to say. "Still, I am going to call the doctor."

"Yes, but before" she pulled him to her. "Could you please call my mother?"

Rich looked at her in wonder.

"Ask her to come see me now." Isabel was calm. "As soon as she can."

"Are you sure?" Rich knew about her relationship with her mother. She told him about their reunion. "You did not see her for years."

"Yes, I know, still . . . Tell her that I need her here, with me. You can find her phone number in my little notebook."

Rich nodded. "Will do."

"Then bring the doctor."

He called her mother at midnight. She was there at first morning light.

*　　*　　*

"Isabel, what are you doing?" Her mother sat near her "I heard everything from your doctor. You have to stop the pregnancy otherwise you will not survive."

Isabel smiled. "You sound as I always remember you; strict and down to business. Thank you for coming to see me." She reached out and held her mother's hand.

Her mother was not ready for this but held her hand firmly. She felt that something was wrong. "What is going on Isabel?"

Isabel took a deep breath. "For the past few months I had plenty of time to think about life Mother, my life." She laughed bitterly. "They say that pregnancy changes our perspectives, well, I guess it does." She looked straight into her mother's eyes. "I have something to tell you."

Her mother did not say a word. Instead she held her daughter's hand.

"I am very sorry." Isabel cried quietly "I am very sorry for what I have done in my life. I should have not been so merciless. I should have thought about all the poor boys and girls I brought into hell. I am so sorry."

Her mother listened silently.

"I want my baby to live, at any cost. Even the cost of my life mother."

"Isabel . . ." her mother voice shook.

"I will not survive this pregnancy mother. I know it."

Her mother was shocked. "What? Wait, I am going to call the doctor now."

"No," she stopped her. "I already talked with the doctor. "We will deliver the baby by tomorrow mother. I want you to be there, with me and Rich."

"Yes, I'll be with you my child." Her mother burst into tears and buried her face into Isabel's stomach.

Isabel was relaxed. She laid back and closed her eyes. "Thank you Mother."

Her mother raised her head and wiped her tears. "Isabel, I want to tell you something also."

Isabel stopped her "I forgive you Mother. I forgive you."

They both remained silent for a while.

"You never know when something is wrong until your guts tell you." Isabel was in deep thought. The sun sent her warm beams through the window and she loved it. "You never know that everything is dark until light is presented."

Her mother nodded "Yes . . ."

"You never know what you are doing to others until you have a child and are able to see through its eyes."

She paused for a few moments.

"I am asking you to raise this child mother. Rich will not know what to do. Let him visit, let him support the baby but I want you to raise the baby. Can you do it for me?"

Her mother lowered her eyes. "After what I have done to you?"

"Make it better mother, here is your chance, make it better with this one. Think as if this baby is a second chance with me."

Her mother's voice shook when she raised her wet eyes and answered in a steady voice. "I will."

"Thank you."

"Thank you." Her mother gave her a kiss on her forehead.

"I am hungry. Could you please bring me something to eat?" Isabel sounded happy.

"Sure, this is a good sign." Her mother released a sigh of relief. "I'll bring you something from the cafeteria."

When she was back Isabel's bed was empty. She dropped the tray and panicked. She ran to the first nurse she found. "Isabel, where is she?"

"She was taken to the delivery room few minutes ago." And then she added to the rushing mother "Delivery room number seven."

*　　*　　*

When she arrived there was already a full medical team, working with Isabel on the birth.

"Mother, I am glad that you are here." Isabel grabbed her hand as her mother sat near her.

Rich was on Isabel's other side and tense with stress.

"Hello, I am Professor Green and I am the head of the obstetric department at the hospital. Since this is a rare case, I'll deliver the baby." His smile disappeared. "In case of any detected distress to the baby or to the mother we'll immediately switch to a Caesarian procedure. We will not take any risk."

They gave her drugs to accelerate the birth and within an hour Isabel was in advanced labor. Although under epidural sedation she was still in severe pain but handled it bravely. Even the medical team was amazed to see how she squeezed her lips and suffered terribly without any sound until the moment of birth. Isabel then released a high pitched scream and tightened her grip on her mother's and Rich's hands. Her face sweat and her entire body shook when the baby's head was almost out. A few minutes later and Isabel gave a long scream. The baby was out. The doctor immediately checked for vital signs and they showed almost immediately. The baby started to cry when the first air came into its lungs.

"Congratulations, it is a girl . . ." The doctor told her with a smile. "How do you feel Isabel?"

"I am good, I am good, can I see her?", she mumbled in joy.

The baby girl was put on her chest after a quick cleaning and Isabel hugged her to her chest. Her mother and Rich were happy at her sides.

"See, everything went well." Her mother whispered to her with tears in her eyes.

"I want to name her Light." she told them.

"Beautiful name", the doctor was amazed.

"May I hold her?", Rich asked.

"In a few minutes." Isabel held the baby to her. "You grow to be a good human Light." She talked to her. She could feel what no one else in the room could see. "Be good and gentle. Be wise and considerate." Then she gave her a long kiss "Be a Light to the world." She finished her words, closed her eyes and held her close to her chest.

"BP is dropping." The nurse warned the medical team.

The medical team which had been relaxing rushed back into the room. "Mother and husband, please leave the room."

The mother sent a shaky hand towards her daughter who was laying on the bed with closed eyes, as the medical team started the hopeless fight for Isabel's life, without even knowing it.

*   *   *

"Bad judgment" said the dark angel with sparkling eyes. "Humans tend to make these mistakes quite often. Look at their bloody history."

"Indeed," the light angel agreed "But there is always good to be found in them. There is never bad without good and vice versa."

Another green check mark illuminated and the dark angel looked at the board, completely unhappy. It was clear that he was going to lose. But he did not lose hope to break the count of ten. Now he was looking to find the one necessary example. The one case that evil would win so there would be a red check mark.

"Humans do not know what is good for them. All their lives they do evil and then due to circumstantial influences turn away from me and run to you.", the dark angle hissed. "They are not aware that this is their normal behavior. They are caught in meaningless moments."

"On the contrary," the light angel smiled. "At some moment in their lives, and it does not matter when, they realize the evil of their past actions and are filled with remorse. They want to make up for what they have done. They want atonement. This is a true win of good over evil."

Chapter VII

THE FATHERS HAVE EATEN SOUR GRAPES

$*$ $*$ $*$

Gustav Rhine was happy. He lit himself one of his fine cigars, laid back on his large executive chair and sent circles of blue smoke into the air. He looked out his office windows, down to the city of Zürich and smiled widely. He had all the reasons in the world to be happy. His pharmaceutical company announced today to the whole world the cure for cancer and he immediately became the center of world media attention. He had just finished hours of interviews with all the major American networks and was taking a break before starting few more interviews with major European stations.

"*The world is a bunch of fools*", he thought and poured himself a glass of cognac. "*If they only knew what this new drug that he invented was. Yes, it does cure some types of cancer but the long-term side effects are hardly worth it. Who cares, though? The side effects are such that they can be dismissed as unrelated to the drug*".

He became a world hero on the backs of many millions who will be slowly poisoned during the next few decades. Even if at some point they decide to stop using his medication, it would be after many years and he would probably be the richest person on the planet. This was only partial reality. Another dark secret lay hidden but no one would ever know about it.

He turned in his chair and laughed to himself.

"*If they only knew how I developed it*".

His thoughts sank into the past.

It all started many years ago, actually when he was a child. His father was an unpunished perpetrator of World War II war crimes. No one knew about him since his father had destroyed all his records. His father was Dr. Mengele's closest assistant. Quietly and wisely his father burnt all documentation and records about his existence and escaped to Zürich. Using fake personal identification and a new name he started to practice medicine as a local, anonymous family doctor. Gustav, as a child, did not know about his father's history. He remembered how he wondered once when he brought a Jewish friend home from school and his father took him to a back room and told him in anger to send his friend home. Then he wondered what the problem was but quietly obeyed his father's demand. Many years later he understood his father's importance and his vision of the world.

He would never forget the day that his father took him for a horseback ride in the country. They stopped at a small creek in the woods and his father picked up hands full of red mud and sat him near the flowing creek.

"Today I am going to teach you something very important in life, my son. There may be many people in the world who will never agree with me." Then his father looked straight into his eyes "Some of my best friends were sentenced to death back at the end of WWII for what I am going to tell you now." He'd never forget the distant look in his father's eyes. "If they would have caught me, I also would have been executed."

Then his father nodded towards the creek. "See this creek my son, it is pure by nature. Look how clear the water is. The water has been flowing like this for generations; clear, pure, clean and innocent. These are the German people. This is your country. Clean, pure, perfected, the Aryan race, us." Then he dumped the mud from his hands into the clear water. The water immediately lost its purity and cleanliness and became blurry and muddy.

"These are the Jews. They made the water filthy. They made our country filthy and dirty. Wherever they went they brought scum and filth, and spoiled everything. They are the source of all bad things. Our leader then, the Fuhrer, saw it. He figured it out and created the final solution for this bad race of people. We wanted to exterminate them all."

His father pointed toward the spot where he had thrown the mud. The slow flow had washed away the muddy dirty spot and now the water was almost clear again. "See, fortunately nature has a tendency to clean itself over time." Then he looked at his son "We are nature. We have to clean this mud from the world." He'd never forget his father's eyes expression. They became cold as ice. "We have to clean the Jews from the world. This is our mission in the great work of nature." His father then released a long sigh and looked at the horizon "I was once part of this great organization that our leader created. I helped the human race by conducting medical experiments on Jews. Doing this we killed many of them but it was nothing more than cleaning the muddy water." He then smiled at his son. "This was our great history."

This was the only time that his father talked with him about this subject but he never forgot his father's words. His point of view changed then. From that day on he hated the Jews. He did not even know why, he simply hated them. He saw them as the mud that turned the pure creek to scum and he hated it.

"Mr. Rhine, you are scheduled for an interview in fifteen minutes. Would you like something to eat?" His secretary told him over the intercom system and cut his day dreaming about the past.

"No, thank you Gretta, I'll eat later.", he commented to her.

He stood up and walked in his large office. Memories came again to him.

He had started his own company thirty years ago. He, like his father, had studied medicine at Geneva University, one of the most prestigious in Europe. He graduated as one of the top students. He remembered his first crime against Jews. He was in his second year as a student as he saw a fellow student jogging in the University Park, late at night. She was one of the students with whom he went to classes. Her name was Rosetta Adler and she was one of the most beautiful students in the class. Almost every boy wanted to date her. Eventually she dated a guy named Arnold Rothschild, one of the top students. Both Rosetta and Arnold were Jews. In a quiet, hidden way he developed hatred towards them over time. He avoided talking with them and always watched them from the corner of his eye. He hated them secretly and was constantly hoping to see something bad happen to them.

One night he watched Rosetta marching across the path that crossed the large park. As he looked at her he suddenly felt his anger grow inside him. He discovered something that he never knew. He wanted to harm this Jew. He had the natural right to do so. He was a cleaner, assigned by nature. He remembered well the rush that flowed through him when he found himself running quietly on the park grass towards her. He knew the university campus very well and was familiar with its illuminated and dark spots. He used to jog there. He knew that they would soon arrive at a dark spot in the path. Perfect.

He attacked her from the side. He ran to her, hitting her with all of his body weight. She fell on the ground and he hit her hard on the head. She immediately lost consciousness. He dragged her behind a large bush as he breathed heavily from the rush and excitement of his action. It was his first violent act against Jews and he found himself enjoying it. If only my father could see me now, he thought then as he slowly gained control of his breath. He would be very proud of me. He looked at the unconscious young woman lying on the ground. For a split second his common sense flashed at him.

"What are you doing? This is a crime . . ." he thought to himself but pushed the idea aside.

This is a Jew, filth and scum, something we have to eliminate from our world. By then he already knew history. He knew about the Nuremberg trials and the death penalties for Nazi criminals. He had already figured out that his father was one of the main assistants for Dr. Death, Mengele and he was actually proud of his father. He carefully asked his father a few times if he knew Dr. Mengele and the answer was affirmative. His father always talked about Dr. Mengele with great admiration and respect. Although his father never gave him a clear answer, his hints pointed to the fact that he had worked hand in hand with Dr. Death.

Now he was about to join his father's legacy for the first time in his life. He felt the rage growing inside him towards the defenseless Jewish woman lying on the ground. She started to grunt and move and he knew that soon she would wake up. He quickly took off his shirt and remained only in his coat. Despite the cold night air he did not feel cold at all. He ripped his shirt and blocked her mouth. Then a thought crossed his mind. He tightly tied her hands behind her back and undressed her. As he brutally raped her she woke up. She moved her head to the side but could not produce any sound. As he was raping her behind the bush he looked closely at her eyes. She mumbled in great efforts to scream for help but all could hear was a weak dim noise. Typically, at that time at night no one was out. He actually enjoyed watching her teary eyes begging for mercy as he had his way with her. When he was finished, she closed her eyes. He spit out his words in a harsh whisper, "Filthy Jew."

He stood up and a moment of panic caught him. If were caught he'd go to prison for the rest of his life. He had to kill her so no one would ever know. He wanted to hit her for the last time and just then she opened her eyes and looked straight at him. Her eyes expressed great pain and agony as if asking him why. "Why are you doing this?", her eyes asked. His hand froze for a second in the air but then the vision of his father came to him and he hit her with all of his strength. He dumped her into the deep river and went to his room in the dormitory. He took a shower and looked in the mirror with great satisfaction. He laughed at his image in the mirror.

"Tonight I did my first cleanup father, tonight I started to clean the water. Tonight I killed my first Jew."

"Mr. Rhine, the interviewer will be late. He'll be here in about thirty minutes. He just called. Can I get you anything?"

"Black Coffee Gretta, please." His manners were sharp. "Thank you."

"Of Course", Gretta's voice sounded business-like, to the point, emotionless but that was why he chose her for his secretary. He needed someone like her.

As he was watching the cars and people below in the streets of Zürich he went back again into his memories.

They never found her, his first victim but he did not really care. He felt proud of himself and thought that this was just the first step. His father had worked with a great person, a medical genius who made progress in the medical field for the entire world. It was a shame that the world did not recognize him as a hero for his work. All they saw were his sacrifices, the Jews. He thought then about a greater plan. I can also be creative. I just have to be careful. I can also think about a final solution for the Jews. It just has to be secretive. I'll clean the water without the world's knowledge and when the time comes, the world will thank me. When everyone sees the good that I bring to the world by eliminating all the Jews, they'll thank me and probably make me a hero. First, I have to get rich fairly quick, and then I'll execute my own plan.

He focused on his medical studies and graduated among the top five of his class. His teachers predicted a great future in the medical field for him. With a small inheritance from his family he opened a pharmaceutical company in Switzerland. His first his goal was to make money and he wanted to make lots of money to execute his larger plan. His father had specialized in the gastronomic area and so he opened a company for research and development of drugs for stomach problems. He worked day and night and achieved great success. He hired a few other top graduates and together they developed breakthrough medication for fighting stomach ulcers. He became a millionaire overnight and the road for his big plan was paved.

He went to his desk and turned on his laptop computer. He logged in into his secured network using a code that only he knew. He had paid millions of Euros for a special, highly secured network and server system in a hidden plant. He opened his records and felt a warm feeling reading old documents from the beginning of the plant. He had written those documents more than twenty years ago. Now they were here, in a secured location, a constant remainder of his great contribution to the world.

He smiled to himself, *"What an achievement!"*

He picked a location in a small town about hundred kilometers from Geneva and quietly built his medical plant. It will be a testing and quality assurance plant for our main pharmaceutical manufacturing sites, he wrote on the application to get a license. There will be only a few employees, performing safe, final testing of our products. The site was small, clean and friendly. Even the few employees who worked in it did not know about the underground operation that went on deep under the ground. Quietly and secretly he built an entire medical facility under ground. The facility was built like a modern hospital including all the necessary equipment to conduct surgeries and treatments.

Accessing the hidden facility was done though special elevator that was hidden above ground at the official innocent site. Access to the elevator was through a restricted area. Special keys were made for every person working in the underground facility. The facility had its own air, water and electricity systems. It could function completely independently for one year at a time. It cost him a fortune at the time but he knew that one day it would all be all worth it. The main purpose of the facility, besides research and development of breakthrough medicines was completely different. The main purpose was to renew the glorious medical experiments of great doctors, to bring back the great inspiration and spirit of those responsible for advancing the medical knowledge of the human race, and to revive and continue the work of the medical genius of all times, Dr. Josef Mengale.

He was flipping through historic pictures of some of the large images that he printed at the time. He had paid thousands just to get hold of historic, rare photos from the concentrations camp where his father worked with Dr. Mengale. These images showed the great doctor, his father and patients in different stages of these treatments. Some would say these images were gory and inhuman but for him it was history at its best. He made sure that these rare photos from concentration camps would be in every room of the underground facility. The personnel will be working there needed to remember the glory. They needed to see their heroes constantly in front of their eyes for encouragement and spiritual elevation. After about two years of hidden construction, the underground facility was complete and equipped with everything needed to conduct medical experiments. The medical experiments were not planned to be done on animals but on humans. He spared no expense and purchased the best surgical equipment necessary to conduct advanced experimentation. Here they would continue the great medical research of their heroes and like before, these medical experiments would be conducted exclusively on Jews.

Now all he had to do is finding the team for this facility.

He opened a secured document with an old photo that he took when first hired his first doctor. He lit himself a cigarette and breathed in the smoke deeply. He remembered this guy. He was a great doctor at the time. He was a brain surgeon, one of his best. He was also a great believer in the Nazi idea. This was necessary to be hired. He paid huge salaries but for a person to agree to conduct such research, the money was not the main incentive. Their belief in the future of the third Reich through its resurrection was the main motivation. Their admiration for great leaders and a blind dedication to the Nazi idea was a must. It was not easy to recruit these people in modern days. After all it was a crime that would result in a life sentence to prison. Even he had serious doubts about finding such team. Yet against all odds he started to fill in his underground facility with doctors, nurses and other necessary staff. His gaze returned to the man in the picture. Dr. Otto Grecht, brain surgeon, was one of his best personnel.

"Gretta, I am hungry, could you please get me something to eat?"

"Yes Mr. Rhine, Your favorite sandwich?"

"Please."

"Ten minutes", she announced. He was satisfied.

It took him another year to get an entire team to operate the underground facility and then at last everything was ready. Only one thing was missing. The patients. The money that he made from his the development of stomach medicines exceeded his expectations and he had the entire necessary budget to create a special unit. This group would be responsible for selecting and kidnapping people, not ordinary people, only Jewish people. This military oriented personnel would have to be smart, strong and able to use weapons. They would have to research Jewish people in different towns and cities, select targets according to age group, sex and other necessary requirements to be defined by the medical team. These people would be followed and targeted for kidnapping at certain dates and times. On the target date they would be sedated, kidnapped and delivered to the hidden plant where there they will be put in comfortable rooms, categorized and dedicated to necessary medical experiments. There was a full security team in the facility. Their job would be to treat the patients with a smile and give them the feel that they were in a regular hospital. Of course if necessary the patients would have to be sedated. The patients would remain in the facility until all necessary experiments were completed. Due to the nature of the experiments most likely these patients would not survive but that was one of the main patriotic intents of this facility. No patient should remain alive. It was part of the water cleansing process. The experiments should be more advanced than the old WWII ones, of course. They have better technology today. Gustav was a great believer in progress and technology although the same concepts would be kept. Pain, death or any other damage to the patients was affordable and even welcomed. With the completion of his great underground facility he would be able to secretly conduct medical experiments that no other pharmaceutical group was capable of carrying out. Without any morals, ethics or human limitations and with direct human testing, the road was paved for the world's most avant guarde medical advancements. He'd catch two birds, one, clean the world from Jews and second earn the glory of developing the best medicine in the world. It worked well and after four years, somewhere in a small town in Switzerland, in his underground facility, he started conducting his medical experiments.

He even picked a symbolic name for his facility, The Wolf's Lair.

There was a knock on his door. "Mr. Rhine, your sandwich is ready."

"Please come in. You're right on time I was getting hungry."

His secretary entered the room and organized his meal on the small table in front of the large window. "I also brought you some orange juice", she added with a polite smile.

"*What a perfect assistant*", he thought. "Thank you Gretta." He gave her a wide smile.

She left the room and he enjoyed a few last peaks at historical images from the past. The images showed the patients with their doctors, some laboratory results, success cases and failures also. For cases of failure and death they built an advanced facility to get rid of patient's bodies.

He went to the small table and sat down to eat his sandwich. While eating he looked through the office window and thought about his success. He was definitely lucky. To have this idea of advanced medical experimentation was one of his great inspirations. That is why he is here today. It took him almost fifteen years of research and development to reach the point he was at today. Many people died so he would be able to declare he had invented a drug that can cure cancer. The people were insignificant. They were only Jews. The end result was what counted. Yes, he had a success rate of about fifty five maybe sixty percent but this was great. The long term side effects were not his problem. People get sick anyway. He drank his orange juice and laughed. The most beneficial part was that his achievement was made at the cost of many Jewish lives. "Great added benefit", as his father would probably say. He never told his father about his secret operation. He planned to do so many times but always felt that somehow, he would not be happy to hear about it. He could not exactly point towards it but something inside told him that his father would not be happy. He was sure that this would not be due the loss of Jewish lives but probably because it was a crime in our time and his father would not approve of breaking the law although it served a noble cause. His thoughts went into his parents. His father was very strict with him since childhood but on the other hand knew how to be his friend and spent many hours with him doing sporting activities including horseback riding and hiking in nature. His mother died in his childhood and he did not have much recollection of her. What he knew about her was mainly from his father's stories. He knew that she was a nurse and a very good hearted woman. His father never told him how she died and he assumed from sickness. His father was getting up there in age. He has to visit him. Maybe tonight he'd go and have dinner with him.

"Mr. Rhine, your interviewer is here, should I send him in?" His secretary's voice broke his chain of thoughts.

"In few minutes please, yes." He finished his juice and stepped in front of his office mirror. He needed to look his best. He was a great hero that day.

173

                    *   *   *

That evening he dined with his father at his home. A few years ago he purchased a beautiful home on the river for him. The house was surrounded by a huge green lawn and trees and had all the luxuries money could buy. Money was not a problem and his father was very proud of him as a medical doctor who had gone into the business world. "Utilizing your medical knowledge to make big money is great.", his father used to tell him "I am very proud of you and the ways you are managing your business.", he told him frequently and he was happy.

Tonight they ate a late dinner together and after that sat at the large balcony and drank liquor.

"I am glad that you are here tonight." his father told him in a tired voice. "I know that you have been very busy recently with your new medical announcement. Well done son, well done." he raised his glass towards him.

"Thank you Father. It is my greatest achievement in life." He felt very proud. His father liked his work. He drank the whole glass of liquor and enjoyed the warm, fuzzy feeling that spread inside him. He felt elevated tonight. After few glowing interviews today which included admiration expressed by the world's most prestigious medical community, he felt like the world was rewarding him for his discovery. All of a sudden he felt the urge to tell his father how he accomplished this achievement. He wanted to tell him that he followed his father's ways that he also experimented on Jews. He was influenced by his patriarch and created The Wolf's Lair bunker. He poured himself another glass of liquor and raised it towards his father.

"Tonight father, it is not really about my medical achievements. Tonight I want to tell you some more about this achievement."

"Wait," his father interrupted him with a serious face. "I heard all about your new drug that you developed and I am extremely proud of you. But there is something that I've been holding back from telling you for years now, something that has bothered my conscience for years. It is something that I hope that I still have time to correct."

Gustave got quiet watching his father's face express deep seriousness.

His father sat closer to him and took his hand in his. His head shook slightly as he did not know where to start. He could tell that it was hard on him. Eventually after clear internal struggle his father looked into his eyes and started.

"I do not know if you remember my talk with you many years ago about some ideas that I had then." His father looked into his face trying to see any clue that would tell him if his son remembered their talk. Of course Gustav knew immediately what his was talking about. He was even happy that his father raised the topic. That's exactly what he wanted to brag about.

His father shook and Gustav was not sure if it was due to excitement or age. "Many years ago you were a young child I told you only once, about my duty as a doctor during the war."

"Yes, and I thought that was great . . ." Gustav started.

"No," his father cut into his words. "It was not a great thing and I had hoped all throughout these years that you have forgotten about the conversation that we had then."

Gustav was silent. His father continued.

"I told you terrible things then."

"But the dirty water . . . The creek . . . The Jews . . . ." Gustav mumbled without understanding the change.

His father took a deep breath. "Yes, I believed in what I told you then. I truly believed in it but that was very wrong Gustav, very wrong."

He took a long sip from his liquor glass. "I will tell you bad things tonight and I hope that you will not hate me for them. If you do, I'll understand completely."

"A few years after I talked with you I discovered something about your mother." He looked at Gustav's eyes for a long while. "I discovered that she was Jewish."

Gustav's heart raced and cold sweat covered his back. He felt dizzy and had to hold the handle of his armchair.

His father saw his reaction and lowered his eyes. "It was a shock to me also. Apparently she hid the fact very well during the war. If someone were to have discovered it then, we would all be sent to the camp to die. You mother always had issues when we talked about the war. She would become angry and claimed that the whole Nazi idea was one big fit of madness. I never understood why until one day she told me that she was Jewish. At first, I thought that I was dreaming or imagining but then she described her family ancestry to me in detail until I had no doubt. She was Jewish. Imagine this, she was Jewish and I worked for Dr. Joseph Mengele."

Gustav remained silent as an emotional storm flashed in him.

"That night, after she told me I erupted in anger." He shook even more.

"Are you feeling all right father?" Gustav became concern.

"I killed her that night Gustav."

Gustav remained silent in his seat. This information came as a shock to him.

"I killed her with my bear hands. I strangled her." his father continued with lowered eyes.

"Do you know what this information means for you?" his father continued in cold, sharp tone like a knife that was ripping the thin air. "This means that you are also a Jew."

Gustav stood up in panic. "It can't be father. I mean, how come?" His mouth became dry and his heart raced again. He thought he'd pass out but then sat and enforced himself to relax by breathing in a monotonous way.

"The mother's religion determines the child's religion." His father said "This is of course by the Jewish religion. For Christians it is the opposite, the child's religion is determined by the father. Still, the end result is the same. You are half Jewish."

Gustav did not feel well. He felt hot flashes running through his body. The knowledge that his father killed his mother because she was Jewish and that he himself was Jewish, was too much for him. He wanted to get out of this conversation. "Father, I do not feel that well, can we continue this tomorrow?"

His father gave him a penetrating look. "No, I would like to finish tonight. I have been postponing this conversation with you for years." Gustav poured himself a glass of cold water and sat in front of the sparkly skies.

"Who would have imagined this?", He thought.

"A few years ago I was diagnosed with a serious neurological disorder, something like Parkinson's disease but with a much faster rate of progression. It is deadly disease. I did not want to tell you about it but now time has come." He paused and looked towards the water bottle.

Gustav poured him a large glass of water.

"Thank you," he drank almost half the glass of water in one gulp. "I went to a specialist in neurology, probably one of the best in the world, right here in Switzerland. She is an amazing doctor. She told me the truth, that there is no cure for this illness. All she could do was prolonging my life and make me suffer much less. And that's what she did. She took care of me personally. She made sure that I had all the necessary medications. She made sure that I would be able to live a normal life. I owe her very much."

His father stood up and took his cane. "I need to go to the restroom," he mentioned and then when he passed near him he patted on Gustav's back. "Guess what? She is Jewish also."

When his father returned Gustav sat there with his eyes lowered as his father continued with his news.

"So after years that she took care of me, I told her one day what I'd done in WWII. I told her with whom I worked with and recited my memories about that time. I didn't hide anything. I told her the truth and nothing but the whole ugly truth. I described the horrific medical experiments that we did on live people without anesthesia, without caring about their excruciating pain. I told her about the women we conducted experiments on, the children and many others. You know what she did? She listened to me. She listened all the way to the end and then when I finished she looked at me for long time and asked me only one question and with this question she sent me home."

Gustav looked at him silently.

His father nodded and said, "She asked me 'What is your soul telling you now?'", and with that I went home and did not return to see her for an entire week."

His father raised his eyes to Gustav's "I thought about her simple question all that week. I looked inside myself, deep into my soul and the answer was there. See Gustav, the answers are always there. We simply ignore them for all types of reasons. Circumstances, personal desire, fear, greed or any other human reason. The answer was always there. I knew it then as I knew it all throughout the years. Somewhere along life I turned off my humanity and never turned it back on."

Gustav closed his eyes. He did not want to be there.

"Well, you know what they say, "better late than never". I returned to her after that week and told her that I regret what I'd done back then. I told her that I am very sorry for my actions and I wish I could turn time backwards. I told her that I'd do anything that is in my power to fix it. See, I am sure that I'll not see the light when I'll die. I do not deserve it but at least I want to do one important thing before I die."

He put his hand on Gustav's shoulder. "I want to take back the words that I told you about the filthy creek. I want to take back the racist words. I want to take back the blind hate for no reason. There is no justification for killing or hating people because of their religion or beliefs. There will be never justification for killing women, children or elderly people. All humans are equal before their creator. That woman, the doctor, then told me a story of her own." his father continued.

Gustav raised his eyes. This evening was too much for him already and he became numb. What other surprise his father can bring now?

"Many years ago while she was in medical school, here in Geneva, she was attacked late at night. The attacker raped her and then called her a 'filthy Jew.'"

Gustav's heart raced one more time. "What? What was the doctor's name?" he mumbled.

"Dr. Rosetta Adler" his father said. "Why? Do you know her?"

Gustav's face became pale and he had difficulty breathing. He quickly grabbed his glass of water and used it to stabilize himself. "No, I don't know her." He said in steady tone.

"So she experienced hatred towards her because she was Jewish. She survived the attack." his father continued "Apparently the attacker dumped her into the river but she swam away and was saved. It caused her trauma for many years. She never got married and she never had children because of that night." He took a deep breath.

"Tonight we had the conversation that I wanted to have with you for years now. I wanted to tell you to forget about our talk then. It was wrong, very wrong. Never even think about those words. They were insane, inhuman and worthless."

As Gustav's eyes became glazed his father finished his words. He looked straight into Gustav's eyes.

"I am glad that I had this talk with you tonight."

Then he noticed Gustav's expression. It was one of great internal pain. He became quiet for a while and then added slowly, "Or am I too late?"

*   *   *

Gustav's father died two months later. Gustav stopped working and remained at his father's house for a whole week by himself. He had lots to think about. After that week in which he could hardly sleep at night he reached a conclusion. That night he slept like a baby. The next morning he started to execute his plan, his final plan.

*   *   *

Gustav purchased two small graves in a secluded place, far from anywhere. He buried his father by himself. No other people attended the short ceremony that he conducted. As a matter of fact there was no ceremony at all. Gustav also did not want to write his father name on the headstone. Instead he ordered to engrave in a simple letters to create only one sentence.

"Every new day is another chance to change your life."

The next day he went to visit Rosetta Adler. He stood in front of her in her office and remembered that day. She looked almost like then, older of course but with the same look. She did not recognize him. He gave her a sealed envelope.

"Please accept this small gift from me and my father. In this envelope there is a check for ten million Euros, a small contribution that I hope will help you with anything you need."

179

"But sir, who are you?" She asked him surprised. Then her eyes narrowed.

"Will she remember me?" He thought.

No she didn't remember him.

"Thank you, but please can you tell me who you are?", she kept asking.

He held her hand. "It does not matter. I am sorry. I am very sorry Rosetta."

Then he left her office while she stood there wondering who he was.

He wrote a long letter in which he explained exactly what he had been doing over the years. He ordered that the total profit from his pharmaceutical company be split evenly among all the families of victims were murdered in his facility. They kept full records about all the people. He ordered all of his property to be sold and donated the money to hospitals. He stopped his new drug manufacturing and wrote in detail about the long term effects and a course of direction for continuation of its development. He had no wife or children so all that remained of his money was designated for charity.

He wanted to be buried near his father's grave in another simple grave, to be anonymous, in a distant, secluded location. He planed everything. He even wore a metal necklace with his name tag so his remains could be identified.

On a target date he gathered his team in The Wolf's Lair main conference room. The facility was built from the first with an explosive self-destruction system. At the time it was merely a precautionary mechanism. Only he had the detonation key and access codes. He planned a big party for the evening of the target day. All the facility patients were sent to other hospitals by anonymous buses by early evening time. The bus drivers were instructed to drop them at various hospital Emergency Rooms. Each patient had his medical history, gruesome as it was, attached to a personal necklace. In this way hospitals would be able to treat the patients. One hour after the facility was emptied of its patients, he was about to start the party. The entire medical team was there with him.

"Good Evening to all of the Wolf's Lair facility team. Tonight we celebrate. Tonight we celebrate our great moment. We made history."

The team cheered. They all knew about the new drug that had been released to the world. Gustav raised a toast and at the same time pressed on the remote control button that was in his pocket. From that moment on they had five minutes to escape but all external doors were locked. None could escape tonight. He'd be with them as well.

"Tonight we celebrate several events", he announced and all became quiet.

"First, we celebrate the release of our new drug. Even if it is not perfect yet, maybe one day it will be." The team cheered again and drank from their Champagne.

Gustav peaked into his pocket. About three minutes were left. "Second, we celebrate new life. The life of the patients who left today. They have more of a chance to survive."

All cheered again. The atmosphere was euphoric and no one really cared what he really said. No one really paid attention to his words.

Thirdly, we raise a toast for a chance at atonement." He became serious and the crowd, already dulled by few glasses of Champagne still did not get the meaning of his words. Atonement for our souls. By regretting and changing our lives we may still have a chance to see the light."

There was silence. People tried to process the meaning of his words.

"We have perpetrated horrible crimes in this place. I am giving us a chance to regret. Who regrets these actions? Who regrets our crimes?"

Again there was silence.

He looked at the timer. One minute remained.

"We do not have much time in this world. Who regrets what we have done in here? Look inside yourselves. Look into your souls. Are you regretting what we have done here? I want an answer in thirty seconds, no later than that." His voice was loud and steady. He wanted their remorse. He wanted to hear them say they were sorry.

Slowly people started to speak. "Yes, I am sorry." said one of the doctors. "We really did bad staff here."

"Very good," he answered, pushing more people to express their regrets. "Who else is sorry? Who else?"

Slowly but surely people started to speak their regrets and with every new person that join Gustav became happier.

He looked at the remote. Fifteen seconds to detonation.

In the heat of the moment he yelled at them "Who is willing to die with me for our actions? We deserve to die, don't we?"

The answer echoed back almost immediately. "Yes, we do."

"Cleanse our souls." Gustav opened his arms upwards and everyone repeated after him.

There was a spark and a series of underground detonations occurred. Nothing was felt on the surface. The self-destruction system was carefully planned so that whatever was underground, stayed underground, sealed forever in massive ruins.

*   *   *

One week later a large envelope arrived at the Interpol office in London. The clerk signed on the little note and asked the delivery man. "Who is this for?"

"No particular names", the delivery guy informed him, smiled and was on his way out. "Who knows it may be a shocking news letter."

*   *   *

"Disappointing" the dark angel seemed to be fascinated by the chain of events. "So much talent was lost."

"No, so many souls had a chance to see the light at some point." The light angel illuminated another green check mark.

"You know, it is not clear to me who the actual case was here." the dark angel tried to doubt the results.

"Obviously the father caused a chain of events that caused many to regret.", the light angel answered.

The dark angle raised an eye-brow. "So is this means that the son did not make it?"

"Well, the answer is not in our hands but he definitely made a first step towards the light, creating a group of followers behind him. They all have a great chance of being brought into the light." He nodded and concluded with the biblical quote, "Fathers have eaten sour grapes and the children's teeth are set on edge."

Chapter VIII

SARINA (PEACE)

*   *   *

Cyrus Dominic lit a cigar and sat back in his comfortable seat. The thick smoke filled the small plane space and soon enough the entire cabin was cloudy. It was a fairly small jet carrying no more than thirty people and the small space quickly became smoky. He didn't care much. Nor did the other twenty five people care about the cabin's air quality. As a matter of fact they were taking a nap. They were all soldiers for hire and Cyrus was their commander. Furthermore he took care of his men's personal matters starting with their bank accounts and ending with what food they eat for dinner or where they slept at night. He was their father, their mother and their moral leader. The average person would probably claim that Cyrus was not exactly a positive role model due to his divergent morals and doubtful virtues but for this small community it didn't much matter. They were quite happy and content with their lives. Cyrus provided them with food, places to sleep, women, money and everything else they needed or wanted, so they were satisfied. Cyrus even occasionally took them on fancy vacations and he made sure that they'd have hefty retirement savings accounts.

They were a rough team trained to do the worst. They did not hesitate to murder anyone regardless sex or age. No one cared when Cyrus smoked one of his thick cigars in flight to a mission. They were big strong guys and ignored the smoky air. Some of them even got used to the cigar's smell and liked it.

As for Cyrus, he was a violent man, a convicted criminal on death row who had escaped after three months. He was accused of killing men with his bare hands. He claimed it was for self defense. The prosecutor claimed that killing several men cannot be called self defense but murder. The jury believed the prosecutor. He was sentenced to death. Cyrus did not get upset when he heard the verdict. He was already devising a plan on the way to death row. Within three months he escaped and fled to Canada where he later established an organization called "Metals Only".

"Metals Only" had grown out of an idea Cyrus first contemplated while in the Marines. He knew what he was good at. He served patiently in the Marine Corps for years as a platoon commander. Patiently means that he did not really agreed with the humanitarian approach of the Marines but had to comply with it. On many occasions he would have preferred more aggressive and violent methods but had to control himself. In some cases he couldn't control his nature and got in trouble for his unethical behavior. When he was serving with his platoon in Iraq they encountered a situation in which terrorists were hiding inside a village. His orders were to shoot and kill only if clear identification was made. Cyrus took the opportunity to wipe out the entire village without any clear identification of terrorists.

"It was a dangerous situation", he wrote in his report, "In which we could not identify who was the enemy and who was not. Therefore I needed to take extreme measures and exterminate the entire village in order not to risk my men. The villagers were hiding the terrorists among them and we do not negotiate. There is a price for everything". According to his command the entire platoon, armed with tanks, Hummers and armed vehicles entered the village and killed almost everyone in it, including women and children. Luck was on his side that this event occurred in a remote location and no media reached the site. It was also lucky for Cyrus, that one of the high military commanders was his personal friend and saved him from a court marshal and military prison. Although this friend saved him from doing jail time he could not prevent Cyrus's discharge from the service. The Marine Corps kicked him out. Shortly after that he became a mercenary for hire in the crime world.

He had taken pleasure in his work as a hit man until his arrest and imprisonment. Then upon his escape from death row he tapped the underground connections he had made and created Metals Only, a group of mercenaries of the worst kind. The Metals Only organization was carefully constructed by Cyrus. He picked men who would not hesitate to execute any type of violent operation regardless of how inhuman, for the right amount of money. He selected his men according to these criteria and tested them. Every person who joined his team had to go through a test mission after which Cyrus determined the candidate's position in the group. Those who were capable of executing the cruelest acts were assigned to leadership roles in their bloody operations, functioning as commanders in this small platoon. These men did not hesitate to kill, burn or butcher others using any necessary means. Those did not pass Cyrus's brutality tests were assigned to be assistants, drivers, backup or performers of any other tasks that Cyrus determined. They all had to have strong stomachs and no fear of gory details and scenes. He even recruited a small medical team to support his compact army. After about two years he was satisfied with his unit and disseminated an underground announcement that they were ready for hire.

The first outside mission given to them was by a wealthy drug dealer. He ordered the assassination of a high ranking police officer in New York as a matter of personal revenge. The mission was to kill the police officer including his wife and two children. Cyrus took this mission as a testing-the-water assignment and he was not disappointed. His team operated like a Swiss clock. Under his command, they conducted their operation at midnight. After generously planting a number of C4 explosive devices around the officer's house, they detonated them all at once. Shortly after the explosions were completed they arrived in an official city SWAT team vehicle, fully armed with machine guns and checked the remains of the burning house. The intention was to shoot any survivors but none of the household residents survived the explosions. They quickly left the area before a real SWAT team arrived at the scene.

Cyrus insisted on full control of his people. He orchestrated their lives. He put them all in an apartment complex that he purchased. The apartment complex was modern and offered a pool, tennis court, gym and even an advanced theater room featuring popular movies. Every team member received a Swiss bank account and a substantial monthly salary. Cyrus paid for their food, clothing and all other necessities as long as they remained in his residential complex. Living in the complex was a must in order to be hired. He even provided them with high class prostitutes on a weekly basis. The team owned military vehicles, weapons and even a large private jet which they flew to wherever they had a mission. Cyrus himself lived with his people and they considered themselves a small family.

Cyrus took every dirty mission. The only prerequisite was the price. After few years he and his team had a record of numerous successful operations world-wide and were considered experts in their field. They went into each operation without anything to identify them. No personal ID card, no tags, nothing that could identify them. They all knew the basic rule. In case any of them was captured, he was on his own. There was no room for sentimentality.

Cyrus continued to smoking his cigar, sending thick clouds into the air. They were on their way to a new mission. There was no direct person who hired them for this mission. They had been hired in similar ways in the past. An anonymous person contacted them via electronic media, sending them the mission requirements. Upon Cyrus' review and price demand, a full payment was wired to their account. From that moment they were independent to operate on their own. Cyrus requested detailed documentation about the mission including location, target and satisfactory outcome. He did not care about the purpose of the mission. It was not his business. All he needed to know was the target and if they could expect resistance. Upon payment he launched the operation. He always kept his customers happy and made sure that everything was done according to their instructions.

Today they were flying to the Middle East. In one of the countries in the region they were assigned to massacre a village. The target was properly defined and re-confirmed according to Cyrus's request. He always made sure to get full details, including longitude and latitude coordinates. The village had about one thousand people in it including elderly, women and children. For Cyrus it did not matter. They were all targeted and that was that. He did not ask its source or the purpose or reason for the action. He assumed that it must be involved with some political move or even personal matters of some sort. As long as the dollar amount in seven figures dollars was wired to his account, he made sure that the mission would be done to the best of his team's abilities. They brought all the necessary equipment and weapons to handle their mission. Typically such an operation also required extra payment for bribing local assistants Cyrus had all over the world. His payment-based, trusted assistants were always there for him and his team to assist with landing fields, description of local topography and other vital details they might need.

He remembered their recent operation and smiled to himself with pride. It was something. They had received an order to sink a cruise ship in the middle of the Atlantic Ocean. Even he had raised an eye-brow when he received the email with the directive. *Why the hell sink a fancy cruise ship?* It was one of the largest liners in the world. The instructions were very clear. Sink it in mid sea without any consideration for people on board. They had life boats. They'd manage. At the time he simply nodded and accepted the task. After all he could not refuse such payment. The operation itself was quite simple. They had all the necessary knowledge about explosives so they efficiently connected explosive devices to the ship's perimeter at night and detonated it early morning. They did not take into account that they planed the explosions to be too excessive. The bombs exploded accurately according the computer program sequence and the end results were catastrophic. They were counting on the fact that the ship would sink within a few hours giving the passengers enough time to flee for their lives but the explosions flooded too many compartments at one time which basically gave the ship no longer then thirty minutes to float. This was not the result that they desired. The majority of the passengers did not even have time to wake up from their sleep as they were trapped in their rooms during the rapid sinking of the ship. More than two thousand passengers sank with the ship that morning, creating the largest marine disaster ever, even larger than the Titanic in it's the time. Their mission was accomplished and they received their payment on time but since the entire world had sent investigators chasing after them, they had to go underground for long time. The extended hiding time did not bother Cyrus that much. He was just bored.

He briefly peaked at his watch. They would be landing in a deserted field about ten miles from the village. It would be ten at night, local time. His local assistant had already prepared a large tent for them for the briefing with the regional maps and detailed directions to the village including a fall back plan in case something went wrong. After the short briefing they'd have a quick dinner and leave for their destiny. They planned to arrive at the village by midnight. The villagers would be asleep when they were attacked. Still they'd have to take extra precautions against any surprises. An intelligence agent warned him about the possibility of Israeli forces nearby. He could not point to an exact location as the forces were moving constantly and it would interfere with their operation if the Israelis were to notice. He'd take that into account. They had one hour to complete their mission and leave. By 3:00 a.m. they should be back on their plane and in the air few minutes later. *"It will be a "Piece of cake"* he thought.

They had conducted similar operations before. Some of them were ordered by drug cartels, religious organizations or political groups. They were all successful. There was no reason to believe that this one would be different.

He put out his cigar and lay his seat back. He'd take a short nap. There was a lots of work in front of them tonight and he'd need all of his strength.

*   *   *

They landed in the field exactly as expected and immediately gathered in the briefing tent. It was a dark night which perfectly suited their plans. The absence of the moon would make their approach easier. After a short briefing they left for the village. They progressed quickly as the night providing them with excellent cover. They had the top of the line navigation equipment and had no problem finding their target. They arrived shortly before midnight and gathered outside the village to observe.

Cyrus watched the sleeping village with his night-vision binoculars. He could see some light coming out of small houses but overall the village was dark. He could not see any guard activity but knew that they should always consider the possibility of armed resistance. He sent two people to check the village from the inside as they hid in a thick forest near it. After an hour the search team returned with good news. The village seemed to be unguarded. There were no signs of weapons or military operations. They'd go according to their plan with caution. The enemy may be within. After all, there must be a reason that they were sent to destroy this village. Cyrus calculated that some sort of leader lived in the village with his family. If this was the case there must be some militia or armed people in the village who were hiding. Cyrus well knew the history and traditions of this region. Typically his presumptions proved correct.

They prepared the explosives and quietly entered the village. Then they planted the explosives strategically. The fact that they could get an accurate satellite image of almost every structure in the village helped tremendously. They created an advanced plan for the sequence of explosions. A computer program would detonate each explosive at a certain time in full synchronization with the location of each structure and the estimated positions of victims as they fled. In this way no-one would have a chance of escape. If the bomb at home didn't kill them, other explosions, at different locations, would. It was efficiently planned. After all explosives had detonated they would enter the village quietly fully dressed in camouflage. They'd have their night vision goggles on and would simply traverse the narrow village streets and paths and using guns with silencers, shoot any survivors. The fact that they would be essentially invisible would facilitate their quick cleanup of the rest of the people. Their instructions were to shoot anyone is still alive. Of course there was a margin of a few percent that would flee into the forest or simply survive in some way. This was acceptable to the customers. After all explosives were in place they gathered near the village and prepared their gear to enter the village. None of them carried any identifying symbols of any kind. After the operation was to be completed, they were all to arrive at this meeting spot by 2:00 a.m. At 2:10 a.m. they would leave the site and return to their plane. Those who did not make it by 2:10 a.m. would be abandoned. Those were the rules.

Cyrus made a sign and one of the men clicked a small button on a wireless keyboard. They all knelt in the dark as strong explosions shocked the night air. The sequence of the explosions continued to be heard and they waited for a certain one to be heard. It would be fairly small one. It will be their signal to enter the village. After that one they knew that the chain of explosions was progressing toward the far side of the village. This would enable them to enter the closer part and start to clear it of its residents. After some time they heard the signal and moved in one line into the village. As they arrived at its entrance each person went his own way according to plan. From this moment on, each one of them was on his own. They had to complete their tasks and return to the meeting place by 2:00 a.m.

Cyrus was last. He made sure that all his men quietly disappeared into the darkness and then went his way. It took to him the north side of the village. Some of his men were suppose to go over there before him to clear any survivors. He would move in few minutes after them to do a final check. According to their satellite information it was the most populated area of the village and they planned to give it extra attention.

Cyrus crouched behind a thick bush and listened. The explosions stopped and all he could hear were people screaming for help. The whole village was on fire and the night skies were orange from the flames that were everywhere. He observed the area with his binoculars. Here and there he could see dark images moving quickly between the houses. He knew that these were his people. Each one of them had a team gauge to identify all other people from their group. If they saw a person not approved by their team gauge they had to shoot him or her. It meant this person was not from their team and therefore defined as enemy. He was satisfied by what he saw. There were almost no people escaping from the houses. Occasionally he could see some figures but they were shot almost instantly.

"Good job guys." he whispered to himself as he observed for the last time the scene before embarking on his own incursion into the village. He made sure that his team gauge was turned on and started to move towards the north side of the village. As a fully trained combat soldier he moved quickly towards residential structures. His dark bowed image was seen quickly moving between the homes as he was checked for survivors. Twice his team gauge alerted him with a blinking light but it was always a green light to tell him it was one of his team. All the residents seemed to have been killed by the explosions.

Then he entered a fairly large house. The door was not there, Instead there was a large dark hole. With his gun aimed forward Cyrus entered. There was strong burnt smell and inside was a big mess. Smoke was billowing from burnt furniture and the walls. In front of him he saw a large door. The door seemed intact. Slowly he approached the door and then kicked it. It fell back and a feminine, high pitched scream was heard. He slowly entered the room. What he saw froze him. A woman was lying back on a broken bed. The room was full of ruins. Two illuminated kerosene lamps were on the floor. The flame flickered on the women's face and he could see that she was shaking, probably from fear. Then he noticed another fact. She was holding her stomach with both hands while breathing heavily. She was pregnant and almost in labor by his quick assessment. He quickly looked to the sides and understood why no one could see any light from the outside. There were no windows in the room and he thought that this was odd. Typically this was done to cover a secret gathering place or headquarters. He immediately became alert and held his gun firmly. He was ready to face any surprise but nothing seemed to happen. Only he and the pregnant woman were in the room. His eyes went back to her. She seemed to calm down and was holding her pregnant stomach with both hands. He was wondering if she was injured. He did not have any feelings towards her. He'd have to kill her. He had done it many times before. Then he noticed that her hair looked wet. He slowly moved to his left and saw that all of her head left side was wet. It seemed like blood to him. She must have been hit by something. His look went further to the left and then he identified large, flat brick that had large red stains on it. Probably she was hit by this brick when the explosion occurred. By her position he figured that she couldn't move much. She lay there in a twisted position holding her stomach and breathing heavily.

Cyrus had seen many dying people in his life. In the majority of the cases he was the one who had caused these people to die.

Among them were women, elderly and even children. There was nothing new about seeing another woman die.

Oh Well, he thought, according to her look she is dead anyway, I can leave her to die. But then there was something different about this woman. She continued staring at his eyes stubbornly, like she wanted to tell him something. She was still breathing heavily and he concluded that she was probably in a lot of pain. All of a sudden she spoke to him.

"I know a little English." she said in weak voice.

She was definitely local, he thought, He identified her mid eastern accent.

"I know why you came here." She continued and he was quietly listening. "You probably came to kill my husband. He is a leader of terrorist group. I don't care." Her eyes became sad. "As a matter of fact I even agree with you. His group should be stopped. I saw what they do. It is not nice."

He remained silent. Now he knew why they were here. Who knows by whom they were ordered to eliminate this village? It could be anyone from a rival gang to a government. The customer was completely anonymous but as long as it paid, they did the job.

"Ah." she released a sigh and her face warped in pain.

He needed to complete the job. He aimed his gun at her.

"No, wait." she whispered. "I already got hit on my head. I am not going to live long, I can feel it but . . ." her voice shook "I can help you . . . I can help you and your men."

He stopped.

"How could she help him?"

She looked at his eyes. "I can save you and your men from my husband's trap."

He became rigid. Trap? What trap?

"I will ask for one thing in return please." She expressed her words with huge effort "that you will help deliver my baby. She'll need to come out any moment now. My water already broke in the explosion."

His brain worked fast. She mentioned a trap. He did not see any trap but what if she was right? What if there was a trap

195

somewhere? It could cost them many soldiers. He did not need to help her. He just needed this piece of information.

He leaned near her and looked at the wound on her head. He saw that her entire head was bleeding. "What happened?" he pointed towards her head.

"There was a big explosion and a big stone hit me on the head. I passed out for few minutes but then woke up when you arrived."

He felt her skull. It was seriously fractured. She probably suffered massive brain damage, he thought. Her entire head was sunken on the left side and he could feel the broken skull. He calculated that if she did not reach a hospital soon, she would soon be dead.

"What is this trap?" he asked her.

She looked at him with big brown eyes. "You have to help me deliver my baby first."

"I don't have the time. I have to leave here in fifteen minutes. People are waiting for me."

"There will be no people if I don't help you." she insisted in a calm tone. "There is a big trap for you and your people. I heard about it many times when my husband made his plans. They already contacted their allies. You can find the transmitter in the next room. You will find only its wreckage."

He raised his eyes and saw another door. A quick shot from his silencer equipped gun broke its lock and he opened it. The room was empty. On the far side he could see a large table. Amazingly it seemed like the room was not damaged. He looked around him and saw that it looked protected and lacked windows. It was probably reinforced by heavy concrete.

Then he noticed some debris across the room. When he approached he found some sort of broken electronics. It did look like a transmitter. He had a good knowledge of electronics and could identify coils and other components that could definitely be used in a transmitter.

"What if she was right?"

He returned to her. "I can assume that your husband and his men left already?

"They left shortly after the explosions started." she whispered. "He did not even look at me when they left." She lowered her eyes.

"Where is the trap?" he asked her laconically. He looked at his watch. He did not have much time. He was already behind schedule.

She raised her eyes. Her words came slowly and it was that she would not survive long.

"First you have to help me."

He debated what to do. He could kill her but she was already considered dead. He could leave at that moment but would not discover the trap designed to kill him and his men until it was surely too late.

"You and your men are already dead if you go now. Trust me." She saw him debating. "Tell your men to wait for you. Otherwise they all will be dead.

Cyrus typically had a good sixth sense. This sense had saved him many times. Something told him that she was right. It told him to leave everything behind for a short while and help this woman. For a brief moment he tried to push his internal instincts aside. There was no reason to believe her and the plane was due to pick him up. Still he had this internal instinct. Without even knowing what he was doing he looked at the woman.

"I'll help you."

A tiny smile appeared at the corners of her mouth and then vanished. She did not have much strength and she knew that she would have to preserve it for her last mission in life; giving birth to her baby.

"Tell your men to wait for you near the village." She said quietly.

The seriousness in her eyes told him that she was telling the truth. All his senses told him to listen to her and he did as she asked him. Using his emergency radio he texted all of his men "Complete your task and wait in the meeting place until I arrive. I will be delayed. Wait there and do not proceed." He knew what this meant. If they did not make it to the plane with the margin of time allotted, the plane would leave and they would have to switch to plan B regarding getting out of the area. It was a much more difficult plan but they'd have to do it.

He saw a faucet in the corner of the room.

"Forget everything," she said when she realized what he was looking for. "We don't have time. You'll have to help me with what you have."

He nodded and approached her as she lay on the floor. Cyrus had paramedic medical knowledge and knew the procedure by the book but he had never actually delivered a baby. Then again, there was something different about this woman. It was something that he did not know how to define. Her face was radiating goodness, delicacy and yes, she was beautiful. Her hair was curly and dark, her lips were full and red and through all the filth and soot he could tell that she was beautiful.

"What the hell she is doing in a place like this?" he asked himself silently.

She read is mind and released a bitter laugh "Yes, I was asking myself the same many times the same question. What was I thinking when I was a young student in Beirut University? Don't ask me now please."

"That's how she knows English." He understood.

Surprisingly she gave him her hand. He took her hand and looked at it. It was like a surrealistic image from a different world. In between all the wreckage, the soot, the ruin, in the middle of this bloodshed war, a delicate white, soft hand was extended to him, Cyrus, the cold blooded murderer responsible for all of what was around them. Her fingers were soft and warm. Her short finger nails looked so delicate that he could almost not see the dry blood on them. Instinctively he kissed her hand as a matter of politeness and could smell her hand. It had a smell of paradise for him.

"What is going on with me?", he questioned himself.

"My name is Giselle, what is yours?" She asked him and for a moment he forgot that they were in the middle of a battle field, deep in Lebanon.

"Cyrus." he said fascinated by her big brown eyes.

She seemed to put everything aside and smiled to him. "Thank you for helping me Cyrus. You are probably partly or even fully in charge of what happened here tonight but the fact that your heart told you to transcend all this and help me, shows me that you have good inside you. It is not only because of the trap information. I can feel it."

Cyrus remained silent. He was prepared for everything else but not this. He was definitely not good.

"Yes, you are . . ." She said "Even if you do not think so." Then her face wrinkled in a grimace of pain. "Now we start." She told him and tightened her grip on his hand.

"Maybe she wants to think that about me."

He was not ready for this. He knew how to accept pain silently but he never imagined the strength of the grip of a woman in labor.

*   *   *

"You will have to help me accelerate the process Cyrus." she told him softly.

He knew why. She would not last for long. Her words touched him inside. Cyrus had many women in his life but never a relationship. They were always very pretty prostitutes with whom he only had relationships based on payment. He had never heard any female say his name like that.

She noticed his reaction. "I see that you probably a very lonely man Cyrus."

This caused him to do something that he had never done, not with men and not with women. He lowered his eyes.

"What is happening to me?", he thought.

"I see you were never loved." She stretched out her hand and touched his face. "I am sorry. I have short time to bond with the man that will help me bring new life to this world. I just hope that this man will help me further to rescue this new born from here, from this gloomy reality. What I will do now is to rupture my womb's membrane. I will do it by putting my hands inside me and kind of cleaning myself internally. I saw a roommate of mine doing so while I was in college. This will accelerate the procedure and I should be in labor within minutes. My water already broke,

I can feel the contractions becoming stronger but I do not have the power to push." She gave him a sad look. "Please help me."

"I'll help you." Cyrus said and started the procedure as he had learned only through text books.

Within thirty minutes he could feel the head. Giselle's face was sweaty and he frequently gave her water from his military canteen. She did not scream throughout her labor. When the time came she simply held his hand as her face flushed from her colossal effort and then with the last push she screamed only once and Cyrus pulled the baby out. As he learned he immediately cleaned the baby's eyes and nose and opened all air ways for breathing.

"I don't hear cry, why the baby is not crying?" Giselle said as she shook from the effort.

Just then the baby started to cry.

"Congratulations, it is a baby girl." Cyrus laughed unintentionally. "Here she is."

He cut the embolic cord, closed it with a clip that he had in his medical kit and gave the baby to her mother. He then covered Giselle with his coat. Giselle hugged the baby to her chest and closed her eyes. Cyrus looked at both the mother and her baby and thought that this was something out of this world. Throughout his life experience, his battles, his wars, his adventures and his wildness, he never felt touched like this before. In the middle of nowhere, in the middle of a village whose name he did not even know, which he and his men destroyed tonight, he experienced the event that would change his life.

Giselle opened her eyes. The baby lay quietly on her breast. She offered her hand to him again and he took it with care.

"Thank you for everything." She tightened her grip on Cyrus's hand and then opened her eyes with seriousness. "You don't have much time." She talked straight to the point. "You arrived through the deserted airport not far from here. I know about it. I heard them talking about this many times. Waiting for you there will be many people with missiles and heavy weapons. I suggest that you do not return to this spot. You have to find another way to escape from here Cyrus. Do not go back to the old field."

Cyrus looked at his watch. The team would have been waiting for him for one hour now. They'd never make it in time to meet their plane anyway. Either the plane would leave or as Giselle said maybe it was even destroyed by the terrorists. He'll have to execute plan B. It would be much more difficult but this was their only choice.

"I will not go to the field." He told her "We'll escape in a different way. I already have an alternative plan prepared."

She seemed relieved. "Good," Then she caressed her baby quietly for a while. "I would like to name her Sarina. It means peaceful."

"Beautiful name, Sarina" Cyrus mumbled.

Giselle gave her a long kiss on her forehead then wrapped her well in the little military blanket.

"She is yours now Cyrus, you have to take good care of her." Tears were in her eyes.

"What?" Cyrus somehow did not see it coming. "I can't, I mean . . . I have to take my men . . ."

"She will protect you. Her spirit will watch you and your men and you will make it to safety." Giselle said with sparkling eyes. "Think about her as your mascot."

"But what about you?", Cyrus stopped his sentenced.

Giselle slowly shook her head. "I'll stay here Cyrus I can't go with you anyway." She did not mention what her fate would be but he already knew it. She would stay to die in this place.

Cyrus closed his eyes. Emotions flowed into him, emotions that he had never dreamt he had. He controlled himself in front of Giselle. He was ashamed of the fact that he was responsible for all this. His soul felt a change. He looked at Giselle. He gave her a kiss on her forehead.

"I would never imagine that something like this would happen to me and certainly not in such circumstances." he told her. "Not to me, the rough, brutal, emotionless man." He looked down as tears filled his eyes but then decided that he had no reason to be ashamed of what was happening to him now and raised his red eyes to Giselle. "I am very sorry Giselle for what I have done. I am very sorry for what is happening to you. I am very sorry for all that I have done in the past to other people. I am so very sorry."

Giselle reached out her arm and hugged his head to her chest as Cyrus cried like a child. All these years he had never allowed to himself to cry or to feel. All these years burst out now, in the arms of dying Giselle, somewhere in Lebanon.

Giselle smiled at him. "You are a good man Cyrus, you always had it in you and I am honored to have had this experience with you. Tonight we forged a special bond. I want you to know that."

"Thank you Giselle" he mumbled.

"Now you have to go. Take little Sarina. Be her father and her mother. Love her like she is the only creature on earth, and love her like she is your own daughter."

"Well, I feel like she is my daughter already. I'll take care good care of her Giselle."

He covered Giselle and left her his water and some military food that he brought with him.

"Here our ways separate, but I'll always be with you and Sarina", Giselle said with tears in her eyes.

"I would love to have you with us." Cyrus told her quietly.

He prepared everything for departure and sent a text to his men. "I'll be there within fifteen minutes."

Just before he was about to leave the room she suddenly felt a slight panic. "Wait Cyrus. Can I see her one more time?"

"Of course", he hid the tears that came into his eyes.

She cuddled with her baby for few more minutes. This time it was Cyrus who had to remind her that he had to leave.

She gave him her baby and Cyrus looked into her eyes and kissed her, this time on her lips. "I know it has been a very brief encounter but in this little time that we shared together I fell in love with you. It is tragic. I love you, Giselle."

She wept "I love you Cyrus."

With a broken heart he left her in the room and went to meet his men. There was a difficult task in front of him. This time it was not only for himself and his men. He had to bring little Sarina to safety. He promised that to her mother.

*   *   *

Plan B was an emergency plan that had he hoped they will never have to execute. Unfortunately, they had to. When his men saw the baby girl they said nothing. Every one of them was with his own thoughts. They obeyed Cyrus without any questions or doubts. He was their leader and that was how it would continue.

Plan B was based on reaching to the Lebanon shore and stealing a boat. Cyrus planned to stay fairly close to the shore and contact a friend via his satellite phone to meet them in mid sea. That was why he did not like Plan B. It had too many luck factors. They arrived at the shore at dawn and camped on the beach in a secluded area.

Cyrus knew that babies do not need to eat immediately but he would need to provide her with food soon enough.

"Watch the camp, I am going to take a short hike." he told his men. "Watch Sarina, she is sleeping quietly."

They all knew him very well. If he needed some time for himself that means that he needed to think something through.

Cyrus walked quickly along the beach. The sun was just then radiating its first beams of morning light and the sand was still cold from the night. The wind blew salty sea water on his face and he enjoyed it. He had been in this climate a few times before and loved it. The Mediterranean climate was typically warm that time of the year and the sea water was simply an ideal place for a refreshing swim. Today he did not have time for a swim but he enjoyed the natural beauty of the beach.

"What to do from here?", the thought penetrated him. This was the first time in his life that he did not know what to do. He was not worried about their escape plan. Something would pop up, something always did. He'd find a way to bring them to safety. What he was wondering about was his personal life. He just had an experience that he had never had before. All of his life he had judged events, people and decisions entirely without emotion. Yet something happened to his soul last night. Giselle had said his name with love. He had been a helper in nature's greatest event, the miracle of birth. He had been given a beautiful baby girl, Sarina to be responsible for. He, Cyrus the merciless, the one who never hesitated to destroy and kill complete villages and full populations of men, women and children, had received a gift that just now he started to comprehend. He was given child to raise.

Something had changed inside him last night. He could feel it. He took a deep breath and looked into the blue horizon. The Mediterranean Sea seemed to be talking to him saying, "You will be a different man Cyrus, I have given you a precious gift and you are a new man now. You have my blessings.

Yes, he would change. He already changed. He'd reinvent his organization. He'd stop being a mercenary for hire. He would change their purpose. He would still use his military expertise and resources. After all, these were acquired with blood over the years but he'd exercise their power in a positive way. They would transform from a group of murderers to a group of rescuers and helpers. They had plenty of funds to search the world and look for the weak in need of their help; if in some poor village in Africa attacked by vicious soldiers or if a small tribe in the desert suffered from abuse by stronger tribes. They would help the weak! They would become "The Rescuers".

That was it. The decision had finalized inside him and he was sure, as Giselle told him before he left her, "If you do good, nature will be good to you. Nature will help you."

He knew what to do.

All of a sudden he became alert. A jogging young man was approaching him."

There is no need to get tense", he thought. "I can just be a simple man walking on the beach on this beautiful morning.

The young man approached him and Cyrus looked at the horizon while also watching him. Then the young man stopped just near him and smiled at him.

Cyrus looked at him without any expression.

"Why is he smiling to me?", he thought.

"Cyrus I presume?" the man asked him politely. He had an accent.

Cyrus did not answer. Although he was very surprised he did not show it. He was trained to maintain a poker face. His brain already made calculations.

"*I am not armed but can easily take this guy. What if there are others? Where are they? Is this is a trap?*"

Somehow his gut feeling told him that this man did not bear any treat for them but he was not sure and always calculated for the worst case scenario.

"Relax Cyrus. We were watching you via satellite." The man laughed in a friendly manner. "You did good work." He gave him another semi serious look. "You need a way out, that's why we are here. Let's go pick up your guys." He patted Cyrus on his back and they walked to the camp.

"Who are you?" Cyrus at last said something.

"My name is George and I live in Johannesburg. You do not need to tell me anything about you, I already know everything.", he smiled at him again. All that Cyrus could think about was that he was not as secretive as he thought he was.

They were picked by a small patrol boat that took them to Cyprus where baby Sarina received her first bottle. They were all checked into a hotel near the sea where they rested. The nicest fact was that no one asked from them for any identification. George was with them during all this time, making sure that they got all what they need. They were fed at a fancy restaurant from which they enjoyed the exquisite view of the Mediterranean. They enjoyed a few pleasant days on the island of Cyprus before George arranged their flight back to the U.S.

It was their last day in Cyprus and George came to see Cyrus in his room.

"Thank you for the great hospitality." Cyrus held baby Sarina and was rocking her.

"Our pleasure.", answered George.

"So, who are you if I may ask?" Cyrus raised a friendly question. "We were completely taken care by you guys but never knew who were?"

George was quiet for a moment. "Consider us your customer. You all have a pleasant trip home." he commented and then left.

Cyrus never saw him again.

Cyrus changed their entire organization. All the team members agreed to the change. Now they all were fathers to a baby girl and this changed their entire point of view about life. They all loved little Sarina like they never loved anyone else before. As for Cyrus he was the happiest man on earth. Sometimes when he and little Sarina were alone he thought that she had her mother's eyes; big beautiful brown eyes. He would then release a long sigh. In the very short time that he knew Giselle, he developed feelings towards her. When he was thinking about her, his eyes would fill with tears. He would never forget how he had to leave her to her death in that dark room.

Nature has mysterious ways.

About year later Cyrus had to fly to Dubai. He was invited to a good friend's wedding. The affair was extravagant and rich as any royal wedding and Cyrus had a very good time with his friend. On the day of his flight back he left the hotel early. The airport was not too crowded and he stopped in one of the airport toy stores to buy Sarina a toy. He bought a pretty doll of Jasmine from the Disney tale. The doll laughed and giggled when someone pushed her belly. He smiled to himself. "They didn't have such toys in my time".

His thoughts turned to Sarina and he felt warm fuzz inside him. He missed her so much.

Then he looked at his watch. It was time to go to the gate. His flight was leaving in forty-five minutes. As he walked towards the gate through a long corridor he noticed young woman walking towards him. She carried a small suitcase and looked like a typical traveler. His attention then turned towards the huge beautiful photos of Saudi Arabia that were in the hallway. The photos were very large yet very detailed and showed vivid scenery of desert and modern cities.

They did an amazing job building a beautiful city in the middle of the desert, Cyrus thought. Right then the woman who was walking the opposite direction, passed near him. His eyes briefly saw her image and she looked at him. They continued walking to their destinations and slowly both stopped.

Cyrus' memory was jarred to attention. *"Where did I see these beautiful eyes before? Do I know this woman?"*

She passed him and then stopped.

"Where have I seen this man?"

They both turned around at the same time.

Cyrus looked at her as his heart raced from excitement. *"Can it be?"*

"Giselle?" he mumbled but already knew the answer before she called his name.

"Cyrus?" tears quickly came into her eyes.

They started to walk towards one another.

"But, I left you there." He said as he increased his pace.

"Cyrus? Is that you?" she also increased her pace.

They met in the middle and he looked deeply into her eyes.

"Yes, it is you. I'll never forget your eyes. You are so beautiful." He could hardly talk.

"Cyrus," she smiled and it illuminated his world "It is you." Tears of joy fell on her cheeks.

They hugged in the joy of reunion.

"But how did you manage?", he mumbled.

"I survived," her eyes sparkled with eternal joy "remember, you left me with water and food. I laid there for a while. I thought I would surely die but then a miracle happened. In the morning I felt stronger. I decided that I could not let myself die like that, even with my injuries. I gathered all my powers and went outside. A helicopter that flew above saw me. They landed closer to me and took me to a hospital in Israel where they worked on me for many days."

"Amazing! We were rescued but by Maronites who had hired us to get rid of the murderous terrorists destroying their country. We were taken to Cypress and flew to the US from there." Cyrus was amazed.

Then she remembered something and her lips shook. Cyrus already read her mind and was smiling widely. "Sarina . . . Did she . . . make it?" She was afraid to ask but when she saw Cyrus smile she covered her mouth as she was shaking from crying.

He hugged her to his heart. "She is alive and well. She is wonderful although a little bit of a control freak but her pediatrician tells me it is natural for young girls raised by fathers."

She could not speak so he took her into his arms. "I'll tell you everything on the way to the United States. Let's go and change your flight."

She did not say anything and simply let him led her to her baby and their new life together.

*　　*　　*

"Stupid little thing called love." The dark angel mocked the lyrics of the song. "Love is the great flaw of humans. It is superfluous. Worthless emotions have always been a good way to drag people into my world." He hissed with anger. "This time it caused the opposite. "Worthless. Completely worthless. Give them a few years and they'll separate. Humans rarely stick to their vows of love."

"Nevertheless", the light angel smiled "there are many happily married couples who live together all their lives. Every case is individual."

The dark angel looked to the side as eight green check marks were illuminated. It was despicable in his eyes and he made faces at the score board. "Humans kill, cheat and lie for what they call love but is it really for love or superficial passion? How many love stories will really make it in time of trouble? Almost none." He waived with his hand and booed. "Take for example Samson and Delilah, what was the end then? That was love for you, nothing but another fake reason for doing evil." Then he smiled evilly "That's my type of love."

"Jacob worked for Rachel for fourteen years, married her and lived happily ever after." The light angel nodded. "Now that's what I call love."

Chapter IX

BENJAMIN

*   *   *

Carl Hanz was a head hunter. He considered himself more like a skull hunter since his targets were to be killed. He has done this type of job almost since childhood, as he defined it. He was always into hunting. It is funny, because Carl did not look like a hunter. As a matter of fact he looked like a typical engineer. He was of average height, with a nerdy looking hair style and glasses. He had all the features of an average engineer whom no one even notices. This was one of his strong cards though. No one ever suspected him of being who he was.

His methods were sharpened since he started working as a skull hunter during college. He found friends who introduced him to this path. He was in an electrical engineering program and thought that it would be a great cover for his real work. He graduated summa cum laude on the dean's list. The he found a job almost immediately in the city of Schenectady, N.Y. as an electrical engineer. He loved the east coast weather; especially the distinct seasonal changes and so established his residence in the region. He rented a small apartment, bought a small car and occasionally even had a local girlfriend. All this was to cover his real job. Carl had a charming personality and he often used it in order to go for few days' vacation when he needed to perform his other jobs.

He started with simple jobs like finding people but very quickly found the channels to perform the high paying jobs; assassinations. Again it was pure luck when at one time someone wanted him to find a person. During the meeting the customer who was a beautiful, wealthy woman asked if for additional sum he'd make sure that that person will disappear. Carl could not pass up such an opportunity. That person was the woman's old husband. He received a very fat lump sum and was rewarded with have an enchanting, sexy vacation with the wild widow.

That was his first experience and he simply fell in love with his job. He even had a nick name for it, skull hunt. With the years he gained robust experience in this type of work and earned a high reputation within many organizations. Rich private people such as high-class criminals knew about him and often gave him jobs. He also received a nick name. He became The Engineer. The F.B.I. had been trying to put him behind bar for years. Hence Carl knew how to leave no marks at the scene, unless of course he wanted to do so. Carl was a smart man and knew all about forensic methodology. Therefore he was always very meticulous in performing his jobs. There was never any evidence of his visit at the crime scene. His crime scenes were always perfectly cleaned like a precise work of engineering.

He had no fear about the victims. Even older policeman and high-ranking F.B.I. agents were fascinated when an important criminal was found dead. Not everyone had the guts to assassinate these people. This was considered tempting fate but for Carl everyone was the same target. The head of a large crime organization or a simple husband cheating on his wife were the same for him. He always used the same method. He had a small, silenced Logger that he used at the right moment. His innocent appearance and his sharp moves in an out of the scene turned him into one of the most deadly killers ever. He enjoyed his reputation and he successfully turned into fortune and glory.

He managed his banks account overseas as the balances grew to sums that would not shame any celebrity but for Carl this was not big deal. Yes, he enjoyed the increasing savings in his bank accounts but continued to go to his daily job, pretending to be an average person who makes the world a better place.

* * *

It was Friday night and everyone in the plastic plant was about to leave early. It was a tradition at the plant in Albany, N.Y. Happy Hour was something that had been scrupulously observed every weekend for the past twenty years and this weekend there was no reason not to continue. Don Sayer, the company's CEO, relaxed comfortably in his chair and looked through the large one-way window into the plant. The manufacturing hall was huge and he could see all the personnel cleaning the machines and preparing to go home for the weekend. People like to work in my plant, he thought with joy. He liked to keep his employees happy. His idea was that happy employees make better products. They are dedicated and self motivated. Most important of all, they were happy in their personal lives. A happy employee who is satisfied with his job and its compensation, will stay with that company forever. That was his motto and he always made sure to pay nice salaries, a bit more than the industry standard. It did not cost much for the company but kept employees happy. He held social events including meals provided by the company in order to create a family atmosphere. A few times a year he company catered social events for the employees and their families and he provided paid vacations and other benefits. The end result was impressive. The plant's production was always above expectations. Employees went the extra mile for the company and the overall atmosphere was of a large family. The board of directors was of course, the happiest of all watching constant growth in the company's profit and success.

Don was satisfied. He looked at his watch and debated if he should go to the happy hour with the guys or skip it and go home. The weather was supposed to be great this weekend and he planned to take his family to Lake George. They loved to swim there and enjoyed the small resort town of Lake George. That's why he loved this place. He was married to his high school sweetheart and they had two great children. He and his family liked to live in a small town near the big plant. They lived in the enchanted small town of Amsterdam, N.Y., a beautiful, quiet place, between tall green trees and meadows. Maybe on Sunday, after church, he'd continue writing the book that he started few months ago. Writing was something that he discovered recently and it had become a big passion in his life. The more he thought about the weekend, the more he became eager to start it. First he'd go to the happy hour event with the guys. After all, traditions must be kept.

He gathered his notes into his briefcase, cleaned his desk and was ready to leave the office. Like every day he walked through the sky-bridge on his way to the parking lot on the other side of the building. As he walked he looked down onto the plant. It was empty. Everyone had left for the weekend. When he arrived at the far side of the bridge he looked down at the huge tanks of melted plastic. These tanks were always filled with melted plastic compound. They had to be heated to the exact temperature of hundred and fifty degrees Fahrenheit. Otherwise this type of plastic would congeal. This was the plastic that flowed through pipes into huge extruders to create tubes, cans and containers for food industries. They developed a unique polymeric formula to create this type of plastic and registered about dozen patents for it. He noticed that one of the large tanks was open. He could see the hot plastic vapors coming out of the big tank.

"That's odd", he thought. *"These tanks are not supposed to be opened for longer than a few minutes at a time. Otherwise there is a risk of coagulation. Especially now, just before the weekend, they are supposed to be closed and sealed. Is there any maintenance work that I was not aware of?"*

He stopped just above the huge tank and looked to see if there were any personnel near it.

"Don Sayer I presume?" A person approached him with a smile.

Don looked at him. He did not know him. He was average with glasses. He looked like one of his engineering team.

"Yes. Are you new here?" Ron asked in surprise.

"Actually, I am not, but I do have a question, if you please." He pointed down to the tank.

His manners were perfect and Don had no reason to suspect anything. He bent down slightly and that was all Carl needed. All he had to do was push Don lightly. This caught Don by surprise. He lost his balance and fell over the bridge directly into the boiling plastic. He even did not have any time to scream as the bubbly plastic swallowed him whole.

Carl looked down with satisfaction. Then he checked if anyone was around. No one saw him. The place was empty. He had already taken care of the cameras that were everywhere. All he had to do was to shut down the video system via remote control. It was a piece of cake. He already knew everything about Don. He was a successful C.E.O. of this plant, with a wife and two children, loved by everyone. "If he was such a positive person who would want to get rid of him? Maybe an ambitious board member? Someone else who wants to take his place? Who knows?" He wondered for a moment. Then again it is not his job to analyze reasons. Someone wanted him dead and was willing to pay generously for it so it was done. He texted the message about job completion to the customer and took a final look at the plant. The plastic below continued boiling. On Monday the staff will probably discover the gruesome scene. Until then Mr. Don Sayer would likely be declared missing. Again, it was not his problem. He was never there.

*   *   *

Erica Sanchez was devastated. She had just received a phone call that her husband had been killed in a car accident. She immediately called her mother who lived in Maryland and told her the news. Her mother had said that she'd take the first flight she could get and probably arrive by evening. In the meantime her good neighbor and friend Heather was with her and her baby boy, William.

"I can't believe it". Heather's eyes were red from tears. She had known Erica and her husband Steve since they moved in about ten years ago. Steve was serving as a high officer in the Miramar air force base in San Diego and Erica was a senior secretary in a Hi-Tech company. They were a nice couple and Erica had just delivered a baby boy three months ago. Her had husband left for the base this morning and a few hours later she received a call that he had died in a car accident. She was sitting with her baby boy William, rocking him while big tears flowed from her eyes. She was unable to talk. Heather brought her water occasionally that she drank slowly. Little William enjoyed lying in his mother's arms and opened his eyes widely, observing objects in the room. Typically he would be in a day care but Heather brought him to his mother when she learned about the accident. His presence helped Erica to stay focused.

"My mother is flying to be with us and will probably be here within a few hours." Erica told Heather.

"Sure," Heather nodded "I'll stay with you until she arrives."

"Oh, no need sweetie. Erica gave her a faded smile "You can go home for a little while. I know the boys are coming home from school." She knew that Heather's two boys were coming back home soon and they would need their mother.

"Are you sure? I can work something out."

"No, thank you Heather, you can go now. You have already been here a few hours and my mom will be here shortly."

"OK, if you insist, but give me a call if you need anything and I mean anything." Heather gave her a hug and gave little William a kiss and then left.

Erica remained in her rocking chair while little William fell asleep with the soothing movement. Erica thought about their life together. They had a good life, not spectacular but a very good life overall. They had all that a young couple would want to have; good jobs, stable incomes and a promising future. Yes, they also had a few crises in their relationship but who doesn't? This was life. They overcame it and were quite happy together until this happened. She shook her head in disbelief. She just kissed him goodbye this morning, when he left for work as she did every morning. She wondered for a moment how this thing happened. Who was involved in the accident? Where was it? The police officer told her on the phone that someone would come to tell her all the details. They were working on piecing together the details of what occurred after the accident.

She heard a knock on her door.

"Come in please", she said.

The door opened and a man entered the house. "Oh, I am sorry if I am interrupting." he apologized.

"No, it is O.K. Please sit down. I am Erica, his wife and this is our baby William. The baby is asleep now and when he is asleep, it is very hard to wake him up. Trust me." She looked at her sleeping baby with love. "We always say that he sleeps like the dead." She smiled and then her smile disappeared when she realized the meaning of what she said. Her face became sad and she burst into tears again as her body convulsed, crying.

"I am Detective Paul Young, ma'am and I am very sorry for your loss." The man stood there quietly.

"Please sit down Detective Young," she wiped her nose. "Excuse the mess."

"Don't worry about any mess ma'am, and you can call me Paul." He seemed very polite.

"How did it happen?" She asked. "I mean, he was not a bad driver."

"We actually suspect sabotage in the brake system, activated remotely. From initial findings it seems like someone implanted a small devise to explode the braking system at a critical moment on the highway. Someone knew very well what they were doing. The device could be activated electronically." Then he looked straight into her eyes "Erica, do you know if your husband had any enemies?"

She was shocked to hear this question. "Absolutely not! Everyone loved him, at the base, friends, here in the neighborhood." Her eye-brows slanted upwards in surprise. "Are you sure it was sabotage?"

"Well, we are not fully sure but that is what it looks like from initial forensic analysis of the car. His brakes were disconnected at the exact moment he moved into high speed. As a result he immediately lost control and the car flipped a few times at high speed. He died instantly."

Erica had hard time grasping the information. *"Who would do this to him?"*

Baby William woke and started to cry.

"He is hungry. I need to make him something to eat." Erica prepared to stand up and make a bottle.

"Oh, I'll help you." The detective immediately volunteered. "Where is the bottle?"

"Thank you, they are there in the kitchen" Erica pointed "But do you know how to make the baby formula?"

"I have one of my own ma'am", the detective smiled to her "Trust me I am the one who wakes up at night."

"How sweet." Erica smiled. It gave her a moment of light. "Please use three spoons of formula with six ounces of warm water. The heater is to the right of the fridge."

"Bottle for the baby, coming up." The detective seemed to be very helpful and it actually made her happy for a few moments. She was exhausted emotionally and physically.

The detective brought her the warm bottle within few minutes and she started to feed baby William. He was always hungry when waking up from his sleep and ate with great enthusiasm.

"Thank you very much Paul." Erica smiled at him.

"Don't mention it. Would you like something to drink? I am sure that you did not eat or drank anything for the past few hours."

"No, actually, I would appreciate a glass of orange juice. I have some in the fridge. I did not drink or eat since noon time, since I received the news."

Without any words he went to the fridge and returned with a large glass of orange juice. "Sorry, it took me few seconds to find the O.J." he apologized with a shy smile.

"Don't worry about it. Thank you." She was very thirsty and finished the juice quickly.

"I was very thirsty without even noticing it." She finished feeding the baby who was now lying calmly in her arms.

"So, why do you think someone would want to have Steve killed? I mean this is so farfetched. Is this murder case now?" She asked in great surprise that showed in the expression on her face.

"I don't really know." The detective sat on the coach in front of her. "Do you have any idea?"

She nodded, "Not at all."

"Hmmm. Do you have any enemies Erica?" He asked her, looking straight into her eyes.

For a second she got scared. Suddenly Paul did not look that nice detective anymore, or maybe it was her mistake?

"Me? Of course not. This is also absurd. Why someone would want to kill me or him?" She was surprised to think in this direction.

"Excuse me for asking but are you sure? Any ex-lovers? Were you cheating with someone who might have been jealous?" Paul was insisting now.

She looked at him "No, no one at all." Then for a split second a thought crossed her mind. She did have a short affair last year with a man. She and Steve had a bad year and almost split. Then she met this man at a bar and one thing led to another. He was hot tempered and refused to end the relationship when she wanted to do so. Wait." She raised her head to look at Paul.

"Yes?"

"Well, I had a minor affair when we were on bad terms but that was many months ago, almost a year. We almost broke up then." Erica apologized in discomfort "But he did not look like a killer."

Paul nodded "What was his name?"

"Armando, but . . ." She mumbled.

"Latino?", he asked.

"Yes. He had arrived from Spain not long before we met. He was a wealthy business-man. I met him only few times when he came here for business."

Paul was quiet then he said, "Well, it may be it." He stood up and straightened his clothes. He did not really need this information. It was for his curiosity only. After all, even for him this murder case was hard to explain. "This man seemed to have fallen desperately in love with you so when you left him he decided to go to the extreme. I mean killing a man and hurting the entire family for a broken heart." He smiled at her, cleaned his glasses and was about to leave. "Again, I am sorry for your loss ma'am. Please call us at any time you need anything."

"Yes, thank you." She thought that something was weird in what he said but had a hard time remembering what it was. All of a sudden she felt tired, very tired. She looked at her baby. He seemed to have fallen asleep.

The detective left and she remained there. She was almost asleep when a loud knock on the door woke her. "Yes, please come in."

A policeman entered. "Good afternoon ma'am, my name is Paul Young and I am with the police department. I am truly sorry for your loss."

She was confused. Was this policeman just here few minutes ago? She looked at him but this Paul Young looked completely different then the first one. She felt dizzy.

"Are you O.K. ma'am?" The policeman rushed to help her.

"Yes, I am", she mumbled just before collapsing into Paul Young's arms.

"*That was easy*", thought Carl as he started his car and drove away. "*He had the exact opportunity that he wanted. Just a few drops of the deadly poison in the baby's bottle and his mother's juice and now the entire family is dead. There is no antidote for this poison and even in case they end in the hospital they simply will not have enough time to save the mother or the baby.*"

He had to ask the wife about a possible enemy just for his own personal curiosity. After all, they seemed to be a really nice family but then again, this was not his business. He had received an order from a man with a Spanish accent to eliminate the entire family and that's what he did.

He was just doing his job.

*   *   *

Carl was on his way to New Orleans. He loved visiting New Orleans. Just walking in its streets and listening to street artists was an enchanted event for him. This time of the year the weather was nice in New Orleans, not too hot and not too cold, just in the low seventies, perfect. He planned to stay in town for few days. At night he'd have dinner on the famous boat that sails on the Mississippi river. He'd get the private booth with the best wine and steak and observe the stars flickering above the river. He could sail like this forever.

He considered his trip a personal challenge. An anonymous customer requested a hit on a very peculiar person; a known church man in New Orleans. When Carl heard what the job was he raised an eye-brow. The price must be doubled he said immediately. Not that he cared much, after all, he was not religious man but still for the concept of killing a priest he thought that the price should be doubled. Not for what he thinks but for what the people think. The customer agreed but would only pay after the priest was proven dead. Typically he would not do the job until the full amount was paid but this one tested his is capabilities so he took it as a personal challenge. For the first time in his life, he'd do the job first and then get the payment. It seems like the customer had serious doubts as to his capability to execute this job. He was determined to prove him wrong.

He took a taxi to the hotel and relaxed until the evening. He decided to enjoy his first night in the city. At night he went to one of the city's famous jazz clubs and remained there until early morning. The next day he went to see the church. He was amazed to see its size and beauty. For an hour he walked through it and observed the amazing religious artifacts and details. Then he saw one of the priests. He did not know how is target should look. The man who contacted him just gave him a name. He planned to use all of his well mannered tricks to identify the man. He saw a tall, large man standing on the alter reading a large book. The man was dressed in an impressive red and white gown and wore a large necklace with a metal cross. He was praying quietly while Carl observed him.

"Can I do that? This is a holy man. Hey, I am not religious. There is no such thing anyway. It is all man-made. All the rest is done for money."

The priest finished his prayer and raised his eyes from the holy book. His eyes met Carl's. For a moment Carl's felt like those eyes were penetrating his own soul, observing it inside and out. A moment of fear caught him but he overcame it quickly. The man smiled at him, almost like he knew him.

"Excuse me father I am looking for priest Benjamin." Carl kept his manners.

"Just Benjamin?" the man had a deep, pleasant voice.

"Well, this one can be a good singer. He has a good voice. Maybe everyone in New Orleans can sing." he thought to himself.

"Yes, that's what they told me. They say that everyone will know who he is just by his first name. I guess there is only one priest Benjamin in here?" Carl smiled.

The customer told him to look for priest Benjamin saying there was only one Benjamin there and he'd find him.

The man looked at him for a while and smiled a wide smile. His smile illuminated the entire Church. His eyes sparkled and it seems like everything else was sparkling around him, the candles, the walls, the colorful windows, everything sparkled.

"Indeed there is only one Benjamin here. It is me my good man. What can I do for you on this lovely day?"

"Bingo" he thought.

"Oh, I thought to ask you few questions." Carl was not ready to approach him now. Typically he planned every detail of the operation and how things would be done. He liked clean scenes.

Benjamin looked at him thoroughly. "Well, I tell you what. I have tonight free, How about we'll have dinner together?"

A thought passed in Carl's mind. "Excellent idea, please allow me to invite you for a dinner cruise. Dinner on a boat on the mighty Mississippi river, my treat."

Benjamin smiled widely. "We've got a deal. Tonight, dinner on the Mississippi. I'll be there."

"Thank you father", Carl thanked him with a smile.

"It could not be better than that".

*   *   *

They had dinner on an authentic steam-boat. The night air was clear and the boat trip was to be about three hours. Carl thought that was not enough time to enjoy the tour and atmosphere. Dinner was excellent, as usual. They had medium-rare fillet-mignon, done to perfection. On the side was served New Orleans' famous mashed potatoes with steamed buttered green beans. Carl ordered the best Merlot one could get in New Orleans to accompany their dinner. The wine was smooth and added another level of culinary pleasure to their meal. The desert was Boston cheesecake and hot apple pie served with a huge scoop of French Vanilla ice cream. Simple, authentic southern food was Carl's favorite.

"So, what brings you to New Orleans?" Benjamin asked with a large smile.

"As usual, business." Carl nodded and returned a wide smile of his own.

"What type of business are you in?"

"I am in the electrical engineering field, microchip design." Carl knew his material.

Benjamin's face expressed his curiosity. "I don't know of any engineering corporations here."

"It's the Design Automation Conference." Carl took a sip from his wine. "The conference is held every year in a different location. This year it is in New Orleans."

"Ah, understood." Benjamin seemed to be satisfied with this answer. "And why did you search for me?"

"That's a different story." Carl's face illuminated. "A good friend told me about you and your wisdom and recommended me. 'When you go to New Orleans you have to see father Benjamin' he told me. 'There is a lot to learn from him.' So that is why we are here."

Benjamin looked straight into Carl's eyes and nodded quietly. Carl got a feeling of discomfort that like Benjamin did not fully believe him.

"Maybe it is just the way he looks at people." he thought.

"So please tell me some wisdom Benjamin." Carl raised a toast in the air. "I would like to hear something that I never heard before. I have to warn you though, I am not a religious guy but my parents took me to church few times when I was young."

Benjamin drank from his glass of water and laughed loudly. "It will be an honor Carl to show you the way tonight."

He then gave Carl a thorough look and Carl felt like his soul was wide open in front of Benjamin.

Then Benjamin began.

*   *   *

"I'll let things enter from one ear and get out of the other", thought Carl quietly.

"So here we are today looking and searching for the meaning of life." Benjamin started. Although Carl did not want to really listen to him he got carried away since Benjamin was an exceptionally charismatic person. When he talked everyone listened. Tonight his audience was Carl.

"I will not talk with you about deep religion today, oh no." he said with a smile "Tonight I'll talk about humanity. Tonight I'll talk about how people treat other people. Tonight I am going to talk about considering others." Carl wondered where he was going with these words but remained attentive.

Benjamin leaned forward and straightened his eyes deep into Carl's. "It all began when people lost the meaning of human life. Every person has a meaning for his life. Every person's life is his most valuable asset. Life is given to us by greater power and we have to appreciate it." Then he gave Carl a wide smile "Let's not forget the sixth commandment which is a very strict one, 'Do not murder'. Every person's life counts, every person's soul is secret."

Carl moved in his seat with discomfort.

"I need to execute my play for Benjamin. I have a job to do", he reminded himself.

He'd wait for an opportunity.

Benjamin continued with his lecture and Carl started to feel that it targeted him. It was like he knew Carl.

"Taking someone else's life is strictly prohibited. Not only from the humanitarian side of it but also because we do not have the right to do so. Not even our own life. We did not create life and therefore we have no right to take it from someone else, under any circumstances."

Carl listened quietly. Without noticing he became transfixed on Benjamin's words.

"Sometimes evil takes over humans and lead them to wrong paths. Some humans have souls that can fall for evil temptations but they'll always have the chance to redeem themselves at some point in time." Benjamin continued with passion. "Remorse and regret are always part of changing as long as the soul is seeking for the truth."

Carl's eyes did not even blink. He listened, hypnotized by Benjamin's words.

"Only humans can make the difference." Benjamin continued with passion. "If a person violated the sixth rule only his great desire to change can make a difference, otherwise it is worthless and soon enough he'll continue committing more violations. A true belief is necessary. A true belief in the good and the greater power that sees everything we do."

Carl wondered. Benjamin's words seemed to fit his life perfectly. What was going on? Did he know about him? Did he know what he had done in the past?

"One may ask himself, 'until when?' ", Benjamin continued "Until when will I continue with this way of life? How many times will I continue to sin? Will there be an end to all this? Many individuals are caught up in this life style for so long they do not even know how to get out of it." Benjamin stressed every word. "They have forgotten the light. They got so far away from it that they simply forgot about it. But the light is always there even after many years of sin. The light is always waiting to be given a chance. A chance to illuminate the darkness inside. The chance for atonement."

Carl listened silently as every of Benjamin's word penetrated his soul.

"So the question remains, are you going to give light a chance? Are you going to face the fact that you have sinned? And the most important of all, Are you going to change?"

Benjamin became quiet and observed Carl. "Excuse me I have to go to the restroom. Nature calls. I'll be back in a sec.", he laughed to loosen up the tense atmosphere and left the table.

Carl woke up from his trance.

"Here is your opportunity. Quick before he'll comes back"

For a second he hesitated. *"What is happening to me? It's my job and I am here for that".*

Quickly he pulled out a small vial and poured a few drops into Benjamin's wine. A few drops were more than enough. There was no antidote for this poison. Once it is in a human's body there is no way back. There was no way to reverse the process. It was a death sentence.

Benjamin returned and sat in front of him. Then he was quiet for a while just before he said what he said. "I have preached in front of many sinners. My goal in life is to bring people back from the darkness. To show them the light." Then he said something that caused Carl to quiver. "Do you need to be shown the light Carl?"

Carl was caught completely by surprise. "Not really, I am good thank you."

Benjamin looked at him for a while. "Are you sure?"

Carl remained silent. Again, he had this feeling that Benjamin simply knew everything about him. But how could it be? He never saw or heard about him before.

"Then let me start." Benjamin nodded, noticed his hesitation. Benjamin talked about life and beyond. He talked about love, passion and all the beautiful things that life offers. He talked about forgiveness and mercy and he talked about many other noble virtues that people should appreciate. He talked for almost two hours and when he finished Carl remained speechless. They sat there for a while, each with his own thoughts.

"Well, I believe that I can enjoy my wine now." Benjamin smiled and took his glass.

"Stop." Carl grabbed Benjamin's hand just before he took a sip from it.

The moment was intense. Benjamin looked at Carl silently.

"Don't drink that wine.", Carl said in a low voice.

Benjamin put the glass on the table. "Look for Benjamin, there will be only one in this church." he said in a low voice.

Carl stared at him, astonished.

"You'll get your payment after the job is done." Benjamin continued.

"It was you?" Carl's heart raced. "You hired me to murder you?" I don't get it.

Benjamin's smiled and leaned towards Carl. "I was a criminal once, many years ago. One father showed me the way back and since then I vowed to make my life a mission. A mission to change people who are doing wrong. I found out about you from a friend. This friend knows many people who are doing wrong. I select a name and I work on the case." He released a long sigh "I do not succeed every time. Sometimes I lose to evil but many times I win." A wide smile spread across his face. "I like when this happens."

"But, I could kill you. If you were to drink this wine, you would be dead in short order." Carl could not comprehend. "You are . . . You are risking your life."

225

"True. Sometimes I have to but it is worth it. Look Carl, I know who you are. I know your reputation and your side work. You have done it for many years now. You heard me tonight. What are your thoughts?"

Carl lowered his eyes. "Yes, I've sinned Benjamin. I have sinned many times."

"You can change it right now!" Benjamin talked loudly and with passion. "The light is always there, you just have to go for it."

Carl looked towards the dark Mississippi river. Benjamin's words touched him inside in a way that nothing ever did before. All of a sudden he wanted to change. He felt the desire to change. He took a deep breath, took Benjamin's glass of wine and threw it overboard.

Then he filled a new glass for him and raised his. "I want to go to the light Benjamin. I want to see the light."

Benjamin smiled with great satisfaction. "Hallelujah!"

*   *   *

"I knew that religion would pop up here at some point." The dark angel, said, underrating the transition.

"Religion is advocacy of good." replied the light angel. "It is an integral part of many human lives."

"The man was right. It is manmade tool to control others.", the dark angel argued contemptuously.

"Maybe, but the fact still remains, without religion there would be much more evil in the world."

"That is exactly what I have been trying to achieve", came the retort and the dark angel's face became grim upon seeing the ninth green check mark illuminated.

Chapter X

SPELL

*   *   *

"Franz Mauer, Attention" The commandant screamed and I stood erect without even blinking.

"You are re-located to Poland."

"Ja Herr Obersturmführer." I responded loudly.

"Will you serve your country faithfully there, as in here, the battlefield?" He screamed again.

"Ja Herr Obersturmführer."

"And will you serve faithfully your Führer?"

"Ja Herr Obersturmführer."

The lieutenant looked at me thoroughly and seemed to be satisfied with my responses.

"Good then, go to your barracks and pack. You are leaving tomorrow. Dismissed."

He left and I remained standing straight like a tree near our camp flag. After a few minutes I noticed that I was the only person still standing there. A slight wind started to blow from the north. I allowed myself to look up, where our national flag started to flap in the wind. I loved our flag, the Nazi flag. The colors are vivid and match the symbol inside, the Swastika. I smiled towards it. I was a fairly new soldier and had spent only few months near the Polish border and now they wanted to move me. I was good with that. I accepted any job in the war. I'd do everything to make my country win. I fought against Yugoslavia for a while. I even received a medal for my bravery. Nothing really scared me, I do not know why. The sounds of flying bullets near me just didn't do anything to me. I saw many friends get very scared hearing explosions and bullets but somehow to me it did nothing. Even my commandant always said to me that he did not understand why I was not afraid to die. He said that though, that this stupid characteristic of mine, this quality would help me to become someone big one day. Who knows? I may be able to be in command one day. A few days ago they let me know that my help was needed in some camp inside Poland, a concentration camp. This may be a much easier job, just watching prisoners and performing some camp tasks. My commandant told me that

I may be a great fit for the camp. I have no fear and no feelings. I didn't understand exactly what he meant by that but who cares. I'll happily obey all my commanders' orders. I love my country and I love my Führer. I'll do everything that is needed to make our country win.

Some soldiers were passing near me. They gave me a funny look and continued on their way. I have to go to the barracks and pack my stuff. I am leaving tomorrow to a new camp. Wait a minute, what was the camp name that I am going into? Hmmm . . . I forgot its name. The commandant mentioned it to me few times but somehow I did not pay attention. After all, for me it doesn't matter much where I am going to serve my country.

I saw Corporal Miller walking nearby. I thought he might know.

"Hey Miller," I yelled to him and approached him "Do you remember which camp I am being transferred to tomorrow?"

"He smiled at me and lighted a cigarette "Franz, you are an idiot as always. You are going to Auschwitz tomorrow." He shook his head, made some funny move with his hand and left.

"Why do people always laugh at me?"

I walked towards my barracks. Now I knew where I was going to be moving tomorrow. I never heard about the place but what can it be? It is only a prisoner camp. I hope I will not be bored there. Another soldier passed near me. I didn't know him. A thought crossed my mind so I called out,

"Hey, I am being transferred tomorrow to Auschwitz. How is it? Did you hear about this camp?"

The guy just nodded. "Oh yes, you'll like it. I'm sure you will."

My heart filled with joy.

I was going to Auschwitz.

*   *   *

Auschwitz was much different than what I imagined. I arrived with dozen other soldiers and they immediately put us in an orientation course for a few days. During those days I learned many facts that I never knew. For example, I learned that the Jews are one of our nation's deadliest enemies since they are enemies from the inside. Not like other visible enemies like the Russians that we can fight and handle face to face, the Jews were destroying us for many years in a hidden way. They stole from us and from our ancestors. They lie and they cheat. They are weird in their beliefs and need to be eliminated from our society. They are the source of all evil in the world. I also learned that Gypsies, black people and homosexuals are very bad for our nation. All these people were prisoners here in Auschwitz.

On our second day we learned that our great leaders came to conclusion that the people who are causing direct damage to our society should be exterminated, yes, killed. Our hero, the Führer even thought about an impressive idea how to get rid of all these people. It's called the Final Solution. That means to kill them all. To create concentration camps and death camps to gather all these bad people and kill them systematically. We built gas chambers, we built crematoriums and we are doing massive executions in order to kill as many of them as possible on a daily basis. They even made a daily quota of how many need to be killed. I was amazed to learn about this. Our nation is well known for its precise clockwork and machinery but this time we have implemented systematic murder methods.

On the third day they took us out to the camp and showed us how to treat the prisoners. The instructor took us to a line of Jews that was waited to go to the gas chamber. "See'" he told us, "These Jews are waiting for their turn to enter the showers. They think that these are showers but actually they are gas chambers. When these Jews will enter the showers gas will be blown in and they will all die. Then other Jews will take out their bodies and put them into the crematoriums for burning. This is an efficient system.", he explained and I was amazed. Then the instructor called to one of the Jews that were standing in line. When the Jew reached us he pulled his gun and shot him in the head. "These are not humans, they just look like are.", he explained us. "These are Jews. They are like the worst roaches, insects, rats, things that we need to exterminate." Again, I was amazed to see that. I would never imagine something like this would happen to the German country; that we will have enemies from within. Then he brought a few other Jews in front of us and asked us to shoot them. A few of the soldiers did not want to shoot them even after he commanded us. They were sent to the doctor. When my turned arrived I did it without any problems. I shot the young Jew. He was a young boy, maybe sixteen but I remembered all what they taught us and shot him in the head. The instructor was very happy with my performance, I could see it. After that they said that we were ready to start and I was assigned to be under Untersturmführer Gunter Amon. He was in charge of a process called selection. This process, they explained to us, was for distinction between the prisoners who could work for our nation and those who were not capable of working. This was a very efficient procedure supervised by our great medical stuff. Those who were not capable of working were sent to death. It made sense.

That evening they gave us a graduation party and even invited women from the nearest town. We ate and drank until late at night and the next morning I started my service in the concentration camp of Auschwitz.

*   *   *

It was a cold morning when we brought a few small tables and chairs in front of the prisoner's barracks. Some other soldiers and I were ordered to gather the prisoners in front of the tables in long lines. The doctors would be arriving soon and examine the people's health. I went to my assigned barracks and shouted to get out and stand in front of the tables. I saw that a few of my friends hit the prisoners on their way out of the barracks. I remembered that these were not humans. They were our enemy of the worse kind. I hated them for that. I started to hit the people and scream at them as they got out of their beds. It was very cold out and most of the prisoners had almost no clothes. No one cared including me. They deserved to suffer. They deserved to die. They were our enemy. I saw them coming out of the buildings, young faces, children and older faces, all looked horrified, many looked sick and starving. Honestly, they already looked like ghosts. They were the living dead. They deserved it. They were evil and for this they would pay. Motivated by my unexplained anger towards them I picked an older man took him to the side, yelled at him and then shot him in rage. No one said anything. Proud of myself I continued to arrange the prisoners in their lines. That felt good.

Then one of the other soldiers walked to me and told me something in private. "No need to kill anyone now. Remember some of them are good for work. You killed an old man, he would be probably being sent to die anyway. Wait until the doctors make the judgments." He pated my back and left and I went to guard the line for the doctor. I had become too ecstatic about killing Jews.

I watched how it was done.

The prisoners were moving slowly forward. The doctor would sign one at a time to stand in front of him. Then he checked him briefly, told him to turn around, to cough and to do few other activities. Then he marked in the paper and signed to which line he should go. I must say it was accurate, effective and conclusive. I felt proud of our system.

After the selection was complete another soldier and I were to bring the group of prisoners to the gas chamber area. There was another Jew who was on our side. He talked to the group and explained to them where we were going. He explained to them that we would now go to the showers. Slowly we escorted the large group to the shower buildings. The showers were large rooms with pipes and shower heads on the ceiling. I knew that there was no water in these pipes. This was just to convince the prisoners that these were real showers. It was explained to us that if the prisoners were to know that these were not really showers but death chambers they may start a riot that would be hard to control. The psychological aspect was very important in the execution of the final solution.

They explained another fact to us. In order to make the daily quota of dead Jews they had to execute them in massive grave sites. For many German soldiers and officers it was too hard mentally. That is why they invented the gas chambers. The top Nazi leadership had to come with a better solution in order to minimize the German soldier's exposure to horrific scenes. It was a clean, distant and impersonal extermination method. I escorted the group of about five hundred people to the showers and instructed them to gather near the facility.

One of the soldiers gave them a speech before they went inside.

"On behalf of the camp administration I bid you welcome. This is not a holiday resort but a labor camp. Just as our soldiers risk their lives at the front to gain victory for the Third Reich, you will have to work here for the welfare of a new Europe. How you tackle this task is entirely up to you. The chance is there for every one of you. We shall look after your health, and we shall also offer you well-paid work. After the war we shall assess everyone according to his merits and treat him accordingly."

"Now, would you please all get undressed? Hang your clothes on the hooks we have provided and please remember your number [of the hook]. When you've had your bath there will be a bowl of soup and coffee or tea for all. Oh yes, before I forget, after your bath, please have ready your certificates, diplomas, school reports and any other documents so that we can employ everybody according to his or her training and ability. Diabetics, who are not allowed sugar, report to the staff on duty after your baths".

It sounded like sincere concern to me.

Sometimes we even gave them bars of soap for better cooperation on their side. After they were all inside, I closed and sealed the large metal doors. I signaled to the chemical expert and he put on his gas mask and went on the roof of the building. I watched from the button how he carefully handled the Cyclone B gas ampoule and threw it into a hole in the ceiling. Then he closed the opening and removed his gas mask. A loud generator was activated and I knew that this was done so the screams of the people inside would not be heard. Still I could hear the panic and horror of the people who died inside. I looked around me and at my comrades, the other soldiers. They all stood there, smoked, talked and swore at the cold weather. For them it was another task. Soon there would be other tasks to do. They explained to us all, this is death camp, it generates death and it does it very efficiently.

After lunch we were assigned to perform another selection, this time at women's barracks. Again the scenario repeated itself all the way to the gas chambers. The camp had a few gas chambers due to the fact that after each session a few hours were needed few hours for the gas ventilation. By the end of the day I was exhausted. The battlefield was easier for me. There I would have moved forward and fight, here I had to be constantly on alert that someone would try to escape or attack us. After all, we were surrounded at all times by hundreds of prisoners.

The next day I was assigned to assist in massive executions. We were escorting many prisoners to mass graves, aligned them and shot them into the graves. I had never seen so many dead before.

The rest of the week we escorted groups to perform labor outside the camp. After a week they sent us to talk with psychiatrists. They wanted to know how do we handled being in a concentration camp. When my turn arrived I claimed that I was proud to serve my country in this war and I am looking forward for our victory. When the doctor asked me what I feel about Jews, my answer was immediate. I hate them all and they deserve to die. They are our enemy and not only ours, the entire world's enemy. We will cleanse Europe and the entire world of them. The doctor seemed to be happy with my answers and sent me back to the camp where I continued with my assignments. After few more months I felt comfortable in Auschwitz. It became like a home to me.

*   *   *

About six months into my service at the camp, resistance organizations had developed. These organizations helped prisoners to escape the camp. One day a group of prisoners that were kept separate from the others in order to work in the crematoriums attacked our S.S. soldiers with makeshift weapons; stones, axes, hammers, other work tools and even homemade grenades. They caught our S.S. guards by surprise, overpowered them and blew up a few of the crematoriums using explosives smuggled in from a weapons factory by female inmates. They were joined by another group of Jews who worked in another crematorium who also overpowered their guards and broke out of the compound. Hundreds of prisoners escaped. This was our hour. We soldiers who came from the battlefield got to prove our military experience. We made a strategic plan for their capture and within few days we captured them all. It felt good to exercise my military education and knowledge. Of course, we executed all the escapees down to the last one.

One day we were ordered to execute a few barracks full of Gypsies. We woke them up early in the morning and led them to massive graves where we executed them. Later we were ordered to search their barracks for hiding people. As we went into their barracks we heard babies crying all over the place. The Gypsies mother's probably knew that they are led to execution and hid their babies under the beds. We found dozens of them. We were ordered to throw them alive into the massive graves. Some of the soldiers practice shooting them in the air just before they fell into the grave.

At some point the orders from our headquarters were to increase the daily quota of dead. They wanted to accelerate the process. More crematoriums were built and we were very busy hauling several shipments per day to the gas chambers. We rushed the killing process. There were times that many shipments of Jews arrived by trains every day. We did not even have time to register them correctly, as we typically did. We led many of these shipments directly from the trains into the gas chambers. These people will never have a record. No one will know what happened to these people, a senior officer told us one night at dinner. Then he laughed, "But then who needs to know about these people? They are just Jews, sub-humans." All the soldiers joined in the laughter, including me.

Then something odd happened. It was something that I could not explain to myself or to others.

I stopped laughing. All of a sudden an image floated into my mind, an image that caused me to stop laughing. An image of this mother with her three children. They arrived from Hungary and I told them to progress directly to the showers for cleanup. The mother and children looked at me, as I smiled with kindness. They had total trust that I was leading them to safety. They had total trust that I cared about their cleanliness after the long trip on the train. Somehow they even smiled to me. The thought of shower and water probably even charmed them. But it was the mother's eyes that looked inside me. Something struck me internally. I could not explain what but something started to bother me inside that day. I tried to look inside myself without any success. Was it fear? Was it the desire to go to war again? Did I miss the battle-field, my natural habitat? Did the Jewish mother do anything to me? Well, it can't be, I led her to the showers and never saw her again, exactly as I did with many thousands of other Jews.

"What is going on?", I asked myself.

*   *   *

I went to visit my family. We lived in a suburb of Berlin and I went for a whole week of home visit. My mother and father welcomed me like a hero. Mother prepared a huge dinner for me and father showed me all the newspapers that described our victory in detail.

"So what is your new assignment son?" My father inhaled deeply from his pipe, blew the smoke into the air and looked at me with admiration. "Where did you say you are now?"

"I am in Auschwitz, Father. It is a concentration camp. Do you know what a concentration camp father is?" All of a sudden I wanted to see what they knew about this camp. We were instructed not to disclose the nature of our work in the camps, even not to loved ones and close family.

"Well," he smiled kindly at me, all relaxed in his seat "It is a prisoners' camp. P.O.W.s if I am correct?"

I nodded slowly. "Yes, something like that."

"So do you like it there?", my mother beamed at me. "Eat your potatoes."

I looked at my plate without any desire to eat. "Yes, it is fine mother. Military work, you know."

My mother sensed that something was bothering me. She grabbed my arm and looked at me closely. "What is wrong dear? What bothers you? Is it too much blood for you to see?"

"Oh, stop filling his head with rubbish for crying out loud," Father interrupted "He was in the battlefield almost eight months. There he faced bloodshed, not here. This is just a prisoner camp, probably too boring for him. Am I right son?" Father opened the newspaper and stuck his face into it.

"Actually it is not boring Father", I reported. "And it has much more blood then the battlefield. As a matter of fact I never saw so many dead people throughout my field service."

My mother covered her mouth with surprise. "But how come?"

"This is not an ordinary camp Mother." I took a deep breath "It is a death camp."

The pipe fell out of my father's mouth. "What do you mean son?" His look was serious.

"I mean that this is a death camp. Did you hear about death camps, Father?" I stressed each word on purpose. I wanted them to know the truth.

Father put the pipe back in his mouth. "I heard about it but I thought it was just rumor. It can't be that our great nation is involved with such actions."

I nodded quietly. "Yes, it is. I am there. I see it every day."

"I heard from Martin, our neighbor, that they have something like that. He claimed that a few escaped from these camps and told their stories to the big world. No one seemed to believe such nonsense. It was insane. You know Martin. He always thinks that the government is one big conspiracy." My father laughed neurotically, trying to overcome the tense atmosphere that was created.

"I am afraid to say that Martin is entirely right and even does not even know the sheer size of the operation going on in these camps." I insisted.

Both of them became quiet and I debated if I should tell them the truth or not. I was really afraid for their health if I told the truth. My mother was the one who made the decision. She sat in front of me, held my hands and asked me straight "I want to know."

I raised my eyes to my father, "Father?"

"Tell us the truth son, and only the truth." My father answered bravely.

"I serve our great country with pride. I did it in the front line and I do it now in the concentration camp. In the battlefield I fought against our enemies in Czechoslovakia, France and Poland. We had great victories." I talked with great enthusiasm about my military experience. I was really proud of them. "I am proud to be part of our country's victory."

"These are words that I like to hear." my father's face became happy.

"Then they moved me to a concentration camp. A labor camp for prisoners, they called it." I stopped here. Both my parents stopped their activities and looked at me, concentrated on my face.

"This is not only a labor camp. It is also an extermination camp, a place where we kill and eliminate our prisoners."

"That happens in wars." My father nervously filled his pipe. "Every military takes the enemy's soldiers as prisoners. If they found a bad one, they killed him. War is like that."

"The only difference is that these are not soldiers that we take as prisoners."

"What do you mean?" My mother focused her terrified eyes on me. She felt that something was wrong, very wrong.

As for me, now that I had started to tell the story, I wanted to continue telling it. This was my way to look inside myself and check what I feel and what I have felt for the past months that I served my country in Auschwitz. Now I wanted to tell them the truth. Furthermore, I had to.

My father took a deep breath and poured himself some spirit. He had to be prepared. My mother just sat there and stared at me.

"These killings are systematic. These are eliminations of non-military personnel; unarmed people, including women and children."

My father and mother looked at me without any expression.

I continued my story.

I told them the truth and nothing but the truth. I did not hide or smooth over scenes. I told them all that I had done and what I had seen for almost a year in Auschwitz. It took me almost two hours and when I was done they both sat there without any response.

"I heard stories about this but always refused to believe it. Yes, we all heard the propaganda about Jews but from that to your description of events in that place, is a world of distance." Father looked upset.

"I believed what they told me and I obeyed my commandants. I murdered many Jews, Gypsies and everyone else that they wanted me to kill." Then I lowered my eyes to the floor. "Only recently something happened that made me wonder."

When they both stared at me, I told the story.

"It was a very busy day in Auschwitz. We had received an order to expedite the executions. The administration wanted to kill many more per day. We were receiving several train shipments each day from all over Europe. The one in mid-day was from Hungary. A large group of Jewish people arrived from locations throughout Hungary. When I took them off the train cars I noticed a mother and her three children. They all looked at me like I was their savior. After so many hours in the dense car with so many people, without food, without water, without toilets, I can imagine what they were thinking. We gave them a good story that we were going to take them to the showers and after that a warm meal and drinks would be served." I nodded when I realized the horror in our actions. "We gave them false hope, false hope for those who were going to be murdered. We were leading them to their death."

I paused. My parents remained silent. But this was not the end of the story. The worst part was still coming.

"So I told them that lie and they looked at me with big eyes, all three of them, the mother, a short woman with really beautiful eyes, her son, probably four or five years old with his innocent look and the daughter, probably eight. The children looked at me in total trust. They believed me. The boy even smiled at me. He probably thought that I was a brave soldier brining them to safety.

Do you know what I have done? I led them to the showers. With a big reassuring smile on my face I took them to take a shower, a shower of Cyclone B gas, a shower of death. I took them to their death with many hundreds of other innocent people who were led to these gas chambers." I straightened my eyes into my father's. His face was pale and he remained speechless.

"Are you sure son, I mean, can it be that these were maybe real showers?", he mumbled.

I laughed bitterly. "As sure as the other group of prisoners who were waiting to take out the bodies within an hour or so. It was all very real, maybe hard to comprehend but very real."

My mother sank her face into her hands and shook as she cried. "And you had to serve there for the past year. I can't believe it. You were such a good boy. You had such a good soul." She then looked at me. What did they do to you?"

I sighed "Well, at the beginning I was at the front line. This was war. I fought against other soldiers, I shot canons, and I shot my rifle. It was war. Yes, I saw dead soldiers but this is the nature of war. Soldiers die. Then I was transferred to the concentration camp." I took a deep breath "Here I faced something entirely different. At first they gave us a whole lecture about why Jews are our worst enemy. It was very convincing and I saw them as real enemies. They even implanted in me an unexplained hatred towards them. I killed them. I shot them; elderly, women and even young children. With every kill I had some satisfaction. I had killed our enemy, the one who wants to kill us, exactly as I did in the battlefield. But with time my mind could not deny what I was witnessing. The selections, the summary executions, the brute force against civilians and simple people started to look not right to me. Yes, I am a simple soldier, a corporal. I have to obey orders. I am a slow person, I know that I do not grasp things sharply but even for a person like me it was eventually too much. I started to understand what is going on. Then started the massive executions and the grotesque scenes of hundreds of bodies inside a big pit . . . Something out of this world . . . Something started to spark inside me. This is not war; I said to myself, this is massacre, but why? Why do we do this? Every week they took us to hear a motivational talk by doctors.

Now I realize that they wanted to check if we were still sane. Yet, they continued to push into our heads the Nazi ideas, justifying what we were doing."

My father and mother remained shocked.

"You know, I may not be that bright of a man. I am aware of that, but I do believe that one day the war will be over and with such horrors that we are doing, I tend to believe that we will lose just because of these horrific actions of ours. The world will not let us do this for long time. There will be escapes that will tell the world about what has gone on in the camps. There will be rebels who will try to escape. These camps will be exposed to the world and when this happens our entire nation will be condemned forever."

I took a deep breath of air again and nodded. "I am just a simple soldier. You are hearing about this camp from a soldier's point of view. Unfortunately, we, the simple soldiers are doing the dirty work. We kill, we murder, and we lead the people to their death while officers watch and give commands. Yes, some of them are performing what I called individual contributions and also kill but the majority of the work is on us."

My mother brought me a glass of water and I drank it in one gulp.

"Thank you mother." I smiled at her. "So you see, here is your son, a hero of war. A hero of World War II."

We all sat there without speaking any words. I knew my parents. They were the most patriotic people in the world but they still had humanity inside them. They could not agree with all that I told them. It led me to the thought that probably many German people simply did not know what was going on. They gave their trust to the bloodlust of a dictator who lead Germany into madness.

"You know what I do not understand is how come most Germans did not resist this madness. Even if it took some time, how come so many thousands, hundreds of thousands soldiers, officers and officials did not see what we were doing? Everyone really thought that murdering civilians was not really war? Even if they were the enemy of the state, was it not enough to have them in labor camps? They could work for our country and rebuild it for us. But inventing gas chambers, crematoriums and other mass killing methods for a defenseless crowd? This is an idea of an insane person." I looked at their eyes "Only a mad person would imagine such things.

My father sank his face into his hands and my mother simply cried. No one said a word.

"You have to be careful expressing your opinions, son. You know", my father started. "I am sure that those who express negative opinions about our government will be severely punished."

"Yes, of course, I'll be killed. They kill everyone who resists the Reich", I said bitterly. "But of course, no normal person would join the Reich by his own will when such knowledge is revealed to him.

The atmosphere was tense, more than that, it was despairing. The knowledge that our great nation was in the hands of psychopaths hit my parents with all of its might. I could see on my mother that she was now mainly worried about me.

"Don't worry son, soon the war will be over and these horrors will be over for all of us." My mother held my hand.

I held her hand with love and smiled at her. "Well mother, I'll always love you and I wish you were right but think about all the simple soldiers like me, thousands of them, young people who obeyed their orders blindly, many soldiers who had to massacre innumerable victims. What do you think will happen to them when the war is over? Even if in the best scenario they will not be tried and executed, what do you think will happen to their souls? To their minds? They are already as if dead, Mother. Beside a few who were probably crazy even before the war, the majority are like me, good, simple people who had to serve their country." I nodded with a grim expression. "Even if they are not killed, even if they somehow escape and flee to other countries, will they be able to have normal lives after all they have done? After all they have seen? It does not matter if they wanted to do it or obeyed orders. The results were the same. It is like our leaders put a spell on our entire country. I saw so many soldiers, officers and German citizens in the streets of Berlin all screaming 'Death to the Jews', 'Kill the Jews'. I didn't see a single person, not even one, stop and question what was going on. I understand that everyone was afraid to be killed but still I would hope to see someone, some underground organization, another government maybe that would say this is outrageous. This is some kind of bad dream, a hallucination of the worse kind. It is like we are all under some spell, like we are all under a horrific spell."

I said that mainly to myself then to them. After that I sat there and thought about the consequences of my speech. I wondered about myself. What really happened to me? I felt well, physically and mentally. I always had a defense mechanism to protect myself from responsibility for horrors that I did not want to recognize. I had an internal voice that proclaimed my innocence and provided some excuse for any wrong I had done. My sanity had a self-protection mechanism but what I was worried most of all was my sense of justice. I had developed something that had become strong and dominant inside me, something called a conscience.

"What you are going to do?" My father's words broke my line of thoughts.

I looked at my mother and her face expressed her quiet but determined question."

Yes, what are you going to do?", she asked me with her eyes.

I shook my head slowly. "I don't know, I really don't know."

*   *   *

It was a hard week for me and my family. My father and mother were very depressed after my camp description. My father did not know what to advise to me and this was probably the worst thing that could have happened to him. All my life he had always offered advice and I must say quite wisely. He was also very patriotic. He loved Germany and always preached to me about how important our country was. That was the main reason that I always wanted to serve in the military. I learned to love my country and to obey its leaders. Now it seemed like I had broken the entire family myth. We all realized that the country was in very bad hands. Worse, both my parents knew me very well and I could tell they were afraid how I would handle my conscience. Our dinner talk was mainly my mother's insistence that these events and my involvement in them were beyond my control. I was just a soldier who obeyed orders and nothing else. I already knew that she was trying to convince me that whatever I participated in was not my fault. My father silently supported her. I felt like I had destroyed his world. He stopped talking much and turned inward. My mother hovered above me all the time. I could see that she was very worried for me.

As for me, now that I had admitted to myself and to my parents how I felt I was numb inside. I knew that I was only few days away from returning to the camp where I would have to continue with my duties, those duties that took my soul away.

I was waiting for a sign, something that would guide me in terms of what to do and where to go.

I loved my parents and I loved my country. I hated all the rest of my life.

*   *   *

After a weeklong vacation I returned to the camp. Having been in touch with my real feelings about my duty it was extremely hard to fulfill my daily tasks. One morning while I was shaving, I looked at myself at the mirror. There I was a Nazi soldier starting my day. I wiped my face with a towel and put the Nazi helmet on my head. I was sure that the images of Nazi soldiers with helmets on their heads would become a symbol of atrocity, grotesquery and evil in generations to come. I was one of them.

My soul was tormented. My conscience was suffering. I could not function as I was required to do anymore. Like a zombie I walked between the prisoners looking at their faces. Their skinny, starving, scared to death expressions reminded me of all those I had killed when I was flushed with hatred against them. I had been sure that they were my enemies. But how could I? How come I didn't see beyond? I didn't have the answers. Not for myself and not for the world. I just knew that I had committed terrible sins against humanity and that I had to look for a way to come to peace. I had to find a way to express remorse and regret. After all that I saw, after all that I had done during my service in the camp, my soul was already dead. All I had to do was to somehow use it to save others.

I wrote a long letter to my mother. I explained my feelings to her and told her my intentions. I did not know when this opportunity would arise, I wrote her, but I intended to find it. When it came, I would do what my soul told me to do. "I am very sorry, Mother. This is the only way I will be able to continue. Who knows, maybe some miracle will come and fix everything in an amazing way. I love you Mother. Please always remember me as your innocent child since I still am inside."

I kept the letter near my bed in the barracks. It was waiting for the right day to be sent. Soon enough that day arrived.

*   *   *

It was another shipment from Hungary. A train full of men, women and children arrived early in the morning. It was a cold day and while the people were coming off the train one of the officers arrived shouting "We need people to go cut wood for heating. We are out of wood in the officers' quarters."

An inspired spark ignited inside me. I knew the procedure very well. Typically prisoners were taken to the woods, just near the train station where they had to pick up fallen trees with their bare hands. To some groups they gave some tools to cut logs but typically the order was to get wood with their bare hands. I quickly looked towards the wood. The morning fog still covered the thick woods. It would slowly disappear by late morning. Perfect.

"I'll take the prisoners to get some wood." I yelled loudly towards the officer. "I know where good logs can be found. I'll take one more soldier with me."

The officer looked at me as I smiled at him and waved with my hand. He thought that I was an enthusiastic soldier looking to get promoted.

"Very good, do that and then bring the people straight back into the selection area." The officer was quite happy to know that his quarters would be heated soon.

"Hans, come with me. Let's take the entire group to the woods." I called to another soldier.

Hans was a short, chubby soldier. I didn't really know him personally. "Should we select only men?" he asked, surprised that I wanted to take so many people.

"No, let's take them all. This way we will be able to get more wood faster." I gestured with my hand as if to say I was I was in the know. "I did it before, trust me. It works very well."

"All people getting off the train follow the soldier in the front." I signed towards Hans who started to lead the people towards the thick woods.

Gently I directed men, women, elderly people and children to walk in the direction of Hans. The people were cold and I smiled and encouraged them as much as I could. Cold is their least worry, I thought. It was a large group of people, maybe few hundred. Since I took command no one asked any questions. No one wanted to be out in such a cold weather so when I took over the group of people, everyone left for their other duties.

My soul rejoiced with every minute that this large group of people moved further away from the camp. I felt happy. I felt that this was the moment that I waited for. I already had a plan. We entered the woods. The fog made it hard to see but I directed the people even further deep inside until we arrived at a large clearing. I instructed Hans to gather everyone into the center.

"Say, aren't they are too many?" Hans whispered to me. "We are only two."

"No worry Hans, I know what to do." I smiled at him with confidence.

"People," I started "Before we go be back to the camp, we need to gather some woods to heat your barracks. Please search around you and pick any wood that you can carry."

Part one of my plan was already complete. The people looked at me in surprise but then started to search around for wood. They may be still under the impression that they are going to be relocated, as our propaganda told them. I was hoping that the smart ones would be already flee quietly into the woods.

I needed the time to talk with Hans.

"Hans" I pat on his back "I need to talk with you"

Hans seemed surprised.

"What do you think about our service here in this concentration camp?" I asked him directly. I had to try.

"We serve our country . . ."

"Aha . . . and what are we doing in this camp Hans? Are we fighting other enemy soldiers? Are we in a constant battle?"

"No, we are obeying our great leadership. We are performing the Final Solution." He seemed not to grasp my words.

I wanted to lead him in a certain direction. "People die in wars Hans, soldiers, maybe civilians who are subject to bombing but what are we doing here Hans, on a daily basis?"

He gave me a frightened look. He was scared by the direction that I was leading him.

I stood with my hand on my gun.

"What is the fate of these poor people that are now collecting wood for us? What will happen to them when we bring them back to camp Hans?" I insisted with a smile.

He looked at them in discomfort. "They will go to the gas chambers."

"Or mass graves." I continued with an even wider smile on my face.

"What do you think about this Hans?"

"They are Jews. They are nothing, sub-human. This is the right thing to do, to kill them." He almost whispered when he slowly grasped what he said.

I looked at the group and identified two children. Probably brothers, one looked about eight and the other maybe six years old. "You two come here." I called in the tone of a Nazi soldier that Hans was used to hearing.

The two children approached and stood in front of us.

"Look at them Hans." I told him quietly now. "These are two children we are going to send to the chambers. Look at them carefully Hans."

Hans looked at them with hesitation. Then he looked at me.

"Tell me what you see Hans."

I had to prove to myself that I was right and the majority of the people were just obeying orders because of fear for their lives. I had to prove to myself that not everyone was insane.

He remained silent. I knew that this was my moment to reach his inner being. "Tell me what you see Hans." I screamed at him.

His body started to shake. "I see two children. Two Jewish children."

"These are children Hans, innocent children who did nothing to anyone, children like you and me when we were young. Did they commit any crime Hans?"

"No."

"Did they do anything wrong Hans?"

"No."

"Yet we are going to take them and many others to the gas chambers?" I hit him with these hard words. "Does this sound normal to you Hans?"

He started to get my idea. His face showed the shock of realization.

"So what we are doing here is brutal murder Hans. We are killing men, women and children for no reason. This is not war. This is massacre. This is mass murder of people."

I let my words to sink into him.

"When this war ends, like every war in human history has ended Hans, and the world sees these camps and these gas chambers and crematoria, what do you think will happened then Hans?"

He just looked at me with frightened eyes. Then he looked back at the children.

"You both can go back to collect woods children." I told them softly.

"We will be all prosecuted and punished, most likely by death and you know why Hans? Because we deserve it. We are doing horrific acts against humanity. We are committing unforgivable crimes. We have been mass murdering thousands or even hundreds of thousands just because they have different beliefs or belong to different races."

Hans was shaken.

"We are participating in probably the worst evil that the human race ever performed, Hans. But this is only one side of the story. What about the other aspect? Your soul? Are you capable of sleeping well at night Hans, knowing that today you led hundreds of innocent people to death? Do you even grasp the horror in the meaning of what I just said? We are murdering people every day."

I finished with him. He was shaking like a leaf in the wind. He was clearly broken. I felt sorry for him but I also felt satisfied. I was right. People can see the truth.

"What should we do Franz?" he asked me almost in tears.

"I do not know what you are going to do but I have a plan." I told him with determination. "I intend to let all these people escape to the woods. That's why I brought them here." I took a deep breath. "Then I'll go back and tell my officer the truth. I'll be put on trial after which I am sure they will execute me. I'll die but at least I'll die when my soul has known remorse and I'll have saved a few hundred innocent people here. They have better chance of survival in the woods then in the camp at Auschwitz."

Hans looked at me with frantic eyes "But, but . . . this is . . ."

"Yes," I released a sigh. "I give you two options. You can go back to the camp now, and it will all be on me." I raised my gun towards him "If you'll try to do something stupid now, I'll kill you. I have nothing else to lose. Or you can help me and we will both go back to the camp and face the consequences whatever they'll be but you'll be able to look at yourself in the mirror. What do you think Hans?"

I could see the conflict within him. To make such a decision a person needs a strong persona. Not everyone can do it.

"I killed people Franz," he told me and shook his head. "I killed many people, even out of rage. Without any reason, I hit them, beat them to death or simply shot them." He looked at me and I could see tears in his eyes "Why did I do that? You are telling me why I did that. Now that you have told me I can see the truth. It's like you gave me a strong smack and woke me up from a night mare." He lowered his eyes.

I put my hand on his shoulder. "I did the same Hans. And also I didn't know why I did it. Maybe because I believed the pervasive propaganda about the Jews, maybe because seeing the madness around us actually turned us into mad people. That's what I think happened. We were exposed to madness of such a degree that it warped our minds and our way of thought. That was what led to a change of our behavior. Under normal circumstances you and I and I am sure many other soldiers, would never do something like this. Massacre of people, horrific acts against humans, it is all madness. It's not real. It's like a really bad dream but I want to get out of it with some dignity. The only dignity is to save people. See, I think that our souls are already dead inside. Even If we would have survived after the war, what do you think your soul would do to you for the rest of your life? Just think about it."

Hans nodded quietly.

I turned to watch the people who were still collecting wood. "We are already dead. We just don't know it. Now I want to save these people."

Hans looked at me and wiped his tears. I observed his young face. He must have been eighteen or maybe nineteen, a kid. Still he was a dead kid, a casualty of war.

"Our commanders took young people like you and me and made us expendable. You, I and many of our German soldiers are casualties of war, Hans. Even if they are alive. They are casualties of war."

"I am with you Franz." Hans said with great determination. "I am with you."

I nodded. "Are you sure?"

"Yes, I am sure." he promised me. "Let's let these people go free."

"People, stop all of your wood gathering and stand in the center please." I called them.

They gathered in front of me and Hans.

I took a deep breath. Maybe some of them already knew the truth but for many it would be shocking news.

"People, I have some bad news and some good news for you." I smiled and lowered my gun. Hans stood quietly near me.

"The bad news is that you have arrived to Auschwitz, a death camp. Here they kill Jews. The plan is to bring you into gas chambers where you will all be killed. Another method is to shoot you into massive graves. Some of you, the healthy and capable ones, maybe will be kept alive for hard labor but under inhuman conditions." I had to shock them in order to get them to believe me.

The people looked shocked. Some of the women cried but they all continued looked at me.

"This is the blunt truth." I said sadly. "I wish it were different. I wish that it would be as they told you, a simple re-location but this is intended to be your last station. No one gets out of here alive." I released a long sigh. "My name is Franz and I am a Nazi soldier. They moved me to this death camp about eight months ago. I served my country on the battlefield and since then in the camp. As a soldier I obeyed orders. I led thousands of people to their death. I shot innocent people, I killed and I murdered. One day when the war is be over, the world will see all this and Germany will be condemned forever. But beyond Germany every person has to live with himself and his own deeds. Not that long ago I looked into myself and what did I see? I saw madness, I saw massacre of innocent people, thousands, many thousands and who knows when this will end."

The people were in awe. They stood there lacking the ability to speak, listening to a simple Nazi soldier tell them the horrific truth was something that they were not prepared for this morning. Based on the rough journey that they had to Auschwitz by train they could tell that something was wrong. No one delivers humans like animals. My words probably confirmed their instincts or rumors they had heard.

"I reached a decision with my friend here, Hans,. We cannot continue with this. We cannot continue with the killing and brutality against innocent people like you. We cannot participate anymore in these of actions. We are going to set you free now. I recommend that you escape far away from here, deep into the woods. Find the Partisans who are fighting the Nazi army. Run to other countries. Do anything you can to survive. This is the best we can do."

Some of them cried. I felt tears welling up in my eyes also.

"Someday, all this will be over and every human will be able to live freely again."

We stood there quietly for a while.

"What will you do?" a young boy asked me. I noticed that it was one of the boys I called to come forward before.

"We will go back and face a court martial. We will probably be executed. After all that we saw and experienced our souls are already dead anyway." I gestured with my hand and lowered my eyes.

"You are very brave men." one old man approached us. He got closer to us. He had a white long beard and a good smile. He looked like a religious leader of some sort but I was not familiar with the subject.

"You are brave men and by saving all of these people you are saving you souls." he nodded.

"Thank you but we have already perpetrated many horrors." I mumbled. "We can't return the wheel back although I wish I could."

The man looked at us quietly. "I'll say a prayer for you both until the day I die." He gave us a kind encouraging look. He could not make any promises that were not in his hand but as for him, he would pray for us until his last day. I loved that.

I started to cry. Hans also lowered his face, chocking in tears.

"You don't have much time. I am sure they will arrange to have search teams sent after you. You have to leave now and move quickly." I urged them "Good luck to you all."

"May I shake your hand?" the old man asked.

I was moved inside me. "Are you sure that you want to shake my hand? They have many humans blood on them."

"Not today. Today you are a savior of hundreds of people." He smiled "Today you are a different person. Yes, it will be an honor to shake your hand and your friend's."

The old man approached us and shook my hand. One after another, men and women, even the young children arrived to shake our hands. Tears were in our eyes as the line of people slowly moved forward. We didn't realize how many people were there.

The last one was a middle aged woman. She looked at me with kind eyes. She could see the tears in my eyes. She could feel my inside pain.

"You're so young. I wish you did not have to go through this. I am sure that your mother will be very proud of you."

She hugged me and then Hans.

They all left in a rush and we remained there alone in the woods. I looked at Hans. "Ready?"

He gave me a confident look and said "Ready!"

*   *   *

We were put in military prison awaiting court martial. While in prison I wrote my memoirs of what I'd been though for the past year in the Nazi army. I figured I'd probably be executed and wanted these memories to be sent to my mother.

After few days I was brought in front of the court. The court assembled consisted of four high ranking officers.

"Why did you let the Jews go?" the highest ranking officer asked me directly.

I looked at him. He looked like he could be a good man. He had grey hair and soft blue eyes. His facial features were regular and he radiated the aura of a good father. I felt comfortable to say what was on my mind, without feeling restrained by military titles or manners.

"A few months ago I received a transport in Auschwitz." I started calmly. "I led the people out. We received a few shipments like that every day. The order was to accelerate the Final Solution. I am sure you know about it." I even allowed myself to be ironic towards him. At that point I considered myself dead anyway. I had nothing to lose.

"Among those people were a mother and her three children who had just arrived from Hungary. While escorting them to the gas chamber", I paused to let the meaning of my words to sink in, "they looked at me. I stopped and looked at them. She was a short plump woman with her three little children who held onto her quietly."

I looked at the other people in the room. "A mother and her children. Then, with a smile as I was taught, I promised them

253

hot soup and bread afterward and led them to the gas chamber where they were murdered.

Now you are staging a court martial because I did not kill people? Tell me what is wrong with this picture?" I asked them. "A mother and her children were led to death. What had they done? The fact that they had different beliefs entitled the Reich to sentence them to death? That is murder."

When I saw their silence, I added "You used to be humans before you were Nazis, weren't you? We are not fighting a war in the camps. We are not doing any good for our country in these killing fields. This is the truth and you know it." I continued. "On the contrary, we are condemning our country forever. What do you think will happen when the war is over one day? What will happen when these camps are discovered? What will happen when the massacres and horrific acts that we have been inflicting on humans are exposed? Our country, Germany, will be condemned for generations to come. How could we? How could we enact this madness? Murder, humiliation, medical experimentation, the worst of the worst that can be done to humanity have become normal to us. Don't you see it?"

I looked at them in question. "Don't you see it?" I repeated, demanding answers.

The highest officer blinked a few times. That's what I was looking for. This was a sign of humanity. From my point of view, I won.

As I expected I was sentenced to be executed for acting against the Reich.

After three days I was brought in front of an execution squad. As I was put against the wall, I asked for a last request. The commander in charged considered my request and amazingly enough, allowed me to do what I requested.

My request was to take off my uniforms and remain with my underwear.

When I stood there, only in my underwear, the commander couldn't hold himself from asking me why I requested something odd like that.

My answer was clear and straight. "I am very proud of our country, Great Germany but I don't want anything to do with the Reich. It is a shame for me and for our country."

I stood there with pride and waited for the bullets. I was ready but the bullets did not arrive. I heard some talk. All of a sudden my blindfold was removed. I saw the commander and another person.

"Come with me." he said with severe look.

My father had pulled some strings and I was saved from my sentence at the very last minute. A high ranking military friend of his arranged that I be transferred to a military mental facility where I stayed until the end of the war. Hans, my friend, was executed.

After the war, they checked my story and released me as a free man. Today I live in Berlin and work as a bus driver. I give volunteer lectures at universities and colleges about the war and what I have done there. Whenever I tell my story everyone is fascinated by it and considers me a hero. I do not think that I am a hero but a man who woke up from a very bad dream.

Every weekend I visit my parents' graves. They were buried side by side not too far from my apartment. Almost every day in my mind's eye I see the old man who gave me a kind smile that day in the woods. "I'll say a pray for your soul every day, until the day I die.", he told me, shook my hand and disappeared into the woods.

I'll never forget him and I hope that he did not forget to say his prayer for my soul.

*   *   *

Ten green check marks appeared on the score board. The light angel released a long sigh and gazed at the ten cases they had witnessed. The dark angel also looked at the cases. He had nothing to say.

"The world is not such a bad place after all." The light angel asserted with a smile.

The dark angel remained silent.

"We need to present our findings."

"I already saw everything." a loud voice was heard.

A bright beam of light opened from above and illuminated the scoreboard with the ten green checkmarks. Each checkmark glowed brightly, emphasizing the brilliance of each case and its result. The beam of light radiated joyously, celebrating the very happy event.

The light angel and the dark angel looked at board that sparkled with thousands stars.

Then the verdict echoed throughout the heavens.

"The world goes on."